FABLES AND SPELLS

Collected and New Short Fiction and Poetry

adrienne maree brown

Praise for *Fables and Spells*:

"adrienne maree brown is a force of nature, a stream of wisdom, and an oracle for our times. Luminous creativity permeates this work. While acknowledging the deep despair the world grapples with, adrienne maree brown reminds us that all of nature is adaptive and that witching is, and always has been, the way to alchemize the complexities we are confronted with. These spells are cast with our wellness centered and our humanity uplifted."

—**Chani Nicholas**, *New York Times* **best-selling author of**
You Were Born For This

"I felt such a deep connection to myself and my community while reading *Fables and Spells*. It gave me permission to feel like I knew it all and also nothing ... like I'm tapped into an energy so rich and abundant but also so depleted and tired. The stories reminded me that we all have the capacity to heal and destroy."

—**Juju Bae, host of** *A Little Juju* **Podcast**

"*Fables and Spells* is potent ancestral cartography. It is a deep well of truths, musings, maps, medicine and healing extended from adrienne's ancestral throughline connecting to our own amplifying the ways we engage in witching for love, liberation and change."

—**Omisade Burney-Scott, author of**
Black Girl's Guide to Surviving Menopause

"What an exquisite gift this cauldron of *Fables and Spells* is! adrienne maree brown re-enchants our practices of deep listening and spell crafting, calling us to drink deeply and imagine more wildly. A prophetic voice for our time, adrienne (once again!) channels mycelial and celestial wisdom into remedies in the form of radical tales that guide the way to the world we dream of and grief and praise songs that help us realign with life itself. Full of both urgency and a sense of deep time, this is a book for our altars and our go bags in a world on fire, one you will return to again and again, the pages stained with potion and candlewax."

—**Dori Midnight, community care practitioner**

Fables and Spells: Collected and New Short Fiction and Poetry
Emergent Strategy Series No. 6
© 2022 adrienne maree brown
This edition © AK Press (Chico / Edinburgh)

ISBN: 978-1-84935-450-9
E-ISBN: 978-1-84935-451-6
Library of Congress Control Number: 2021935968

AK Press
370 Ryan Ave. #100
Chico, CA 95973
www.akpress.org
akpress@akpress.org

AK Press
33 Tower St.
Edinburgh EH6 7BN
Scotland
www.akuk.com
akuk@akpress.org

The above addresses would be delighted to provide you with the latest AK Press
distribution catalog, which features books, pamphlets, zines, and stylish apparel
published and/or distributed by AK Press. Alternatively, visit our websites for the
complete catalog, latest news, and secure ordering.

Cover Design by Herb Thornby
Inside cover illustrations by adrienne maree brown
Printed in the USA on recycled, acid-free paper.

Contents

Fables & Spells for Emergence

Fables & Spells for Grief & Endings

Fables & Spells for Celestial Bodies

Fables & Spells for Love

Fables & Spells for Liberation

Introduction

It can take a while to recognize what you are when the lineage has been swept away. I reach back for the tools I was given to be in and shape the world, and at first, I cannot find them. I hear the smooth instruction to love myself and many iterations of instruction to surrender my power to others, to trust someone else to stand between me and the divine, translating, interpreting, directing the exchange. But under all of that there is a feeling that cannot be denied—a direct feeling of connection and invitation to the natural world. It is both within me and between me and life. This feeling courses through me when I hold space, hold change, when I doula, when I work as a healer—and when I write.

I call it witching.

Witching is a practice of engaging the essential, natural world with magic and supernatural intentions. Throughout history there have been many names for witches and the work of witches, including shamanism, sorcery, healing, herbalism, midwifery and doula labor, conjuring, rootwork, ritual and spellcasting. There are lineages that provide a lot of guidance for the developing witch, and there are intuitive paths where the practices are shown, felt, called. I am definitely an intuitive witch—I answer the call and I trust the love in the universe to guide my actions. And I use my witching for liberation.

This act of witching is about putting our attention behind our intentions. And being willing to invite and shape the unseen forces

1

of the world (which go by many names and beyond all comprehensible names) to align with the highest good for ourselves and the whole.

There have been negative connotations and fatal consequences for witching, especially as organized religions have taken the center of common societal space. Many people have died for these good intentions, for trying to help, for having this sense in themselves of the parts of the world that are material but not visible, the realm of the energetic and interconnected. I am so grateful I was born in a time when I can embrace my practice publicly, even as I learn it. I think perhaps we witches are workers of the mycelial realm of humans.

As is my way, I was practicing before I claimed any language for it, and I brought many questions to those with more established practices of witchcraft and divinity. I finally gave in to my witchy ways when I looked at my life and realized I was casting spells, channeling nature, divining with tarot, creating altars of earth, crafting rituals, and practicing astrology. Being a witch isn't the only way I tap into the limitless capacity of the divine, but it is undeniably powerful in my life, and a way that I recognize and am recognized by others who are earnestly attempting to change what is ours to change.

As such, I wanted to uplift the pieces of my work that are doing active, intentional work to cast spells and create meaningful change, as well as stories in which I explore the lives of those discovering their magic. My witching way has always included writing. I rarely craft my poetic writing—I feel and channel, I get taken over by the need to express something that feels true, and I listen, editing and shaping as I write it. For that reason, I have always hesitated to call the work poetry. I am surrounded by people I think of as *real* poets. I see the labor they put into each of their choices, and I respect it, I honor it. What I do is different. The labor I put into my work is clearing everything out of the way until I can listen. The work I do is to look at the moon, or a body of water, or some creature other than human, and wait until I understand something.

The work I do is to repeat the instructions of love that want to be heard, over and over.

The stories in here may not fit strictly into the category of fables, and the poems may not all be spells, but that is also *my* way—I get rebellious around boxes and labels. These are all spells to me, and they have been cast.

As you read, I encourage you to listen for your own spells. I do know that reading your spells out loud increases their power, and reading into a candle increases their intensity, especially for release. Pay attention to the state of the moon when you choose to cast spells, as that energy of darkness, waxing, fullness, or waning will imprint on your magic. Folding a long-term spell and putting it under your bed helps you activate your dream shifting labor. Listen to your instincts as your read these spells and write your own. I hope something in these pages touches your untamed nature, reminds you that you, too, can shape the world around you.

Fables
&
Spells
for
Emergence

radical gratitude spell

a spell to cast upon meeting a stranger, comrade, or friend
working for social and/or environmental justice and liberation:

you are a miracle in motion
i greet you with wonder
in a world which seeks to own
your joy and your imagination
you have chosen to be free
every day, as a practice.
i can never know
the struggles you went through to get here
but i know you have swum upstream
and at times it has been lonely.

i want you to know
i honor the choices
you made in solitude
and i honor the work
you have done to belong.
i honor your commitment
to that which is larger
than yourself

and your journey
to love the particular vessel of life
that is you.
you are enough
your work is enough
you are needed
your work is sacred
you are here
and i am grateful.

trust the people

trust the people who move towards you and already feel like home.

trust the people to let you rest.

trust the people to do everything better than you could have imagined.

trust the people and they become trustworthy.

trust that the people are doing their work to trust themselves.

trust that each breach of trust can deepen trust or clarify boundaries.

trust the people who revel in pleasure after hard work.

trust the people who let children teach/remind us how to emote

be still and laugh.

trust the people who see and hold your heart.

trust the people who listen to the whales.

trust the people and you will become trustworthy.

trust the people and show them your love.

trust the people.

love is an emergent process

i stand before my love
and let the tendrils unfurl
in every direction
i am whole
and becoming

time is one instance
examining itself
mirrors
seeing each other
and blushing
into eternity

i am the ant who carries
grandfather to the grave
in my palms
you lift the next day's meal
enough for everyone we know

we in rhythm

leaving home
and returning

on the wind
love can't look away from itself
vibrating in the cell
fluttering breathless
into sustained migration

i feel you

like dust feels water
and remembers
the home galaxy
it appears nothing is new
never was
and nothing is truly massive
when seen in its wholeness

until i took this breath
repeating the miracle
i didn't know i would say it
could not have known...

i look to the sky
taste the wind on my tongue
and fling myself
into the pattern

when i forget –
when i think the end is near
i realize my insignificance
as important as yours
and begin
to love
again

The River

Something in the river haunted the island between the city and the border. She felt it, when she was on the waves in the little boat. She didn't say anything, because what could be said, and to whom? But she felt it. And she felt it growing.

Made a sort of sense to her that something would grow there. 'Nuf things went in for something to have created itself down there. She was a water woman, had learned to boat as she learned to walk, and felt rooted in the river. She'd learned from her grandfather, who'd told her his life lessons on the water. He'd said, "Black people come from a big spacious place, under a great big sky. This little country here, we have to fight for any inches we get. But the water has always helped us get free one way or another."

Sunny days, she took paying passengers over by the Belle Isle bridge to see the cars in the water. Mostly, you couldn't see anything. But sometimes, you'd catch a glimpse of something shiny, metal, not of the river—something big and swallowed, that had a color of cherry red, of 1964 American-made dream. These days, the river felt like it had back then, a little too swollen, too active, too attentive.

Too many days, she sat behind the wheel of the little boat, dialing down her apprehension. She felt a restlessness in the weeds and shadows that held Detroit together. Belle Isle, an overgrown island, housed the ruins of a zoo, an aquarium, a conservatory, and the old yacht club. Down the way were the abandoned, squatted towers of the renaissance center, the tallest ode to economic crisis in the world.

She had been born not too far from the river, Chalmers, on the east side. As a child she played along the riverbanks. She could remember when a Black person could only dock a boat at one Black-owned harbor. She remembered it because all she'd ever wanted was to be on that river, especially after her grandfather passed. When she was old enough, she'd purchased the little boat, motor awkward on its backside, and named her *Bessie* after her mama. Her mama had taught her important things: how to love Detroit, that gardening in their backyard was not a hobby but a strategy, and to never trust a man for the long haul.

Mostly, she'd listened to her mama. And when she'd gone astray, she'd always been able to return to the river.

Now she was forty-three, and the river was freedom. In that boat she felt liberated all day. She loved to anchor near the underground railroad memorial and imagine runaway slaves standing on one bank and how good   terrifying, but good—that water must have felt, under the boat, or all over the skin, or frozen under the feet.

This was a good river for boating. You wouldn't jump in for any money. No one would. She felt the same way about eating out of the river, but it was a hungry time. That morning she'd watched a fisherman reel in something, slow, like he didn't care at all. What he pulled up, a long slender fish, had an oily sheen on its scales. She'd tried to catch his eye with her disgust, offer a side eye warning to this stranger, but he turned with his catch, headed for the ice box.

She was aware of herself as a kind of outsider. She loved the city desperately and the people in it. But she mostly loved them from her boat. Lately she wore her overalls, kept her greying hair short and natural, her sentences short. Her routine didn't involve too many humans. When she tried to speak, even small talk, there was so much sadness and grief in her mouth for the city disappearing before her eyes that it got hard to breathe.

Next time she was out on the water, on a stretch just east of Chene Park, she watched two babies on the rocks by the river, daring each other to get closer. The mothers were in deep and focused gossip, while also minding a grill that uttered a gorgeous smell over the river waves. The waves were moving aggressive today, and she wanted to yell to the babies or the mamas but couldn't get the words together.

You can't yell just any old thing in Detroit. You have to get it right. Folks remember.

As she watched, one baby touched his bare toe in, his trembling ashy mocha body stretched out into the rippling nuclear aquamarine green surface. Then suddenly he jumped up and backed away from the river, spooked in every limb. He took off running past his friend, all the way to his mama's thighs, which he grabbed and buried himself in, babbling incoherent confessions to her flesh.

The mother didn't skip a beat or a word, just brushed him aside, ignoring his warning.

She didn't judge that mama, though. Times were beyond tough in Detroit. A moment to pause, to vent, to sit by the river and just talk, that was a rare and precious thing.

Off the river, out of the water, she found herself in an old friend's music studio, singing her prettiest sounds into his machines. He was as odd and solitary as she was, known for his madness, his intimate marrow-deep knowledge of the city, and his musical genius.

She asked him: *What's up with the river?*

He laughed first. She didn't ask why.

Here is what he said: *Your river? Man, Detroit is in that river. The whole river and the parts of the river. Certain parts, it's like an ancestral burying ground. It's like a holy vortex of energy.*

Like past the island? In the deep shits where them barges plow through? That was the hiding place, that was where you went if you loose tongue about the wrong thing or the wrong people. Man, all kinds of sparkling souls been weighted down all the way into the mud in there. S'why some folks won't anchor with the city in view. Might hook someone before they ghost! Takes a while to become a proper ghost.

He left it at that.

She didn't agree with his theory. Didn't feel dead, what she felt in the river. Felt other. Felt alive and other.

Peak of the summer was scorch that year. The city could barely get dressed. The few people with jobs sat in icy offices watching the world waver outside. People without jobs survived in a variety of ways that all felt like punishment in the heat.

Seemed like every morning there'd be bodies, folks who'd lost Darwinian struggles during the sweaty night. Bodies by the only overnight shelter, bodies in the fake downtown garden sponsored by CocaCola, bodies in potholes on streets strung with Christmas lights because the broke city turned off the streetlights.

Late one Sunday afternoon, after three weddings took place on the island, she heard a message come over the river radio: four pale bodies found floating in the surrounding river, on the far side. She tracked the story throughout the day. Upon being dragged out of the water and onto the soil by gloved official hands, it was clear that the bodies, of two adults and two teenagers, were recently dead, hardly bloated, each one bruised as if they'd been in a massive struggle before the toxic river filled their lungs.

They were from Pennsylvania.

On Monday she motored past the spot she'd heard the coast guard going on about over the radio. The water was moving about itself, swirling without reason. She shook her head, knowing truths that couldn't be spoken aloud were getting out of hand.

She tried for years to keep an open heart to the new folks, most of them white. The city needed people to live in it and job creation, right? And some of these new folk seemed to really care. But it could harden her heart a little each day, to see people showing up all the time with jobs or making new work for themselves and their friends, while folks born and raised here couldn't make a living, couldn't get investors for business. She heard entrepreneurs on the news speak of Detroit as this exciting new blank canvas. She wondered if the new folks just couldn't see all the people there, the signs everywhere that there was history and there was a people still living all over that canvas.

The next tragedy came Tuesday, when a passel of new local hipsters were out at the island's un-secret swimming spot on an inner water way of Belle Isle. This tragedy didn't start with screams, but that was the first thing she heard—a wild cacophony of screaming through the thick reeds.

By the time she doubled back to the sliver entrance of the water way and made it to the place of the screaming sounds, there was just a whimper, just one whimpering white kid and an island patrol, staring into the water. She called out: *What happened?*

The patrol, a white kid himself, looked up, terrified and incredulous and trying to be in control. *Well, some kids were swimming out here. Now they're missing, and this one says a wave ate them!*

The kid turned away from the river briefly to look up at the patrol, slack-mouthed and betrayed. Then the damp confused face turned to her and pointed at the water: *It took them.*

She looked over the side of the boat then, down into the shallows and seaweed. The water and weeds moved innocently enough, but there were telltale signs of guilt: a mangled pair of aviator glasses, three strips of natty red board shorts, the back half of a navy striped Tom's shoe, a tangle of bikini, and an unlikely pile of clean new bones of various lengths and origins. She gathered these troubled spoils with her net, clamping her mouth down against the lie "I told you so," cause who had she told? And even now, as more kinds of police and Coast Guard showed up, what was there to say?

Something impossible was happening.

She felt bad for these hipsters. She knew some of their kind from her favorite bars in the city and had never had a bad experience with any of them. She had taken boatloads of them on her river tours over the years. It wasn't their fault there were so many of them. Hipsters and entrepreneurs were complicated locusts. They ate up everything in sight, but they meant well.

They should have shut down the island then, but these island bodies were only a small percentage of the bodies of summer, most of them stabbed, shot, strangled, stomped, starved. Authorities half-heartedly posted ambiguous warning flyers around the island as swimmers, couples strolling on the river walk paths, and riverside picnickers went missing without explanation.

No one else seemed to notice that the bodies the river was taking that summer were not the bodies of Detroiters. Perhaps because it was a diverse body of people, all ages, all races. All folks who had come more recently, drawn by the promise of empty land and easy business, the opportunity available among the ruins of other peoples' lives.

She wasn't much on politics, but she hated the shifts in the city, the way it was fading as it filled with people who didn't know how to see it. She knew what was coming, what always came with pioneers: strip malls and sameness. She'd seen it nuff times. So even though the river was getting dangerous, she didn't take it personally. She hated strip malls too. Then something happened that got folks' attention.

The mayor's house was a mansion with a massive yard and covered dock on the river, overlooking the midwestern jungle of Belle Isle, and farther on, the shore of gentle Canada. This was the third consecutive white mayor of the great Black city, this one born in Grand Rapids, raised in New York, and appointed by the governor. He'd entered office with economic promises on his lips, as usual, but so far, he had just closed a few schools and added a third incinerator tower to expand Detroit's growing industry as leading trash processor of North America.

The mayor had to entertain at home a few times a year, and his wife's job was to orchestrate elegance using the mansion as the backdrop. People came, oohed and aahed, and then left the big empty place to the couple. Based on the light patterns she observed through the windows on her evening boat rides, she suspected the two spent most of their time out of the public eye happily withdrawn to opposite wings.

She brought the boat past the yard and covered dock every time she was out circling the island looking for sunset. As the summer had gone on, island disappearances had put the spook in her completely, and she circled farther and farther from the island's shores, closer and closer to the city.

Which meant that on the evening of the mayor's August

cocktail party, she was close to his yard. Close enough to see it happen. Dozens of people coated the yard with false laughter, posing for cameras they each assumed were pointed in their direction. Members of the press were there, marking themselves with cameras and tablets and smartphones, with the air of journalists covering something relevant. The mayor was aiming for dapper, a rose in his lapel. As she drifted through the water, leaving no wake, the waves started to swell erratically. In just a few moments, the water began thrashing wildly, bucking her. It deluged the front of her little boat as she tried to find an angle to cut through. Looking around, she saw no clear source of disruption, just a single line of waves moving out from the island behind her, clear as a moonbeam on a midnight sea. She doubled the boat around until she was out of the waves, marveling at how the water could be smooth just twenty feet east.

She looked back and saw that the waves continued to rise and roll, smacking against the wall that lined the mayor's yard. The guests, oblivious to the phenomenon, shouted stories at each other and Heimlich-maneuvered belly laughter over the sound of an elevator jazz ensemble.

Again, she felt the urge to warn them, and again she couldn't think of what to say. Could anyone else even see the clean line of rising waves? Maybe all this time alone on the boat was warping her mind.

As she turned to move along with her boat, feeling the quiet edge of sanity, the elevator music stopped, and she heard the thumping of a microphone being tested. There he was, slick, flushed, wide and smiling. He stood on a little platform with his back to the river, his guests and their champagne flutes all turned toward him. The media elbowed each other half-heartedly, trying to manifest an interesting shot.

That's when it happened.

First thing was a shudder, just a bit bigger than the quake of summer 2010, which had shut down work on both sides of the river. And then one solitary and massive wave, a sickly bright green whip up out of the blue river, headed toward the mayor's back.

Words were coming out her mouth, incredulous screams twisted with a certain glee: *The island's coming! The river is going to eat all you carpetbaggers right up!*

When she heard what she was saying she slapped her hand over her mouth, ashamed, but no one even looked in her direction. And if they had they would have seen naught but an old Black water woman, alone in a boat.

The wave was over the yard before the guests noticed it, looking up with grins frozen on their faces. It looked like a trick, an illusion. The mayor laughed at their faces before realizing with an animated double take that there was something behind him.

As she watched, the wave crashed over the fence, the covered dock, the mayor, the guests, and the press, hitting the house with its full force. With a start, a gasp of awe, she saw that the wave was no wider than the house. Nothing else was even wet.

The wave receded as fast as it had come. Guests sprawled in all manner of positions, river water dripping down their supine bodies, some tossed through windows of the house, a few in the pear tree down the yard.

Frantically, as humans do after an incident, they started checking themselves and telling the story of what had just happened. Press people lamented over their soaked equipment, guests straightened their business casual attire into wet order, and security detail blew their cover as they desperately looked for the mayor.

She felt the buoys on the side of her boat gently bump up against the river wall and realized that her jaw had dropped and her hands fallen from the wheel. The water now was utterly calm in every direction.

Still shocked, she gunned the engine gently back toward the mansion.

The mayor was nowhere to be seen. Nor was his wife. And others were missing. She could see the smallness of the remaining guests. All along the fence was party detritus, similar to that left by the swallowed hipsters. Heeled shoes, pieces of dresses and slacks. On the surface of the water near the mansion, phones and cameras floated on the podium, the rose from the mayor's lapel lay, looking as if it had just bloomed.

The city tried to contain the story, but too many journalists had been knocked about in the wave, felt the strange all-powerful nature of it, saw the post-tsunami yard full of only people like themselves, from Detroit.

Plus, the mayor was gone.

The crazy, impossible story made it to the public, and the public panicked.

She watched the island harbor empty out, the island officially closed with cement blockades across the only bridge linking it to the city. The newly sworn-in mayor was a local who had been involved in local gardening work, one of the only people willing to step up into the role. He said this was an opportunity, wrapped in a crisis, to take the city back.

She felt the population of the city diminish as investors and pioneers packed up, looking for fertile new ground.

And she noticed who stayed, and it was the same people who had always been there. A little unsure of the future maybe, but too deeply rooted to move anywhere quickly. For the first time in a long time, she knew what to say.

It never did touch us y'know. Maybe, maybe it's a funny way to do it, but maybe it's a good thing we got our city back?

And folks listened, shaking their heads as they tried to understand, while their mouths agreed: *It ain't how I'd have done it, but the thing is done.*

She still went out in her boat, looking over the edges near the island, searching inside the river, which was her most constant companion, for some clue, some explanation. And every now and then, squinting against the sun's reflection, she'd see through the blue, something swallowed, caught, held down so the city could survive. Something that never died.

Something alive.

Call the Water

"You, fix it! Mami-o, call the water. Come, please fix it."

Maria was the oldest woman on Vinewood, maybe the oldest woman in southwest Detroit. Her street was residential, but there were also a million little hustles happening on front porches, in backyards, on the corner. She knew every dream and failure. She had outlived everyone she had ever loved and most of those she hated. Now she stood with an empty jar in her tilted tiny kitchen, every inch of her brown surface pleated by life, eyes sharp and pleading.

Maria was part of the fabric that had held every child in this neighborhood, had watched each one come home from the hospital, go on a first bundled stroller ride, catch their first school bus, bring home their first dates, lose their parents to age or the million cancers. Maria knew how to break fevers, calm colds, bring sleep, and give warnings even teenagers would heed. Maria had been steadier than Sinti's own distant grandmother; the old woman knew there was magic in the child, magic in the woman.

Sinti wished she could fix everything for Maria. The world was full of problems even water could not heal. She felt small, and young, even on this side of menopause.

Sinti could still feel her blood grandmother at her back in the bathroom, drooping ancient hands cupped around Sinti's small ones, as Sinti had played with the water caught in the sink. She hadn't known she was doing magic, not then. She'd simply swirled her fingers, inches above the surface of water that had a slight soapy sheen to it. She'd simply swirled her fingers and the water had danced up towards her hands, tornados upside down trying to touch her. Her grandmother hadn't spoken words, hadn't said Sinti was special, or not special. That had come later.

Now Maria wanted Sinti to call the waters, too parched for doubt. The water woman decided to try, even though she'd never intentionally done her water work around anyone that wasn't her grandmother. It still seemed like a private act, a hallucination or a prayer or witchcraft. She felt possibility alive in her. She stepped past Maria to the dry, useless sink.

It had been seven years since water flowed freely in this house. Seven years of citizens punished for political incompetence. Of bottled rations and dry nights, of Maria, like everyone else, getting used to the dusty sour smell of her dry body.

Sinti leaned down close to the faucet until her own warm, aged cheek went soft against its cold metallic bend. She made a wet sound that no one had ever taught her, a hushing behind her pursed lips, a sound like water flowing over a cliff far away. She brought her hand up slow, moving water lightward from a buried spring, moving through earth and salt. She slipped her left fingertips gently against the knob marked cold, following a shadow of feeling. She didn't turn it, she caressed it, letting her fingers move over the grooves, tracing the distinction between clear plastic and the silver heart of the knob, feeling that it could move, would move once there was something to turn for.

She pulled, up and also somehow out from within, pulled with her own longing, and Maria's longing, and the city's longing.

And waited.

And pulled.

And waited.

And then, between breaths, the rumbling was felt more than heard. She could feel that what was in the earth was coming up, glad to be called on.

Everything in Maria's kitchen was old and mismatched, backwards, mislabeled. Sinti looked at the deep sink under the pale flowered curtains that might have been yellow once, at the chunky faucet, its singular pearly knob that had a big "H" on it for hot water, even though only cold ever came out.

Sinti twisted the knob open in case Maria was watching. Because then, of its own will, water was thundering through the faucet. Sinti moved her own mouth to it, opening, licking, and then letting the freezing water fill her cheeks, swallowing as fast as she could until she couldn't take anymore. She stepped back, wiping her mouth and nodding so Maria knew it was good, drinkable.

Maria smoothed her thinning white hair back, half smug, half awed. She stepped over and put her jar under the faucet to fill. She opened a low cabinet full of empty wine bottles, mason jars, pitchers. Maria pulled them out and stacked them on the counter.

Sinti wanted to tell Maria that there was going to be water now, that it was plentiful down in the earth. But the normal hesitation came...would this work? Would it work if she wasn't around? Would people be excited for her gift or burn her alive? Was it legal? The questions that kept her magic small closed in around her. She didn't know enough about her own magic to make such a commitment, so she helped Maria fill every container in the house. They moved as one body through the railroad of rooms overcrowded with furniture that had been replaced but never really removed, side stepping archives of the street newsletter Maria'd produced for years, a sweet gossip rag that no one read, fresh or dated. In each room there were empty containers, in each room they left water.

"Let me check now," Sinti said, reaching to turn off the knob. She wanted to know if the flow would be available now whenever Maria wanted it. But Maria grabbed her wrist.

"Wait," Maria said. "Others are thirsty. Can we let it run?"

"I think it will flow now." Sinti felt her feet get more solid on the ground, tipped her chin up. "We don't want to waste it."

She found certainty in her voice that had no roots in her gut. Hopefully this spell didn't rely on certainty.

She turned the knob. Together the women watched the raging water slow until it was mere droplets pooling at the edge of the metal, and then, finally, stopped.

Maria looked at her, face an arched mystery. Sinti felt the weight of Maria's eyes on her as she turned the knob the other way, opening.

The water came out strong. They both exhaled.

She tested the knob a few times, closing, opening, closing. Then she stepped back to make room for Maria to try it.

It worked. It worked each time.

Maria smiled at the water, then turned to smile at the water woman already slipping out the door.

Sinti looked back and put a finger to her lips.

Maria just smiled, committing herself to no secret keeping.

✤

The City of Detroit had sent the notice to everyone: no more private water access in homes.

That was the language the city officials used, perverting the meaning of everything.

The socialists had spent the last decade succeeding in local campaigns against privatization, in favor of public ownership of everything that was a basic human right—water, yes, and fertile land, air, health.

But the mayor had been one year into his term and emboldened by federal austerity measures to address the debt to China. He was regressive, and so was the money he rode in on. Water was the thing they could control that everyone would pay for.

The socialists had spent the two months between the posting and the actual water shut off trying to figure out new campaign language that explained the economics of this latest water grab.

Sinti kept her distance, then and now—she agreed with them

in theory but bristled with introversion at anything that required showing up to meetings and rehashing arguments she'd landed in herself when she was half this age.

She didn't need teach-ins or presentations to know that there would still be private water access in certain homes, certain neighborhoods. The enclaves with the waste-gates built up around them: Boston-Edison had water. Indian Village had water. Most of midtown and downtown had water.

You had to go through extensive financial screening to determine if you were the kind of person who would be willing to pay the exorbitant fee for water flowing into your home. If you weren't, you got denied housing or evicted. But if you made it through the gauntlet of credit checks and bank account reports, then you were awarded the kind of home where, when you arrived and turned on the faucet, it worked.

The undercrused pipes were sourcing from dwindling lakes further north. Everything was drying up so much faster than anyone had expected. The water that came out of the working faucets needed to be filtered at least three times. The water elites created a system that involved a filter on the faucet itself, boiling the water that came out, and then pouring it into a filtered pitcher.

Pouring, processing, and storing water was a weekly activity for the extremely wealthy. While there was no way to justify the limited access, it gave her some small respite to know that water wasn't an easy thing, even for them.

✣

Sinti'd never had that problem. Her water never stopped, it came to her as Detroit water always had, cold and clean on the tongue.

She'd ignored the emergency-red, all-cap notices in her mail, and then the signs posted on the front door of her small house. She lived in a two-floor, stand-alone Victorian, nestled and resistant between two newish apartment buildings on the gentrified east side.

Her father had left her the house, paid in full. Other than her life, this was the most meaningful gift she'd ever received from him. Her father had painted the porch "tokyo tangerine" and "flamingo fuchsia" to please her mother. He gave her a hibiscus house when he couldn't give her the fidelity she craved. The rest of the structure was a sallow brown.

She composted organic waste into rich soil. The city fined residents for any overt form of rain catchment, but she cultivated rain-fed crops and fruit trees in the backyard overlooked by neighbors in the apartment buildings, who tried to be nice, to swallow suspicion. They failed. She was strange, always had been. But she smiled at them when she remembered to.

Two blocks south got her to the water's edge, where she could walk the mile along the river to her boat most of the year. Three blocks directly away from the water got her to the bus line.

Before the water shutoffs, people loved to go on her boat excursions, to feel the rhythm underneath them, to see the parts of the city that still had access to electricity explode into color at sunset.

That was before the wave, before the crisis all the time everywhere. Now no one trusted the water.

But she got by.

The city wanted to make sure everyone knew the exact date when private water access was ending, for them to feel their power. She'd felt something else; she'd felt like the water knew her and would find a way to her.

A decade earlier she had watched water change the face of the city with massive and isolated waves that swallowed many of the modern day colonizers. Now the water's absence was changing the city again.

The day of water shutoffs had come and gone, and at first, she'd thought they had failed to shut hers off, that they hadn't reached her little block yet. But then she'd begun to notice the sort of signs that never get printed on paper, the indicators that her running water was a very rare exception: people with homes began to look like the homeless, those lifelong Detroiters who had been pushed out of every part of the city, slowly, over years—dirty, dusty, ashy. Everyone smelled like a body, even when they tried to cloak it with perfumes and deodorants.

On Fridays when recycling was picked up, a new pale blue bin was added just for water containers. They rolled out a new fine for selling water that wasn't bottled by the city, said it was for the safety of the citizens, that only they could guarantee quality water. Then they introduced another fine for mixing water jugs in with the rest of the recyclable containers—the city had to gather the containers back to distribute their precious overpriced water.

Her neighbors were regularly seen carrying jugs of water home from the nearest gas station. The stations now distributed water that cost more than gas—you could bring your own containers, jugs, bottles, or buy it prepackaged in plastic that was getting recycled over and over.

She'd quickly realized that if she didn't fit in, she would become a target. She'd kept personal cleaning to a minimum, let the dust build up on her face, the black settle under her fingernails. She'd cut her short hair even closer when she couldn't handle the dirt in it.

At least once a week she made sure to go refill a jug. She let her eccentricity see to the rest.

✲

But Maria told.

Of course she did. Just her closest friends, but every closest friend has other closest friends. Secrets are just a matter of proximity and connection.

The water woman couldn't explain what had happened, that she had called upon a deeper water, an abundant water, a freshwater sea under the earth. Maria couldn't explain it either, she just told people that, like any problem, it could be fixed.

Who was Sinti to deny anyone water? Once a day they would show up on her sorrel-colored porch, sometimes familiar, then, more often, strangers who had heard of her from someone else who had heard: she knew a way to make the water run, clean and free.

Each time, her task was easier, the water came faster. She perfected her method—she would get under the sink, letting her soft belly and raised knees fill the cabinet door so people couldn't see what she was doing. She took to carrying a wrench hooked in the belt of her coveralls. She hoped people would think she knew some way to turn the wrench and change the source of all life.

That would be easier to explain than what was happening.

✤

When the administrator came to the door, he wore a strange uniform, his beige pant legs gathered into a white boot scuffed with tar. The outfit was bright and militant, as if he was running undercover ops at the Taj Mahal. He stepped into her house. She didn't point out to him that there were no shoes allowed inside.

"Ma'am. Name's Maxwell. Yours?"

She blinked at him.

"Ok. Fine. Ok, I am going to cut straight to the point here. It's implausible, but—you running a black market for water?"

She felt her body chill a bit. She expected a fine for turning on what the city wanted off. At the turn of the century, she had done a direct action to turn on heat in her cousin's building when the city shut it off; she and a friend had gotten caught and set on payment plans for disobedience. The judge had seemed personally offended that she, a Black girl, would take anything so freely.

Maxwell had the same perplexed, hurt look on his face. How dare she?

"Excuse me?"

"Have you been stealing water, ma'am?"

"No. I have not." This felt true. How could anyone steal water?

Maxwell the administrator was blond, his hair long and a bit greasy. Perhaps he also had rationed water.

"Well, we've been watching you. We know you're doing something." He paused to swallow a burp, his bland eyes looking all over her house as if she was hiding a magic water machine in plain sight. "My bad, indigestion. Anyway, lying won't help you now. Just come clean and I will work to get you reduced charges."

She moved towards her front window.

Across the street was Maria's dilapidated building, windows boarded shut where people had left to look for water. The old woman stood wiry and attentive with a small group of gray friends on the sidewalk. That ancient woman felt things, knew things. Had stood there decades ago watching Sinti's father slip their lives from sweetness to suffering.

Now Maria started, as if she felt the attention. When Maria looked up, spotting Sinti there, she got other people's attention. The water woman recognized them as neighbors whom she had helped. Maria punched a fist her way.

Maria was so small. The group was so small.

The administrator was small.

So was she.

The city was small really, on this planet, itself small in the universe. Only the water was vast.

But so many cities had no water left. So many people were gone to thirst. Even Detroit, once the forever freshwater city, was drawing on resources that would be gone in another decade.

The species was not going to make it far on politics, even on science.

"Tell me what you're doing. Tell me what source of water you've found." The administrator did that move where he stepped in front of her, to dominate her line of sight. He had a concave air about him, collapsed and indignant in the tight space between her and the window.

She looked up at him briefly, and then over him, through him, to Maria and her neighbors.

Why was she being so stingy with her magic?

Why was she keeping this good water from anyone?

"I'll show you." She pivoted away from him. She was going to go in the kitchen, but then she realized she didn't need to. She turned and stepped around the useless man. She walked out onto her porch, where she could see Maria, where she knew Maria could see her.

She closed her eyes and spread her hands until her palms were wide, opened to the earth.

She called the water. She pulled.

The peak of the mountain was the core of the earth, the spring was running down, cascading up, pouring down the mountain, ascending to the world. She could see it in the darkness behind her eyelids, blinding cold blue water pouring up through black dirt, spreading like fingers.

She let her eyes flicker open, and saw Maria mimicking her, all the gray hairs across the street, mimicking her, hands open to the earth, shuddering together.

"Ma'am!"

Her body began to shake like waves, like there was a turbulent sea storm inside of her.

"Ma'am that's not necessary. None of this hoodoo is helping your case here."

She felt the water as close as blood in her veins, rushing in every direction, too fast to comprehend. Her body could feel the landscape of the city, flowing under southwest Detroit so powerfully it went further, water mains under Michigan Avenue as it regressed from modern pavement to cobblestone and back again, flowing into gentrified Corktown, up the Cass Corridor to the North End, spread far west, far east, beyond the paltry public transportation, under the streets that no longer had lights, where the popo never answered the 911 calls, where the fire department was only ever in time to douse the ashes, the parts of the city that myopic government had tried again and again to shed or deny. She flowed towards every place there was a heartbeat, into water fountains, bursting up fountains in Hart Plaza, Belle Isle, Clark Park. The water was clean, it was cold, and it was flowing through Detroit now, raging up and into pipes. She heard screams of surprise and joy begin to echo across the city landscape. She opened, and opened, feeling pleasure in this undoing of her solitary self.

She was the blue in the dark.

She was the water that called.

Harness the Water

look
you *have* to *know*
what *kind* of *person*
you *are*
when I'm not *around*
i *need* to *know*
you're making *good*
choices

They were in a cozy underground restaurant in a small town in Italy, down the narrow hall leading to bathrooms. Her mother was beating her with one hand, holding her against the wall with the other, subvocal speech grunting out with her effort to change the child. It was their first time out of Detroit and the girl had done something equally unacceptable and forgettable, such that she couldn't pinpoint exactly why her mother was beating her right now.

But she couldn't feel it. She was flowing down her own body, crashing, and foaming over edges, unstoppable now. She was going to the water.

✢

When she was twelve, her mother Tanya, laughing, pushed her off her grandfather's boat into what looked like a calm and shallow spot in the channel between Saint Claire Lake and the Detroit River. The water was moving deceptively fast, and the girl was instantly out of reach.

Swim girl!

She could hear her mother's quiet choking order, see her mother's guilty eyes glittering dark and focused on her. Her mother was equally terrified of the strong water, and of waking Papa Joe, the girl's grandfather who was napping down in the berth. The girl snatched a breath into her system and dropped down, touching her feet to the river's bottom. She thought something between "breathe" and "flow." The water dipped above her and then opened, parted all the way down to the pale muddy earth. The path ended in a short wall of water on top of which the boat, holding her mother, floated in place.

Her mother stopped screaming with her mouth still gaping open. The girl walked along the sliver of path, looking into the life of the water moving on either side of her. She would later determine that the massive fish she saw were trout. She would later remember that she could see the current moving so fast along her sides, and how everything was moving with the current and she wanted to flow with all of it but knew her mother needed her to return. She would later remember that the water level was above her head, though not by much. She would later remember how uneven and busy the lake floor was under her squishing sneakers. She would remember so much, but in the moment, she just felt ease, she just saw that there were living creatures about, and they were seeing her. She would share none of this with anyone, because her mother would forbid her to tell it. Her mother would cover her mouth with her hand when she even started to speak, because whatever she was going to say had to be a demonic lie, even though they had both been there and seen the miracle.

At the boat she grabbed the bottom rung of the ladder and pulled herself up, her mother looking at her as if *she* was the monster. The water splashed together behind her.

✲

When she was sixteen years old, she understood that her mother was competing with her. She hadn't been able to piece it all together before that, the way her mother would backwards compliment her changing body (*you too young for boobs like that*), but then demand she cover it up like a nun (*put a jacket on before we go in your uncle's house, no one needs to see all that*), would make her sit in the slow boil of the car instead of coming into the store for groceries (*you clearly not dressed to be in a store, I'll be right back*). Their lives had become a game of hide-the-girl, and it became clear only when her mother began seeing a trucker named Carl. Carl scooped Tanya up at a bar by telling her how beautiful she was, how much he wanted her sweet little body. When he was in town, Tanya went to Carl's place for an evening here and there, and eventually some weekends. But one Friday they stopped by the house so Tanya could throw some things in a bag for the weekend.

The girl was used to these lonely weekends when her mother would be gone. They'd started the day after she turned thirteen, "old enough to watch yourself." The girl had learned to process the disappointment, wash her clothes from the week of school and sport, figure out food, read books, watch things that didn't mess with her sleep.

This Friday, Tanya'd expected to take her duffel bag of lingerie and dresses woven with magical spandex and leave a note in an empty house, but the girls' soccer practice was cancelled, and she was home on the couch, reading. Carl came in behind Tanya and seemed surprised to see this Black girl child, his gray eyes looking without shame at her long legs crossed on the couch, her budding breasts in her tank top. The girl tried to arrange herself in some other formation, to make herself invisible. She wished her mother would be disgusted, would throw him out. Instead, Tanya yelled at her for sitting around the house half *naked,* little *whore,* raising a hand until the girl bolted to her room.

The girl had sat on the edge of her bed rocking back and forth, correcting things in her mind, shaking, feeling like she was going to implode. Her mother stood at the door yelling things the girl didn't fully understand. What she did understand is that something had made her beautiful mother feel and act ugly, and maybe it was something in the girl's own skin, in her own body, that made her mother act out so.

She felt a brief and pounding desire to escape herself, and then the yelling at the door changed to both Tanya and Carl yelling about water. The pipes had burst! The pipes had burst in the bathroom and kitchen, and water was spraying everywhere. Tanya was yelling in the chaos, I *know* you did this you *little bitch.*

✣

Like so many witches these days, she didn't know her lineage. Things had happened that were directly related to this soft clear knowledge of the water, her ancestors along her paternal line had long memories of connection with the water that transformed their conditions on land. Somewhere, in the century after crossing the ocean trapped in the belly of a ship that some of them kept afloat while others tried to sink it, the connection dimmed. Somewhere, hemmed into a square of land that didn't even have a creek, working until blood flowed from their hands, her people forgot that they had been given the gift of water.

The gift didn't go anywhere, water forgets nothing.

❋

Her college dorm windowsill was covered in propagating plants, the roots swirling around each other in jars of clear water. It was the first thing she had done when she arrived, go to gather living things to breathe in the room with her, find ways to have water near. She had chosen UC San Diego because she was able to get housing that faced the ocean. Each morning she woke up when the light came and slipped out of her room, up to the "living roof" where she could watch the tides. She rarely missed a sunset; this green sprawling roof was her home as much as the shared dorm room below with its glassed square of sea. She felt a power returning to her with each day that she was by the water, each day far away from her mother. She felt that what moved in her had the rhythm of waves and tides.

She swam in the big ocean, with the salt moving against and through her. She went early, and sometimes at night, so she could dive down as long as she wanted without troubling any other swimmers with their fearful assumptions. The salt cleansed her of the insults and terrors of her mother. The current told her she didn't have to carry anyone else's burdens. The sand offered her gifts, sunken treasures, and lost shells.

She had forgotten most of the water miracles of her childhood, in the normal way trauma obscures magic. But in this practice of giving herself to the ocean, she felt an uninterrupted sense of herself emerge, a self that could extend to the horizon without falling off, a self that could carry an emotion across a continent before releasing it.

❋

Her ancestors knew the ocean before there were tides, before the moon. For what seemed like always, they danced along the edge of the flat, still water until the water danced back. They then harnessed that motion, that power, to generate everything they needed to build, to grow, to journey. Tired of the constant labor, they danced into life a celestial goddess who would pull the tides. She made a mess at first, until they realized that she too needed rest, and together they shifted the cosmos until all the beings were in rhythm with each other, waxing and waning, coming in and going out, building up and bleeding, seeding and harvesting, inhaling and exhaling. That balance is what the water people know.

The imbalance began when people who knew the ways of the water were taken away from the water. And people who knew the ways of air were put in dungeons, and people of earth placed on concrete, working suspended in the sky, and people of fire pulled north into the realm of ice. People of different elements can get caught in only seeing what is wrong with each other.

Tanya, descended from an earth lineage, had been so enamored of the wave that entered her body, full of life. But she was constantly challenged by the water child that came forth from her loins of dirt. In the years of mud, after the man had washed away, she kept trying to make her daughter solid, dependable, controlled. Water is sensitive but cannot be wounded with a strike. Water recovers by returning to wholeness. Her child's ancestors made the whole world dance.

✢

By the time she was thirty, the girl had harnessed the water.

Others called her a healer, because with her hands on them she could return each body to the flow. Every body is water, every body is a vibrant place of life, sometimes caught in stagnation. She knew how to open the channels, she was careful, she practiced boundaried unity with her clients.

She stayed in California, and her mother stayed in Detroit, until more than a decade had passed. Her mother would sometimes call her, meaning to invite her home. The anguish of missing her, the confusion of a child so far beyond her control, would take Tanya's tongue; she would begin to say things she didn't mean and then get lost in anger and the woman-child would withdraw for months, changing and growing and healing herself and others.

When she turned thirty, she had a moon dream. Every so often these dreams would come where she was the moon, and she was so aware of the tides, so aware of the work she was doing, so new, or so full. In this moon dream, she saw her mother, sleeping, a body of fetid water, stuck and full of rot, of things that had died but not been allowed to go back to the sea. When she came to, she booked a ticket home before she had even been able to think.

When she got to her mother's door, she was astounded by the pain she felt. Every joint in her body, her gut, her hands. It was usual that she could feel the pain of her clients. Had her mother always been this walking wound, this sack of need?

When her mother opened the door, her face opened in a familiar way—the wonder of her daughter had always humbled Tanya, frightened her. Tanya remembered her child, pouring out of her hands somehow, splitting the lake, bursting the pipes, becoming a stranger. Before Tanya could say the wrong thing, this grown woman in her Black beauty stepped through the door, closed it and then placed her hands on her mother.

The first stuck place was in Tanya's heart, where there was a fissure that had filled up with loneliness. The second stuck place was along her spine, which had all kinds of aches and bends that were ancient—the dazzling wounds of slavery and white sociopathy. Tanya cried out as this wound flowed out of her. The third stuck place was sensual, was the place where Tanya had been touched too young, had been broken instead of nurtured. Only shared weeping can heal that kind of injury, and Tanya wept into her daughter's shoulder as she caught her daughter's tears, until the pain was shared and released.

The women were there in the foyer for hours, kneeling on the floor, fetal on the floor, wrapped around each other as one body becoming whole, one family coming home. Finally, finally, the healing was done. Without words, Tanya showed her precious child to the bedroom. They slept there, for the first time, in tenderness.

When they woke, there was nothing to say. They had to begin again. They had to meet each other, as if for the first time.

a complex movement

over and over again
it becomes known
the peace we seek
is seeking us
the joy a full bud
awaiting our attention
justice in our hands
longing to be practiced
the whole world
learning
from within

this thrilling mote in the universe
laboratory
labyrinth

internalize demands
you are the one
you are waiting for
externalize love
bind us together into
a greater self
a complex movement

a generative abundance
an embodied evolution

learn to be here
critique is a seductress
her door is always open
so what if you get some
we are going further
past reform, to wonder
this requires comprehension
that cannot fit in words

out beyond our children
beyond the end of time
there is a ceaseless cycle
a fractal of sublime
and we come to create it
to soil our hands and faces
loving loving and loving
ourselves, and all our places

i can't stop being in the present

i can't stop being in the present
noticing how the past tells me what i should care about
and the future tells me what i should fear
and the past tells me what we forgot
and the future tells me what we must dream
but here

i breathe in
noticing the gift i too often take for granted
not knowing how many breaths i have left
i want to spend them loving
being
love

i have done so much, so many tasks
but what matters most
has been the listening
to the thirsting dirt
to the spiraling wind
in the wake of murmuration
to the drumbeat of ant feet moving
abundance with a million hands
the sacred erotic of pollination

the orgasmic opening of mushrooms
pulling the yes for miles underground
the innocent violence of predators
feeding their children
the way the wild wastes nothing
the way the cedar gives me permission
to pray

i thought someone else
had all the instructions
and i, stumbling and following
praying to become worthy
must admit i have been grieving and grieving
all i don't know and don't trust
and grieving so deeply
a world that is still breathing
anticipating failure
in spite of my visions

but when i listen
the universe is reminding me
i cannot be taken from her
i am never untethered from her roots
never beyond the whole
and nothing is lost, it is lived
and we are not here to win
but to experience love
and those who do not know love
are missing life in spite of all other accumulation

and when i listen
the universe is teaching me
that control is impossible
and the season will change
and enough is a feeling that cannot be measured

and the small circle is the deepest
and i cannot teach anyone what i have not practiced
and i cannot change anyone but myself
and i will never feel free in a position of demand
and i am already free
and we all are, and when we realize it
we cannot be contained

and we are never i
even when we are lonely
even when we distinctly suffer
even when we distinctly succeed
we are of lineage
of collective
of era
of farmers' hands and strangers' prayers
of singers with their heads thrown back
we are always dancing with our ghosts
and praying for our great great grandchildren
we are always the harvest

and the future is being decided
the future is being practiced
the future is being planted
in this breath
and this breath
and this breath

so i breathe in
noticing the gift i too often take for granted
not knowing how many breaths i have left
i want to spend them
being
love

if you can't see the small

look here. here.

if you can't see the small
you will keep leaping from built thing
to built thing
begging the sky to rain only on you
you will become a tyrant
reaching, shuffling the cards
until you see only your own vision
massive
but no one else can see it

if you can't see the small
you miss the whole miracle
it is all moments nearly missed, private
impossible to perform, or
perfectly acted, context and all
moments of faith hit the surface
and change it
shivering us open
to love
to our ridiculous longings

adrienne maree brown

if you can't see the small
you may never feel true love
it comes with the slimmest shadow of warning
whisperclacking spider toes up your spine
to love is to truly lose
the only thing you can ever truly have
and never buy
for love, true, the whole surrender kind
starts with a gasp

if you can't see the small
you may never know pleasure
which is not about the immersion
into eternal bliss, no
it's the printed pad of your finger
grazing along my shoulder
as you realize you need to feel me
it is inside, where the sun, wind
rain and earth
have never touched you
but i have

if you can't see the small
you won't know
what the dirt is screaming
one grief at a time
that the whales are singing
warning songs
that there is a shudder
in all of life now
a premonition:
change everything
for everything is changing

Fables

&

Spells

for

Grief

&

Endings

first the unbearable
(learning of egypt)

i hear the condolences first
read the written word, the name, the place
someone is sending love, with rage
with shock, with tears, with analysis
with their people
with all people
and i go looking for the fresh wound

i want to not know
to step from here without this pain
to the next moment, unmarked by blood
looking past the flayed horizon
whispering no. no, not this many, no.

the numbers grow on my tongue
i say them to no one
i read the news to whomever is near
even if they have read
or are reading it
i want to lend my voice
to the spell of awakening
to make every head turn
look, look what we've done

look what we have not undone
what we have allowed and encouraged
what we have invested in
what we forget, what we remember
look who we are now
look who we still are

i want to change the story being written
the history still warm and wet on our fingers
i want to focus on the intimate heartbreak of violation
what stole my smile, my childish peace
boorish men, the mountain of offense
we have all burrowed through
the memories we walk with and the terrors
navigating legacies of genocide and erasure

i know all of the harm intertwines at the root
i know the medicine has to go deeper down
to the core of existence
to the cord between us and god
to the fault lines between us
that make us think: i can be without you

but first, the unspeakable
the unimaginable, the unbearable
we have created hell with our boredom
we birthed hierarchy, greed, and the foolish need
for victory, for righteousness
it is killing us
it is killing everything
eating us up from within
the detonation of cancer in a living body
the cancer of violence in a living world
some days i am nothing more than a prayer
a vessel of tears being emptied

adrienne maree brown

stunned by my own insignificance
our inability to stand in the way of our demons
the brightest truth about us

some days i have to focus on one story
out of the hundreds of deaths
one person telling god everything
feeling the sacred flood all of their senses
planning the next meal's portions
and what to say to their sweet and distant lover
one person remembering they are enough
one person smiling as they gather themselves
for the world outside
enjoying the mundane pleasure of bodies
all around
in and of faith, wearing faith, speaking faith

the doors will open
the violence will burst in
so sure of itself, so wrong
i will learn your name in your absence
perhaps i cannot fathom
the entirety of gore
the scale of destruction we have committed to
but you, stranger of faith
comrade in the act of prayer
beloved to your god, your mother, your son
you i will grieve for
you i will grieve
for all the time and sea between us
i feel the shock of losing you
it is a devastation
i would have loved you
but my species
we are terrified of love.

reincarnation

waves crash in, riverbanks flood
the original souls—a handful in the cosmic sense—
split and fractured for so long
into so many sand particle lives
all feeling some else missing thing some gone
perhaps even half of themselves,
perhaps even more

waves pull away, river narrows, cracks
more soul concentrates in each little riddle of flesh
bringing back more humilities, a variety of heart breaks, the trauma
of true love, of being whole
not thinking of wholeness, but feeling how
you are not wrong, you never were wrong
you were always a child reaching for light

a wave takes flight, a river finds its infinite tail
we realize the total pleasure of minds, desires, histories, dreams,
and futures other than our own
left alone, one would always become god
create another to long for, lean on, snuggle into
and then miss, and return to
and then grieve

adrienne maree brown

addendum:

these newest oldest parts of ourself
remind those coming generations, from within, of truth:
if you cannot grieve you will not survive
life is not promised, death is not fair
the politics of care reveal what people love
don't let those who cannot love lead you
bitterness is only bearable when paired with sweet and with change
it didn't have to be this way—what will you change in yourself to
make this moment impossible to repeat?

The Limits of Blood and Flesh

The goddess appeared last Saturday night on the other side of a drunken and exquisite kiss, and the next morning she was sprawled across my bed when I woke, thick long ebony limbs tangled in white sheets, glowing incantations etched out along her flesh, marking a crown on her bald head.

I was so excited to have conjured her up, minor witch that I am.

Those light scribbles woven around her Blackness were my first clue that this was no ordinary one-night stand. The wildlife was the other.

Perched around my bedmess were at least seven toucans, black chests pompous under tropically bright hooked beaks. One stood claws splayed across the seven tarot decks on the shoe box covered with a pretty handkerchief I called an altar. One stood on my pile of books to read, topped by Jodorowsky's *Tarot*, all of which was tilting under the weight. A third was on my boombox, which I kept because once a year I needed to listen to *The Jets* on cassette tape.

At the foot of the bed, mentioned last only because it was the least believable wonder before me, was a small black panther with a blood-red stripe along its spine, chilling. Imagine how tightly we all occupied the space, which was barely large enough for the double bed and my street-found dresser drawers. Against the Assata

Shakur and Bob Marley–postered tangerine brick of my bedroom, we all looked so Afro-Gaugin.

Now, I know that when you conjure something up from beyond the border, you can't really issue a bunch of boundaries or guidelines around how it comes, even if you are precise. I mean, I'm sure Moya the Blood Witch Queen could get a goddess to show up without an entourage, but I'm just a flesh witch! And a beginner at that.

Frankly, I was surprised my Goddess Solutions™ spell had worked. Not because of any expected failure on my part—I'd cast it meticulously! But I'd cast it in spite of my mentor Ayana's warnings not to practice creation or solution spells without supervision. To be fair to myself, I was in a fit of vengeance after the week's news— two more Black women tased and arrested in downtown Detroit, this time because someone thought they were stealing their own car. This after a year of escalating assaults and violence on our Black bodies, not just in my city but all over the US.

Now, in the spell, I hadn't specified to "come alone" because I thought that was implied. First lesson of goddess spells: no assumptions. I couldn't exactly tell the goddess to send her creatures away, even though I was immediately aware of a previously unknown fear of large birds pooping. But I thought: these birds are too elegant to shit on my carpet. As for the panther, well, I just had to hope he was friendly.

And just so you aren't sitting there worried for me this whole time, these creatures are quite the innocent players in the events of the last seven days, if not flat-out victims.

The goddess on the other hand…

That first morning was as fantastic and clear as the previous night was sloppy and blurred. She kissed me, guava coconut over my tongue, and any concerns of morning breath vanished. My hands went everywhere, just to revel in her smooth surface, skin like mine, but perfect. There was a distinct pulsing heat wherever the light was carved into her. We kissed for a long time before she slid a finger into me, and it felt like she released a beam of gold against that one little big place inside that is so tender and untouched. She seemed genuinely surprised when I burst into peals of laughter at the pleasure of it. Surprise and laughter aren't common in this nerdy young witch's bed, and I liked it.

When I'd recovered, I reached out to please her, but she shook her head, possibly demure. I'm embarrassed in my feminist bones to admit that I can't recall if she'd spoken a word to me in all that time but she did then.

"You brought me here for some purpose?" She asked, her full lips moving slowly as if the words were brand new or time was silly.

"Yeah, yes," I answered, still in the daze of pleasure and possible rejection.

"I'm ready to hear your need." She was looking at me so directly, I couldn't deny the transactional bent of the moment, of her being here. But, I reasoned, it was for a good cause.

"Basically, I wanted to see if you could get rid of racism here."

"Here?"

"Here. Detroit. I mean I figured we could start here and if it goes well, grow from there." I'd felt so confident just a week ago that this was, at minimum, a viable request.

"Race-ism?" She turned her head just a bit, her neck long and firm, her head so smooth it seemed hair had never even contemplated growing there.

"Yes," I answered. "It's this thing, this belief, that makes people think they are better than someone else, or hate someone else, based on their skin color."

The goddess pushed up off the bed onto her elbows, looking down at me, perplexed. It did sound dumb. She reached over and put her hand over my eyes, asking me, "Do you mind if I see it your way?"

I couldn't figure out what she meant in time to answer properly, but then felt something akin to the pressure that comes a second before tears.

A torrent of feelings came rushing up through my body—the weight of danger, constant fear of lynchings old and new, being misunderstood, being made to feel small, dismissed, that my life isn't valuable, that my brown skin, my concerns, my desire to live, were somehow threatening.

It filled up my throat, I couldn't get any air for a long moment. It felt like everything alive and vulnerable in me was being pulled out of my face, eyes, body, into her palm. I started to panic a second before she removed her hand, and I could suck in a deep breath.

I opened my eyes to find hers, wet and wide up close, fast spinning black galaxy pupils flecked in silver. She seemed to be rolling something around on her tongue. She nodded her head and sat up, crossing her legs on the bed. I have to say, for the record, that between her legs was an area as bright as the sun. I couldn't look directly at it.

Then she started singing, loudly.

She had a multitude voice, which I suppose I should have expected. It took me a little while to even comprehend song inside the great noise. Harmonies and solos built up and spun out in tendrils, wrapping back around each other. Her mouth and throat seemed too small for the vast sounds coming through, and I thought briefly about what my upstairs neighbors would think— they were always casting shade in my direction for the enthusiastic magical sex sounds I indulged in this little room, mostly on my own.

Then I looked at her and forgot to care about bothering anyone. The light on her body was glowing brighter as her voice crescendoed, like she might come apart at these lit seams. She could do whatever she wanted—she had goddess privileges.

The toucans came to attention in a different way as she sang. They tossed their bright beaks around and snapped them open and closed, stretching their jaws. They began to flap their wings urgently, lifting and dropping themselves, thrashing the air until the room felt like being inside a down pillow being used in an epic battle. It was hard to see clearly in the flurry, but it looked like the light from her body was lifting, darting like snakes, dashing in and out of the toucans' beaks.

One by one, the birds bounced over and crouched on the ledge of my fifth-floor apartment window, which stretched almost the full length from the ceiling to the floor, the best part of the room. One by one they dropped into flight across downtown Detroit.

The panther stretched, yawned, flicked his tale, and slithered off the bed. He propped his paws on the ledge, sniffing the late summer air, watching the beasts fly off. I stood up beside him, cautious not to get too close, shamelessly naked in the window. His shoulder blades flexed, as tall as my hip.

The silhouette flock of toucans was heading towards the old Michigan Central train station, eighteen abandoned stories of gap-toothed windowless architecture in the heart of Corktown, the center of the city's recent white influx.

The panther rolled his neck and plopped down on the floor, guardianish.

"What's happening?" I asked the goddess.

She stood up behind me and pressed her abundant flesh against mine, an incredibly effective non-answer. She brushed her face into my wild hair, then used a hand to lift it all up so she could do something excruciatingly sweet at the base of my neck.

I couldn't see the toucans anymore, but I'll admit I wasn't really looking.

The birds returned one sweaty hour later or maybe two. I had always prided myself on the witchy tricks I could pull off in the bedroom, levitating my lovers at the moment they peaked, lighting the edges of the bed on fire and holding them by the hair as close to the heat as they could handle, little things like that.

But this goddess wasn't having it.

She'd strung my wrists together tight with a vine she sprouted out of my ceiling fan. I was straddling and grinding her sweet little goddess face, stripped of my own magical intentions, when the first toucan landed back on the ledge.

I won't say the goddess tossed me aside, she wasn't rough or anything, but it took less than a second for the ceiling fan vine to release me and curl in on itself, right out of existence. I found myself flat on my back, alone mid-pleasure, as the goddess rose from the bed, rigid with anticipation—in a way I can humbly admit she hadn't been for me.

She approached the toucan and placed her hands against its massive black wings, looked in its eyes, hummed a little tune. Then she puckered her perfect lips around the tip of its beak, and the beak cracked open and something that looked like a great nothingness poured between them, a space both gray and empty of gray?

All witches know that everything is a somethingness—most of our magic is the manipulation of the tangible unseen.

But this? This looked like the entire world was erased right in the half-inch between the toucan's turquoise and fuchsia beak and the goddess's black lips. New ream of paper bright white-gray nothing. It took only a few seconds before she finished, and the toucan hopped down from the window's ledge into the room, over next to the bed, ignoring me.

The rest of the birds were hovering outside, staying aloft with slow massive pumps of their wings. Each one landed at its turn and gave its blank treasure into the goddess's dark mouth before hopping into the room. When she was finished, and the birds were all crowded in the small spaces around the bed, she turned to me, thumbing the edge of her mouth as if a droplet of nothingness had gone astray.

She said, "It's strangely sweet. Like it can't be wrong, you know?"

I didn't.

"Makes me want more." She smiled at me, looking equal parts innocent and guilty. "I like it."

Her soft belly was a bit swollen now, and she rubbed it with both hands. Then she climbed into the bed, flopping on her back next to me, hands behind her head. We were quiet, her satisfaction tense in the air against my discomfort. After no more than a minute she sat up, flinging her fingers at the great birds. "More."

The toucans looked at each other, their bright heads bobbing as if in contemplation. Then they took off.

Since then it's been non-stop, toucans flying in and out of my room, bringing this harvest to my goddess lover. Lover no longer feels accurate, to be honest. I haven't kissed her since that first delivery. I don't want that stuff touching my tongue! But she doesn't seem to notice my silent snubs, she just feeds and feeds, only slipping a finger along the ins or outs of me as an overt distraction when I remember to ask serious questions such as:

1. How can you enjoy the taste of it?

2. Where are you actually getting this stuff from—is it one person's hate per beak? Or more? Or less?

3. What's left when a person is sucked empty of their racism?

Now, I love a big-bodied goddess as much as the next flesh witch, but I have to say she ballooned in a strange way over this long week. Not like getting fat, but like filling up, the way an air mattress goes from a folded piece of rubber to a bed. It started with her belly and back stretching, her thighs widening, her breasts inflating, dwarfing her grand areolas. Her face gained new resting dimples.

What was filling her to the brim was so much more than fat.

She was taller, wider, her black skin stretching and losing its saturated color like pulled fabric, the glow of her markings fading to dim. Still, she didn't stop. I began to fear she couldn't stop. She was pacing the toucans so that she regularly had fresh...racism?... delivered whenever she wanted.

On Wednesday I spent most of the day in my tiny living room, looking out the window and feeling quite sorry for myself. I'd wanted a quick, tidy solution. But this process was going to take forever! And the goddess was taking up so much space. And, it shouldn't have mattered, but she wasn't interested in me at all now.

The goddess wouldn't tell me where she came from, but she was like a child around basic life skills, which gave me an advantage in creating chores to leave first the room, then the house. I finally left the apartment Thursday, ostensibly for groceries, even though I had a full fridge and no appetite.

I wasn't hungry, but I wanted to see if the city felt different.

Detroit is a fantastic place for young witches for many reasons. One, there are thousands of empty places for practicing spellcasting and new skills. Two, there's tons of fresh water around—conjuring is thirsty work, and the water can help carry things away, cleanse. Three, people almost never look up, so I can fly my dustbuster around most nights without attention. And four, there are a variety of ghost clusters haunting about to help imbue the spells with heft from beyond, and they are *all* gossips.

I got the first inkling that I was in trouble when I tried to communicate with one of my favorite clusters at the corner of Mack and St. Aubin. They haunt a small lot across from the bulk recycling center, "haunting" meaning they move rocks about in mysterious formations, keep an eye on late night walkers, and whisper secrets. I loved the feeling of receiving secrets, wind buffeting from all sides, the words emerging from the din.

But when I came near this time, they went silent, wouldn't show themselves.

Ghost dis? Uh oh.

I went to another downtown haunt, in what used to be Black Bottom but is now a neighborhood of gorgeous, abandoned homes getting arsoned out of the way for the new hockey stadium. The ghosts in this cluster are older, Blacker. I took for granted that they would approve of my work, be tuned into the shift I was sussing out. They must be so much more tired than me.

But again, nothing would manifest to talk to me. I began to have my first serious doubts here about my brilliant scheme. I hadn't thought it through.

I picked up a copy of the *Michigan Daily*, hoping there would be a piece on a mysterious drop in attacks and arrests on Black people, or some other pattern shift to justify the innocent monstrosity I'd created.

The front page instead said: "White on White Crime Hits All-Time High!" More intraracial attacks had happened this week in the Corktown and downtown areas than in the rest of the year combined—muggings, robberies, and an increase in bar fights. Mildly satisfying. But if there was a corresponding dent in white on Black crime, or unfair police arrests, it wasn't registering. I was displeased.

On the walk home I came around a corner and saw what I'd been both seeking and avoiding—a toucan at work. There were three white people standing a half block away from me on the sidewalk, a boarded-up house on one side, a pockmarked street on the other. They stood still, a woman in leggings, two men in suits, heads tilted back, mouths wide open. A transparent flow of that vacuous concentrated goddess food was pouring up out of each of them into the open beak of the toucan, perched on a parking meter. When it was full, it snapped its beak shut and took off. The rest of the racism-substance dissipated in the air, bubbling about and then gone.

The white folks shook their heads, looking at each other with confusion and suspicion. The woman spoke first, "Who the fuck am I? What did you do?" I tucked my body behind the building and watched as they took turns yelling out angry questions, asking where home was, and eventually pushing each other around before parting ways with no shortage of vitriol.

I suspected that whatever my goddess was eating was more fundamental than racism, it was a wholesale removal of these people's sense of self.

I'd like to say that kind of logic is the reason I fully broke with the goddess and my foolish spell, but it's not. I came home, arms loaded with a number of unnecessary groceries that equaled the exact weight of my fear of being caught in a lie. I was practicing ways to ask the goddess to either speed up her work or move along. I put things away in the kitchen and then opened the bedroom door.

Everything I could see was horrific.

The panther was gnawing on someone's sparsely-haired, white and torn off leg, ripping away the khaki pant with such rhythm that the bare foot rocked back and forth.

The goddess had the remains of a bare and withered torso open over her face, her delicate hands holding the ribcage open as she licked inside it.

Several of the toucans were also pecking at human parts on the floor, two of them bickering over a wizened old head. The room stank of decay.

I screamed at the goddess, "What have you done!"

"They brought me a dead one! Less fresh, but oh, he had lots and lots of it." The goddess's eyes and cheeks peeked over the bones, her dark face smeared with blood and nothingness. She might have been smiling, it was hard to tell.

I was so very fucked.

I dumped the clean bones in the trash chute after the animals and deity had swallowed the rest and slept on the couch that night.

By Friday morning she was bigger than my bed, her solid black body spilling off the mattress, her small head and dull eyes following my movements around the room. It still stank, the putrid funk of my guests' dinner, and a new smell which I decided was the goddess's own growing toxic stench—we are what we eat after all.

I told her, unequivocally, no more people eating. Not even racists, not even dead racists. She reluctantly agreed, clearly feeling burdened by my judgment.

She couldn't move much anymore. The toucans would now fly in and climb up the mountain of her body until they could dip their beaks into her always hungry mouth.

I tried to reason with her. "This is not working."

She pursed her lips. "This is what you asked me to do."

I thought, not for the first time, about what I would do if she were to explode all over the room. I'd realized the night before that I don't know any spells for cleaning up organic disasters yet. I didn't even know how to get her out of here. But I mean, how big can a goddess get when the container is still just skin? "I thought you would actually make it *disappear*. Instead, it's just...filling you up, and making you want more and more."

"Nothing just disappears. And I never feel full. I want it all...

but you sent me after something much larger than I expected." Her eyes looked different. When I got closer, I could see that the galaxy pupils which had spun so furiously when she arrived were now slow, almost still.

"I am so sorry," I told her. "I will try to make it stop."

"But I don't want to stop," she said, voice rising like a child's. Then a toucan landed on her with sustenance, and she forgot about me.

I pulled open my bottom drawer, shuffling through my notebooks for revocation spells. After an hour of praying with my fingers, I'd found only two.

The first one, which I hoped would send her home, instead made her have what appeared to be an allergic reaction, the dull light wrapped around her body now sputtering as if its power source was faulty. She complained, rocking her mass back and forth, "That itches!"

The second spell was even worse. It was supposed to contain her power, but it only had the effect of making the goddess and all of her animals really grumpy. The toucans flew right in the window now, skipping the ledge and dropping themselves upon her unceremoniously, scratching up her sacred chest with their four-fingered claws as they poured their spoils into her little cosmic mouth. They squawked and cawed at each other in annoyance, waiting for orders.

With the goddess no longer directing the feedings, the empty fruit of their labor had been overflowing her lips, dribbling down onto my pillows and sheets. In those places, it looked as if spots of the bed were gone from the world, droplets of nothingness. I was going to have to replace everything.

The panther was super grouchy, nipping at anything that came near the window, including me and the toucans. I'd brought him a few steaks and he'd eaten them with disdain, clearly wanting something more reminiscent of whole human. I wondered when he would want to eat me.

I was in way over my head. It was time for help.

I looked in the dresser mirror at myself, ashamed. There, I summoned Ayana, snapping my fingers three times in front of my mouth while speaking her name. She was my mentor, an introverted and crabby witch who had caught me during my moping-on-the-weather-vane-of-my-high-school phase a few years back and taken me under her tutelage.

She tumbled over the toucans, having appeared out of mid-air, gray haired, frail, her black skin mottled in a white Pollock of vitiligo. In her right hand was a steel wand with silvery horsehair trailing down to the floor; in her left was a latte.

She surveyed the room with no amusement whatsoever.

"Listening." She sipped the latte.

"I was trying to eradicate racism and—" Ayana stopped me there, holding up her wand hand as her tight mouth wiggled and her eyes closed. She shook her head. Then she stepped out the window, floating in the air for a second before flowing out of my view. Then I could hear her cackling.

Rude.

The goddess cut her eyes at me. I rolled mine at her. It was our first moment of solidarity in days.

Ayana came back in, skimming over the panther and asking no more questions. She pressed her weathered hands against the goddess's flesh, whispering gently to her. The goddess blinked several times at this touch, and then tried to sing.

A bubble started to push its way up out of her mouth, that nothingness, solid and absent. Ayana cried out, waving her hands in front of the goddess's face, pushing the bubble back in without touching it. The goddess blinked again, tears spilling this time.

I wanted to disappear.

Ayana turned on me, furious.

"Stupid girl!" She clapped her hands above her head and the birds were gone. "If we could just conjure a goddess to swallow this shit," clapping again, now the panther was gone, "do you think that any of us would live in it?" She clapped a third time, and it was us that were elsewhere.

The goddess was still in my bed, but now it and she and the birds and the panther and Ayana and I were in a massive empty building with a concrete floor and an absent roof. Grass was pushing its way up along the edges and a pear tree had grown in through one of the busted windows.

Ayana flung her hand around and the windows went dark.

Then, "Moya, Moya, Moya," Ayana snapping her finger three times. With a rumble, the sky above the roof-free building cracked open and there she was, Moya the Blood Witch Queen.

I was in so much trouble.

Moya's skin was bright green with brown undertones, and she was no less than seven feet tall. She wore a scarlet gown that seemed to flow down and away from her in constant motion as she descended to stand before us. Her face was magnificent, mostly cheekbone and massive green-black eyes.

"Ayana?" Moya sounded interrupted and annoyed.

"We have a mess here, beyond flesh magic I'm afraid," Ayana waved her dappled hand at us.

Moya didn't walk, but rather moved as if on a private cloud. I hoped I was socially invisible to her, but of course she came straight to me, the guilty party, heat rolling over me as she stood near. I was sweating instantly.

"Good intentions," she said after a second, smiling. Then the smile left. "Poor execution. Suspended indefinitely."

She swept one hand over me, top to bottom. I felt a little sting and *poof*, like that, my knowledge of spells was gone. Moya turned away and drifted towards my goddess, who was moaning now.

"Where is home?" Moya asked her.

"I'm hungry!" the goddess answered, eyes rolling back in her head. The toucans pushed up off the ground as a unified group of seven to fetch her some sustenance.

Moya snapped both of her fingers then, back and forth in rapid succession, *1234567*, whispering something beyond my comprehension. The toucans popped out of existence, one by one, each leaving a single black feather to waft to the floor.

"Apologies," Moya said.

Then she bent down and beckoned to the panther, who had been pacing in circles, nosing the toucan feathers. He padded over to her, and she slid a hand down his back, her fingers blending against the red stripe of his back. "Apologies."

She gripped the top of the panther's mouth in her left hand and yanked him up onto the bed, pulling his sharp teeth right up to the goddess's mouth. With her right hand she coaxed the goddess's jaw open, and a half second of chorus came bursting out before the nothingness swelled up, stretching her jaw. Moya took over the song, her own voice loud but minimal after the goddess.

I started to protest, but Ayana silenced me, stitching my lips together with a look. It hurt, but it was not as big as the terror in my belly. She then shook her head a bit and took my hand. I clutched it, grateful.

The nothingness poured out of the goddess's mouth and, as we all watched, between the panther's teeth and down his throat. It was like a dense fog pouring out of her and into him. He wrestled with Moya the whole time, flinging his massive body in every direction trying to break her grip on him. Moya stayed still, holding the channel open.

Then I saw the shift happen. The goddess began to deflate as the panther grew, his belly filling up, his legs extending, paws doubling in size. The goddess was shrinking in the bed, getting darker and darker. The monstrous content was moving from one home to another, emptying her out.

Finally, the panther was larger than the bed, bulbous, with minimal fur covering his body, and the goddess was back to her original soft black body. Moya went quiet, letting go. Everyone was quiet, breathing, waiting.

The panther growled, stretched, pacing around, far larger than all of us combined. The massive building now seemed like a small concrete cage, his sides brushing the walls as he ambled about. Moya kept a red hand extended towards him, her eyes focused, lips whispering protections.

The goddess sat up, slid off the bed, and stretched herself tall, shaking her blue-black body out. She looked remarkably unscathed and unperturbed, gorgeous and humanish again, for which I was grateful. She came and stood before me, placing a hand on my cheek. She smiled expectantly.

I looked at Ayana, powerless. My mentor had no sympathy in her eyes. She turned to Moya, who nodded. Ayana flicked her right hand open and then closed, and my Black goddess was gone.

The panther stopped pacing then, roaring at us, rage and loss in the hinge of his jaws. Even Ayana cringed. I instinctively tried and failed to conjure myself elsewhere. No magic. Now, I thought, we would probably die. And this monster would go terrorize my city, all of those small horrors in this one massive body.

Moya, dress blown back by the terrible panther sounds, reached towards him with one finger extended. He gnashed at her, but she didn't withdraw. He groaned then, a pitiful low sound, rolling his head back. He hadn't asked for this.

She slid her finger right to left in front of his neck, opening him. One drop of blood fell to the floor, then two, and then the monstrous and mighty panther collapsed before us.

The only sounds in the building were the survivor breaths of three witches, still here.

Moya turned to Ayana and me then, a small give at her mouth that might have been a smile in another moment.

She came over to us, placing a hand on both our shoulders.

"Racism," Moya the Blood Witch Queen said, "is not of flesh."

Ayana nodded, looking at me to make sure I understood. I nodded too, wanting to.

"Nor of blood," Moya continued. She lifted her green hands and held them before us, palms up. They looked empty and small. "It is a magic of emptiness and illusion."

She turned and moved away from us, grabbing the panther's big head and turning towards the wall. There was a burst in the room of red smoke, and as it cleared, I saw that Moya and the giant panther were gone.

Ayana turned to me, shaking her head. She grabbed my face and looked hard in my eyes. "We can't disappear it. Only death and time, long slow changing time, can disappear it. It has to be forgotten by facing reality." Her frown softened. "I am sorry I didn't tell you that." Then she pulled me close for a hug. She felt brittle around me.

Just before I could get emotional, she stepped back, coughed into her fist, and was gone from me. The windows were blown out gaps again, and there was a chill in the air.

I stood in the empty building, looking at the bed. I'd be leaving that here for sure. I was a bed-less, powerless witch in Detroit. I felt immensely tired and sad from the lessons I had learned this week, this day. I wondered how long my suspension would last.

I scooped up the black toucan feathers from the floor, they might be useful someday. I climbed out a window and began the long walk home.

being with shadow

did i ever tell you
how everything about humanity makes me
so tender
i could be weeping all the time
my eyes see all the darkness
the shadows crawl across the floor
peek from the corners
laugh when i'm laughing
counting it down
they will take it back with the next sentence

i create troughs
threading away from my heart
spilling down my limbs to pulse out
sole of foot, palm of hand
all wide for the ground
in this way, i can open my eyes
since i was a newborn
people have asked me for direction
and i have almost always felt which way to point
away from me, away, away from me

i hear something coming

which is asking me to receive
to stop letting things go through me
to reawaken the black hole at my center
the part powered by what we lose
what we grieve, and by longing
to reach is to live, to reach is sacred
be attached to aliveness
and nothing else
trust: when life is done, it will let you go

a meditation for jordan davis

we make this offering against our will.
we lay down another young man
        (boy. black boy.)
        on this broken altar
to which we seem chained.

this child
made of dirt and star
        whom we cannot respirit
        with our wailing rage
we lift up, in all grace, to the sky.

follow the bright way home, child.
the mystery reminds us
        we do not know death
        we only know this
mortal ground

this land remains
a field of sunken and bled out dreams
        pierced through by
        bordered by
our night terrors of rhythm, of the dark.

adrienne maree brown

we whisper up his river name
as the moon starts to turn away
        will she raise all these tears into an ocean?
        in some way deliver us
distorted in the pale and shivering gaze?

forgive us, we let our faith go again.
that resilient weed, hope
        crept into us, springlike.
        we grew fertile, foolish, delusional
we, who still cannot protect our babies.

we are who will not forget
we are who will not forgive
        until black is beloved
        in all places—
even deep within ourselves.

we now and again sacrifice
flesh, bone, memory, marrow
        dream, son and daughter, future
        though these sweet ripe lives
mean so little here.

now take this youth to some other ground
fly him to where it is his
        or when.
        blow him to when a black child
can stand, and live.

toyin

if it was up to me
i would reach back through time
push away the hands that groped you
amplify your no into an earthquake
it would open the dirt
all would-be assailants crash and slip down
into a realm of heat and solitude and reflection
to sweat out their demons
as you sashayed to a safe home

if it was up to me
if i couldn't stop the crime i'd pull you close
not asking you to ask what you need from me
cold cloth your forehead
thumb away those tears
place my palm over your trembling heart
remind you that miracles
are stronger than violations
and celebrate however you survived

if it was up to me
we would march side by side
me old, slow, and rolling along

adrienne maree brown

you nineteen, and then twenty
and then fifty and then eighty
those cheekbones high enough to hold ages
feeling the worship due for your labor
sacred child warrior, newly arrowed
you took so many unlived stories with you

if it was up to me
you would get what you deserved
black nights full of pleasure
heart swoons and heart aches
dancing in toyin park all sunday
spirit child i hope you cannot even hear pain now
but if it was up to me, to we who needed you
this would never be the way
you got free

– *for oluwatoyin "toyin" salau*

for george floyd: fire

have you learned nothing from sunsets
flaming the entire sky with soft edges
fuchsia periwinkle whisps
taut and temporary nature taking day
inhaling light

have you learned nothing from autumn
blazing the earth with gorgeous death
burnt orange kiss-red fragility reaching
last chance for the sky, floating, releasing
exhaling life

have you learned nothing from war
inferno dappled muddy hose water, puddled
green edged flames of files, photos, losses
our battleground wherever you make us
defend life

have you learned nothing of justice
the deep ever-changing heart must breathe
the fire in our veins needs oxygen,
do not unleash us if you don't want to burn
we'll keep choosing life

adrienne maree brown

have you learned nothing of love
you on your knees but we the ones praying:
let us never give up on each other
even when grief is the only match for the pyre
we honor life

it is the end of a day, a season, a way, an era
the change is tumult, terrifying and beautiful
we will never be convinced to be expendable.
alchemize every death system, liberate
our divine lives

in the corona

we're all in the corona now
jewels, wet crystal, one structure
heavy and precarious
learning how much we live to touch
our never really seen faces

of a species that won't do things for others
even just wash our hands
i slip into obsession with my spray bottle
ashamed (to maybe kill the ocean a bit to feel some comfort)
but i'm an american (my weapons are organic)

i tie a silk floral scarf around my face
to say: i'm terrified of death
but those ghastly masks are sold out
and anyway i have to be me
right til the end

rumors rumble up through airways
that in the pause, the death and questioning
the earth is able to breath 25% more again
we stifle and stretch her gifts when it's up to us
she gasps while we cover our coughs

adrienne maree brown

thinking of the {3000} dead
isn't this the moment we've expected?
able to fly now we test her gravity
"are we seriously going to die?"
answering, we become split futures for the
best species in the universe
(admit it, you wonder...

when you say there's no one out there, you mean no one better
honey i disagree
i turned back from the mountain when a spider said stop

—better lives all around us)
when my lip sweats it feels worse than danger
and i pull my shield down around my neck

my loved ones whisper to each other
"how will we protect our children?"
"it only eats the infirm and elderly"
"so how will we protect them?"
everyone is ours to carry now
the checkmate generation, trying desperately
to evolve the game

but we don't know another one
we don't even know what losing means
it's almost unimaginable
but it's also already happening
"god is change" "the river is very fast now"

i'm scared / i'm trusting
i'm contained / i'm in motion
we're shook / we're normal
we're here / we're gone
and time goes on

A Multi-Year Conversation with the Dinosaur at Chicago O'Hare Airport and Other Fossil-Beings

October 24, 2015

Me: Wow.

Dinosaur in Chicago Airport: Hey.

Me: I feel a little loopy. Have a three-hour layover here because I missed my flight yesterday...only got a few hours of sleep last night.

Dino: What did you do? When you missed the flight?

Me: First I was in denial, I thought I could make it against all the odds. Then I got really angry, and I snapped on this airline worker.

Dino: I see a lot of that.

Me: I bet. I felt so good, using all the worst words I know as I stomped away. But then I was just standing there breathing and... gaining perspective.

Dino: Airports can be good for that. Everyone is taking a huge risk together, going up in the air. Life is on the line; do you want to fly in a funk?

Me: You know I travel so much I don't really consider that part. Sometimes I tune into the magic part of it, like...woah I am in the sky! And I have started meditating on planes.

Dino: But it's just the way you get around. The business travelers, it's like any other shuttle. The kids and newcomers still have wonder. Travel enough and rage is possible.

Me: Yeah exactly. But no matter how angry I was, it wasn't going to get me home. And I thought about how I had missed my flight—it wasn't that worker's fault. I made a series of flippant decisions and expected my usual travel magic to get me there.

Dino: Travel magic? Explain this—I mostly stand here.

Me: Mostly?

Dino: Long story. Travel magic?

Me: Kind of a series of events of irrational good luck. Traffic opens up, I get randomly selected for TSA pre-check, the airport shuttle arrives right when I get to the door, or they had to hold the plane an extra minute for some reason. Things just align and I make it.

Dino: But not this time?

Me: No. And not last time I flew home either. Last time I got on the slow train, bumped my head, lost my water bottle.

Dino: Dang.

Me: Yeah, it was so sad.

Dino: What do you do, in lieu of magic?

Me: You know...both times ended up being really magical in their own ways. The first time I went to the spa til my next flight. Spa Castle, highly recommend it.

Dino: (shrugs)

Me: Oh right. So yesterday, after I was angry with that worker, I dropped back into myself, my center, and realized it wasn't her fault, she was just doing her job. So, when I was rebooked I walked back over to her and I told her I was sorry for taking my anger out on her, that it was a bad moment.

Dino: What did she say?

Me: She said it happens all the time, just let it go. But she teared up, and I teared up. Like, we were having a real human moment all of a sudden, not in the prescribed roles of travel power dynamics.

Dino: What do you mean?

Me: Well it's this weird thing—like in the moment of interaction there is this temporary power that the airline person has over my life and time, but in the long run, I get to leave and go on about my life, not tied to a desk with no windows, finding my zen with miserable people yelling at me when they miss their planes. There's a balance in there somewhere.

Dino: I think I get that. How did you feel after that?

Me: Light. Emotional. Like everything was ok.

Dino: And was it?

Me: Well, yes. I decided to go back and get more time with my nibblings.

Dino: Your what?

Me: Nibblings. The children of my sibling. Nephews and nieces, but not gender determining.

Dino: I like that.

Me: I got it from my friend Tanuja—actually she lives here in Chicago! Maybe you know her?

Dino: Maybe.

(We watch people for a little while)

Me: Are you always here?

Dino: Kind of. I don't remember being somewhere else in my memories. But observing all of you, I get the feeling I belong to a different time place and sometimes I feel like I'm also there.

Me: Has anyone told you things about yourself?

Dino: Yes...but what do they know? I think it's all theory, all they know for sure is these bones go together. Kids roar at me, as if I can't talk. They learn that from adults. And yet here I am, thinking, feeling.

Me: You're really quite thoughtful.

Dino: Thank you. One more question before you go?

Me: Shoot.

Dino: Why do you keep missing flights home?

Me: Good question.

Dino: Seems like something to understand.

Me: This might not be it, but...last year my friend Charity died. And then on October 5 my friend and mentor Grace died. They were both really big parts of my Detroit experience...and I don't quite know...like I know they are gone, and the city is so full of them, but it's full of grief too. And life, moving too fast for my grief. But...when I travel? I feel like they are still there, and it's just me who's gone.

Dino: I feel that sometimes!

Me: Say more?

Dino: Well, part of me knows that everyone I ever knew and loved is gone. But sometimes I think I am just doing this thing, being the dinosaur that wows people at this airport. And that one day I will walk out of here, flesh and bone, and walk towards the tallest trees, and they will be there, just waiting for me.

Me: Does it make you sad?

Dino: Immensely. It's sad to outlive your loved ones, whatever that looks like.

Me: Especially when it's raining. (points at rain)

Dino: Well, yes. Actually, this season might be the saddest season.

Me: So much loss.

Dino: It's also the most beautiful, from my vantage point. Transformation is the most colorful and alive-looking season. I don't know this for sure but I think it's when we are the closest to each other, this side and that.

Me: I like that.

Dino: Me too.

Me: Thanks for this talk, Dinosaur.

Dino: Thank you for stopping to talk with me. I hope you get home safely. And see your loved ones everywhere.

Me: You too, Dino. You too.

Dec 19, 2016

Me: Mammoth! Hi...um do you know Dino?

Mammoth: In Chicago?

Me: Yes!

Mammoth: Yeah, yeah, he's cool. What's up with you?

Me: If I said World War 3, or apocalypse, would that be in bad taste?

Mammoth: No, no. You can't take these things personally.

Me: Never?

Mammoth (laughing): Well, you die either way. You have to make a case for your existence.

Me: But you don't exist anymore! It takes my breath away. There is this sharp set of photos today of an assassination, two dead men, though one still lives in the pictures. And most of us don't get the implications. And it's those two men and it's everything else too.

Mammoth: Perhaps. You humans use most of your capacity to reason for the most elaborate illusions. You aren't a trustworthy species, not yet anyway.

Me: What do you mean?

Mammoth: I mean don't focus on extinction. Live into your particular purpose, become a trustworthy species, earn your miracles. I am extinct and irreplaceable. And am I not magnificent?

Me: Oh, you are.

Mammoth: So are you. So are humans. Just be magnificent.

Me: But how? And why?

Mammoth: How? You already know. Whatever scares you and calls you. And...you don't get to know why. Don't trust anyone who says they know why, trust me.

amb (with side eye): Just you?

Mammoth: And Dino. 🖤

December 22, 2016, Cincinnati Dino

Me: Mysterious creature free of placard, what are you?

Mcfop: I don't remember.

Me: Oh. Well, what do you remember?

Mcfop: Nothing is real.

Me: What do you enjoy?

Mcfop: Bending the illusions to my will.

Me: Is it lonely?

Mcfop: There is no such thing as a solo dream.

Me: It's very early.

Mcfop: It's also very late.

Me: I wish I knew what you were...

Mcfop: It doesn't matter. All that matters is that I am. And how I am.

Me: And how are you?

Mcfop: Free. And hungry.

(amb shuffles away, shook)

July 18, 2018

Me: Dino! I'm feeling sad.

Dino: Isn't feeling such a gift? You're still alive. You still care about things. I remember that, feeling everything so viscerally, feeling longing and something ahead of you.

Me: There was a lot of death this week.

Dino: The cycle is truly mysterious. Learn to grieve, learn to resolve harm without violence. Death will still come, but it won't be from ego, or fear. Practice is the way to make prayers come true.

Me: I'm freaked out about apocalypse. I know everything had to change, but wtf?

Dino: At least you know what's happening. You can be on the life side of history. Stay humble...the big things don't matter as much as the small things.

Me: ?

Dino: Life is about being honest, courageous, connected. And eating. Those things happen at the level of relationship. All the big horrors end because of relationships healing, mending. Or asteroids...which are still small on a planetary scale.

Me: 😄

Dino: Apocalypse has its up sides too. Some corrupt systems only fail by crumbling under their own weight. It's been coming for a long time. It's time for a growth spurt, to shed the skin of small mindedness. Just don't focus too narrowly on the horrors of the present. If you don't shape the future, there will be nowhere to grow towards.

Me: Say that a different way.

Dino: Dreams, visions...are like sun in the consciousness. The present is giving you spiritual seasonal affective disorder. But the sun is in you, you have to become a light, one of many lights that help the species feel inspired to root down, to conserve the water, to reach up to its highest self.

Me: Like be a plant and the sun at the same time?

Dino: The idea that you aren't these things is an illusion anyway. All separation is an illusion. Death is the end of all that ridiculous loneliness.

amb (tearing up): How can I be part of the light when I'm so scared and small?

Dino: Everyone on earth should be scared right now. Scared is part of caring. So is sadness, confusion. Grief. It's how we love. Don't stop caring about life. Don't stop moving towards life. Look at me...I'm still learning.

amb (hugs dinosaur leg): Later Dino.

Dino: Soon amb.

May 6, 2019

Dino: Well, hello there little one!

Me: Dino! Gosh I'm glad to see you.

Dino: Are you ok?

Me: I'm...yes. I missed my flight and am feeling very negatively towards this airport.

Dino: Is it the airport's fault?

Me: Mostly. But I also know that this airport is slow. You're the best part of it...I didn't give myself enough time for the reality of this place.

Dino: What else is new?

Me: Lol. Oh. Oh, you're asking! Um...abundance. I'm having a very beautiful abundant life. I feel like usually when I see you, I'm kinda sad. There's a lot of complex and tender things in motion around me. But right here (points to self), I'm fundamentally content and just trying to manage for the so-muchness of it all.

Dino: I'm happy to hear that!

Me: How about you?

Dino: I'm also really content. I watch so many transitions. Last year I started seeing what patterns I could see in all of the transitions, got curious again after a century of malaise.

Me: Oh wow...what patterns are you noticing?

Dino: There's a pattern of drama...you all seem to hit emotional highs and lows much faster and louder than i've ever seen before. But there's also a growing pattern of comfort—it's a small increase, but people are offering each other comfort more easily, telling each other what does and doesn't matter.

Me: What do you make of these patterns?

Dino: Awareness is a sword with so many edges. Awareness brings fear, facing reality can be terrifying. Awareness is where agency is born. Awareness can be torture and/or freedom. But kindness eases change. Especially inevitable change.

Me: Dino, do you know Octavia Butler?

Dino: She flew through here a few times...why?

Me: She thought that thought too: kindness eases change. Thanks for the reminder. I haven't been kind enough today.

Dino: Well. When you choose a change, you can begin to be different immediately. I think you all forget that.

Me: You're my favorite dinosaur, Dino.

Dino (blushing): I bet you say that to all your dinos.

Me: I generally love all fossils, whole or partial...but there's only one Dino.

Dino: You're my favorite amb too you know. *hugs*

Me: See you soon.

Dino smiles and nods and goes back to the patterns.

March 25, 2020

Me: Dino? Dino? I'm trying telepathy to reach you because a lot is going on that I could use some ancient insight on. And frankly I don't know when I'll be allowed in the Chicago Airport again.

Dino: I'm here.

Me: Wow! Wow I feel you!

Dino (smiling): I'm always available. But if I explained how, it might mess up our whole thing.

Me: Like I told Santa, I choose the magic.

Dino: Every time. So. Are you here to tell me where the masses have gone?

Me: You noticed?

Dino: I almost exclusively see in patterns these days. The river is a stream, the stream becoming a drizzle.

Me: There's a virus. It passes with no symptoms, hides inside us for two weeks, and it's bigger than our healthcare system.

Dino: Nefarious. Everywhere?

Me: At first it wasn't, but now it really is. So, we're all staying home to try and slow it down while we find cures, vaccines, face masks, ventilators. Thousands of people are dying.

Dino: I'm so sorry to hear that.

amb (hesitant): Is it our asteroid, Dino?

Dino (pausing a moment): You're really scared, huh?

Me: Terrified.

Dino: But...isn't this your thing? Change, apocalypse? The collapse of capitalism? Right relationship to the earth?

Me: Totally. But I don't want to lose the people I love. And I can't make everyone stay home—I've tried. And I don't want to die yet.

Dino (takes a deep breath): It's hard when death comes in big waves. So much grief all at once.

Me: And for what? Earth is getting this brief moment of respite, respiration. But so many bosses are still endangering their workers and plotting ways to capitalize this crisis. Is this the end of capitalism, or the beginning of global authoritarian rule, or extinction, or liberation? What are we meant to learn?

Dino: Woah. Hey now. It generally doesn't help to make too much meaning of things that are still unfolding. From within the storm, vision is limited. And you, my friend, you and your species are in the storm.

Me: But deeper meaning helps me get thru the hard parts of life.

Dino: Hmmm.

Me: I need something to control. A narrative will do in absence of order, safety. I think I'll become useless without meaning. The grief. The fear, anxiety, suspicion, sinophobia. The blur of my empathetic self feeling everything. I need something to root in to.

Dino: I feel your chaos. Perhaps instead of meaning, it's time to revisit destiny.

Me: "The destiny of earthseed is to take root amongst the stars."

Dino: Mmmm!

Me: Octavia Butler wrote that.

Dino: She was always nice to me.

Me: That's amazing. I have been rethinking her destiny. Or our way of understanding it.

Dino: Say more.

Me: I always thought it purely meant space travel. But she struggled with sequels, because no world she found in her imagination was as right for us as earth. And on earth, we are amongst the stars, here and now. This is a perfect home spinning in space. We may even be celestial to someone else.

Dino (mulling it over): Hmmmmmmm.

Me: I think we need to root here. Re-root. Choose here.

Dino: Perhaps. Or maybe all of this, this way of being—on earth or in space—just isn't *your* destiny. Meaning, maybe *human* destiny isn't the most important thing.

amb, sad eyes: Now *you* say more.

Dino: I often think that we are all experiments of an Earth figuring out *her* destiny. She likes living things. She likes sentient creatures that love and make family and eat. In our experiment, she learned she wanted a species that could look up to the stars, defend her from asteroids.

Me: Oh wow. So...our experiment could be teaching her to not let evil people accumulate all the power and money?

Dino (chuckling): Perhaps.

Me: Or?

Dino: Perhaps it's just time to see how what you call evil, what I call wrong relationship, how that can spread, can disconnect a species from its future.

Me: Right. It's like the virus itself, invisible. But making the wrong structures and systems and beliefs so visible.

Dino: We can never teach how evil a thing is better than it will show us itself, with time.

Me: But it's in all of us. Or most, to varying degrees. This I, I, I, exceptionalism.

Dino: Hm.

Me: Sorry. I want to let in new perspective. It's just that all the problems are so big. And intertwined. And I'm supposed to be one of the "hopeful" ones.

Dino: What was that?

Me: What?

Dino: That...tone. You sound...

Me: Sharp? Ugh. Sorry—that happens when I'm trying to be funny but I feel something else. Sad. Scared. Grief.

Dino: Ah humans. Tone is the tip of your internal icebergs.

Quiet together for a while.

Dino: Tell me something. Can you imagine being sad and scared and still feeling hopeful?

Me: It's hard.

Dino: Can I offer something?

Me: Please.

Dino: It's not an asteroid.

amb (shoulders dropping): Oh.

Dino: Hope, hopefulness, that's the realm of the survivors. It's not too late for y'all. Grief shows us what we love, what we most want to protect. It swallows everything extraneous. And so much of what you love is still here. And tomorrow is another miraculous opportunity to change, to protect it.

Me: Dang, Dino.

Dino: Ha. I guess I've been a little scared too. I don't want you to give in, give up.

Me (hugging Dino's telepathic neck for a good cry)

Dino (gently, into amb's telepathic hair): We're all rooting for you, you know. All the extinct ones. We're all at your backs. You humans have so much beauty in you.

Me: There *is* so much superhumanity and kindness and humility and change happening. And humor. And dancing online across all borders. And caretaking. And new kinds of honesty. And heroic communal isolation. And choosing to protect the future.

Dino: Very good. That's life. Grieve like the trees in October. But don't forget you are nature, and spring is certain.

Me: I am glad to know we can be together in this way.

Dino: Me too. Isolated is one perspective of this moment. Deeply connected is another.

Me: Love you, Dino.

Dino: Love you too.

toni morrison, fly

so. you set down all that weight
gave up all that shit?

cleared the ghosts' hands away from your heels?
straightened the wide brims of their hats?
kissed the men on soft smirked cheeks?
danced beyond the reach of your children?

you knew how to end the long tale

precisely

you knew how to meander without waste
you kept our attention on their faces

you heard the black women
folded, almost disappeared between the pages
but you told their stories
and made them our stories

we all learned to love our eyes
we all remembered that we are not wrong

adrienne maree brown

we all looked at whiteness with a withering eye
we all knew the cost of enslavement

we all needed you
we are all grateful

lies

i am stronger than the oceans
in this moment i need for nothing

i am a clear day to the horizon
i can even see tomorrow

i leave my memories in the past
my forgiveness is wholistic

i carry no heavy regrets
my songs have found a resting place

my childhood is behind me now
i can even see god's face

still of it

i am still of it
this world
full of sorrows

i trace the lines back
from my fingertips
to my heart

the feelings all start with distinction
such unique purpose
only to pool and to pulse together

and i want to un-utter
certain passions
in my cellular structure

i taste on my tongue
her absent kiss
the three dead names i always called him
the wet hitch of goodbye
as that failed father enters his prison
the acidic bite in detroit
gasping as hands tighten at her neck

and they bruise her soil
and the sharp raging bitter
of gaza
my god, some god, somebody...

can i blame it on the moon
she thinks we are hers
because we are water
with her ink on our spines

can i blame it on mercury
patterning fuckery
is this envy or legacy
all this human catastrophe

can i recall the prophet
who spoke of joy and sorrow
carving out spaces
from each other's bodies

why don't we find out
there is no place outside ourselves
to put this daunting sorrow
while we breath we are still of it

what is the science
for this bent over grief
crying us to sleep
in this solitary cosmos

can i still wonder
feel wonder
when i am still of it

...

adrienne maree brown

when my breath stops
flood me with joy
i feel room for oceans
here in my veins

the tangerine taught me how to die (or how to open)

thumbnail splitting peel
pulling off her gown in one piece, unveiling
flinging shocks of essence into the air
briefly visible
the bitter scent split from the
sweet promise

but still not open

the exhale of connective tissue
one circle becomes many moons
each part similar (normal)
each piece unique (special)
centered, then piled in my palm
clinging, releasing, wide, falling apart

but still not open

on my busy tongue the taut skinbody
veined and ripe, perfect and ready
(and still not open)

adrienne maree brown

it is only the gnashing of my teeth, the suckling
the bursting of life, lips to throat, the swallow
the total destruction of self for the unknown

now, now we are open

staggering collective emotional burnout

some creatures swallow mulberry leaves
spin silk from their longing to be set free
others cast silk from dark spinnerets
praying fat prey will crash and feed
some swing from branch and vine and sky
with babies who learn young not to let go
others form circles in the ice and snow
protecting their children, whose wings do not fly

we spin in the solitary cage of success
thrash against webs made of concrete and chrome
let go too soon of the wisest hands
always try first to stand here alone
because someone told us this death is our nature
solitude deified to nomenclature
but now we are crawling through our telephones
having suffered enough, we surrender to home

inching there we pass in the dark and fog
last week's collapse strolling back our way
not healed, not whole, but dignified

able to look us all in the eye
burning anguish held, bright flaws dismissed
deep rest affirmed, furrowed foreheads kissed
we all need our mothers, and they're all too far
and we're surprised again at how normal we are

earth do what you will / forgive us

earth do what you will
mother father creator home
full of wrath, molten, tremoring
you show us how to live and to hurt you
all our life, we spiral out from your body
stardust and sea, anemone and feather
flesh and flower, metal and bone

earth forgive us
all children are greedy
we all demand love beyond what we can give
we all expect your miraculous patience
we are nonsensical, ungrateful
we take your hours, wooden toys, all the sweet
the attention, life force, and all your peace

earth do what you will
how long have we terrorized you
we violate your soft/sacred-ness, deny
that you are changed and changing
that your heart is broken, spirit struggling for respite

adrienne maree brown

venom spilling from the wounds, swelling the surface
catastrophic chasm opening within
but earth please forgive us
for we are split as a species
let us who see you and love you
let us join you, we can tell you where the hurt begins
we can tell you where it ends
let us stay and whisper love songs to you
in the turning of the cosmos. let us stay.
earth do what you will
cast us into the endless sky
make us brief

earth forgive us
before we learn to apologize
see us whole

earth do what you will
say finally, enough
take back each perfect gift

earth—forgive us
for we think we are walking
when you carry us

earth do what you will
we thought we could live without you
we have been wrong every day

earth forgive us
every step away from you is an error
even now, we love you

Time Rebel

The Author Corresponds from In-Cycle

"The curse of it all is that we have missed out on the cyclical nature of time, living inside the cycle of the whole earth as a linear species.

"What if we were able to ride the cycle of time more like certain trees and flowers do, perennial? What if we could reconfigure how human bodies use time altogether? There may be a benefit to extended hibernation, for instance, or even a period that looks like death. There may be an abundance to aligning the spring energy of humans for mating and dating, at least regionally.

"If we harness the energy of living into a clearer biocycle, we could, perhaps, approach immortality. And evolve into a species solving for the problems of immortality, versus the current problems of hyper mortality, and construct-instigated mortality, like being killed inside a misguided bioconcept of race, or the false binarized concepts of gender, sexuality, ability.

"A viable theory is that by aligning ourselves with time cycles, we could become more compatible with more planets, relinquishing the idea of a singular home base of 'now,' and embracing a divergent reality of time wherein the present moment is "here," knowing without hesitation that other timelines are unfolding in their cycles. Sage and sweet potato aren't devastated by a cold snap, nor are they perturbed

by the instability of human timelines except where we directly impact land. Plucking the fruit doesn't devastate the tomato vine, or the mycelium behind the mushrooms. I believe we could similarly free ourselves from the crisis of constantly pending death. We could embrace the cycle of life. We could keep going, indefinitely."

Our founder, Aleutius Peddy Getatchew, is a holographic force in the middle of our collective consciousness. We hear her voice, probing possibility, reading from the brief manifesto that seeded our original experiment. We all know these words if not by heart, then by rhythm. She is neutral in the hologram, a purplish tint to her skin and hair, a softness of mouth and nose, an obscuring of identifying racial data that makes it impossible to guess her lineage. We aren't supposed to care, and I suppose in another hundred cycles, no one will.

I care, but I've always been rebellious. Her features, even softened, mirror mine across all time revisions and light years. My name is Alayna Getatchew, and I am the founder's great great granddaughter. My skin is deep brown like hers was, my eyes cornflower blue, my heart curious. I am one of the last unplanned expansions of our space-bound species, the tributary of human life that chose to flow away from the original ocean planet.

We live on Earth-9 as a perennial people, and this ceremony is one of recommitment. Every cycle we come together, we remember our origin story as we celebrate the harvest of this planet, and the harvest of our own energy. We decide to continue the cycle, to hibernate through the cold phase once more. When spring comes, we will decide as a community if we should expand again, and if we do then the child or children of that expansion will be our community focus until they are grown. They will learn the rhythm of life that yields permanence, the passion and hibernation, the centering of life, the relinquishing of competition. The dreams from cold phase which shape our lives during green phase.

Every planet that we can inhabit, every earth, has at least one cold phase and an average temperature range of 10–25 degrees celsius. We intentionally rest when the temperature drops, regenerating our systems enough to move through another cycle. An earth is simply a cycle-based planet, in which life is looping through conditions that repeat at the scale of measurable experience. We have identified seventy-three earths so far, and we have people in cycle on fifty-six of them. Our oldest humans are from the first generation born outside of linear time, 250 earth years ago.

I'm writing to you Original Earthlings about all of this because I want to opt out of the harvest cycle.

I want to die.

And I think the only way to do so is to return to the time construct of Earth-1. I have studied you obsessively. You all made up a starting date and orient everything around it. You know humans randomly selected a time when the cycle of a year repeats, but there's also a sense in the culture that the repetition is both an ending, and a beginning; that something radically different can happen in what you call a January than in a November. I know this is the way of my ancient ancestors as well, though I honestly don't understand it—but I do know that because you live with this sense of scarcity and limitation, you use up your life force so quickly that you rarely get to experience wisdom, spiritual awakening, peace. I would not trade with you if I wanted to live.

To be clear, my desire to die is not a rejection of my people, or of the miracle of life as we harvest it. I really am so grateful to have had such an outstanding life, I have delighted in it. I have experienced love as security, I have been able to heal every rift in me and between me and others as they arose, never needing to rush and be anywhere but loving, I have written two million songs, I have known years of solitude and years of familial chaos and years of easeful, honest romance.

But I think, I suspect, that by creating an extended life that could yield immortality, we may have removed something fundamental to the pleasure of life. It appears life goes on forever. We can do anything we commit to doing, because all things are a matter of practice and innovation, and we have endless room in which to practice and experiment.

But the preciousness is gone.

I read about it. I love the literature from Earth-1 even though my mothers all warn me that it is the love language of arsonists. Love, of a lover, a parent, a child, a friend—love used to be a fire that would blaze without burning out and mark everyone who felt it.

Now everything is so logical, so clear. With every need met we deny ourselves the delicious tension of longing, of not knowing, of savoring the time because it will end.

I am a scholar and this would be a study, the data remitting to my people to understand if returning to Earth-1 and the mortal cycle of time is even possible.

Will you negotiate with me? Perhaps a trade—one for one? One Original Earthling who wants to step outside of time and join the Earth-9 community in exchange for me returning to Earth-1? I don't mind submitting to a year of interviews and observation. But then I want permission to deteriorate, to burn my fire until my future is made of ashes.

The Author Corresponds From Earth-1, Precycle

I don't know what I expected, but it wasn't this.

I thought people on Earth-1 would be like prayers in motion, aware of the sacred brevity of their lives, falling in love and worshiping the birds which fly everywhere so freely.

I thought there would be a humbling emphasis on the lives of newborns and children, a centering of that remarkable wonder of visible need and growth.

I thought everyone would be working together on a unified offer towards the many alien species which wait to meet us.

I thought in the absence of forever, the original Earthlings would be rooted in curiosity and wonder, reveling in the possibility of each moment, each collection of sixty moments, each twenty-four hour cycle. This original planet is still the most generative in the known universe, and perhaps the most beautiful.

But these Earthlings, with some small exceptions, ignore the miracle of place. There is an emphasis on posturing, performance and projection—it is impossible to tell what is real. They are all in constant competition with each other, as if playing a game. But the rules are ever changing and no one seems to win.

The poor think the prize is wealth.

The workers think the prize is power.

The wealthy and powerful are miserable and lonely, and think the prize is fame and recognition.

The famous are hypervigilant, insecure and paranoid. The recognized feel like imposters, and they all think the prize is privacy, boundaries and borders.

The borders are contentious and there's so much unnecessary death.

They still think of themselves more as categories and subcategories than a species.

They don't even realize they are stuck in a loop of ego, of self without larger purpose.

And they are in such a crisis, with so few clues. Yesterday I saw news of a tornado the width of seven city blocks. It looked like half the horizon was spinning into shadow, sucking up homes. Every place on Earth-1 is besieged by extreme catastrophic weather.

The people who took me in here are a group of Indigenous scientists from hundreds of tribal lines. They said that humans have angered the sky. The storms are chaotic and constant, and more and more of human life here is lived underground, searching for freshwater, eating earthworm stew and root vegetables from heirloom seeds.

Everyone has a story to tell me, and I listen to all of it, recording all of it, sending my data home. I ask them why they are using the planet in such a suicidal way, and their stories all tell of how it is someone else's fault. As if that matters.

The terrible and interesting thing I didn't expect to find here is that the humans of Earth-1 have almost used up their collective time. And once they do, their concept of time will die with them. When I realized this I wept, and many times since then, when it is made clear to me again, I weep uncontrollably for days. It is not my own sadness, but the general sadness of this dying race, aware that it is faltering but unable to pivot into even the most elementary collective practices.

The only thing that feels certain here is death.

I feel the deterioration in my bones already, the impact of increased toxins that have permeated even the ether. I feel the weight of collective urgency dragging me forward, and the heft of collective trauma dragging me backwards. I taste in the food the presence of plastic. It won't take long, a decade or two of Earth-1 time, to die naturally. And if the suffering is simply too great, there are other ways.

I am documenting everything precious that remains. There's still so much! The ocean has swallowed many coastal cities, creating these epic landscapes of submerged buildings acting as metallic islands, barnacled, home to growing colonies of birds and sea life. There are ruins in their forests, ruins along their droughted plains, ruins of old highways from the oil age—but there's an undeniable beauty in the reclamation by the wild. On the volcanic and mountainous island I have chosen as my final home, there are these rainbow colored bombastic birds called peacocks, and a fruit called passion.

There is still love. I have found someone undaunted by my story of coming from Earth-9—skepticism is the primary response of most humans, because I negotiated this exchange with the Native Sciences Consortium instead of one of the barely functional nation-state governments. But my lover is from that longer known lineage of Indigenous peoples called Hawaiians, and she believes, and she is patient, skilled at touch, kind. She has lost everyone she loved before me in this lifetime to death. We met on a sand dune, both breathlessly watching their sun come into view. I told her I am excited to die, and she laughed and said, "Me too." I thought I had known romance before but, as I suspected, it is a wildly different experience when death is inevitable. There is an erotic ecstasy that is rooted in how temporary the body is. Her perfect hips will die, my reaching fingers will die, there is only this moment. Imagine how compelling love and pleasure have to be, to keep offering it to each other, keep letting it reconstruct our hearts, even after we have known grief?

Inside the devastation of late-stage original Earthlings, this love is worth all of my research, theory, sacrifice and risk. My founder-ancestor would be mystified by my conclusions, but the pattern suggests, perhaps, that we have to be willing to die to fully live.

The Author Corresponds from Death

We are all one. In many iterations. There is one great cycle that moves from the divine imagination into form. From single-celled organism to whale, from material to spiritual, from singular to complex, from love through love to love. I am ether and energy and heat, but I have been many forms since human and now I am so bright. There is coherence, sentience, even now. We stars are thinking of you.

The Author Corresponds from Heaven

you think maturity is being an elder human
maturity is becoming a black hole
we who are made of stardust die
and the dust returns to dust
folded into or blown over the surface of whatever planet
we have known as home
and the star in us returns to the stars

adrienne maree brown

soul being the bright force of the universe
we materialize and split
materialize and explode
materialize and dissipate
until we learn
to die as if simply falling down
over and over, childlike until we learn
to live as if, precariously, standing

it takes us lifetimes, so very long
to learn
to be
but then life begins
we become our own gravity
collective bodies of soul belonging to each other
we are each other's root in the vastness of space

and one day
when we have done everything a star can do
burn, grow, beam
participate in constellation, burst beyond ourselves
we become so thick with ground
that we finally learn to hold on
to everything
to reality and imagination
in form and ever changing
swallowing only that which is ready to be tasted

inside every black hole is a heaven
a state of being
capable of abundance, solitude, magic and rest
with a boundary
where every construct of time stops
because we need not measure eternity

everything in the known and unknown realms
will eventually be folded into such heaven
the galaxies exist to feed gravity
and gravity exists to hold life

once swallowed
we can be present
by which we mean full on the present
which was never a moment
which was always here
in need of nothing
at peace in the glory
of enough

spell for grief or letting go

adequate tears twisting up directly from the heart
and rung out across the vocal chords until only a gasp remains;
at least an hour a day spent staring at the truth in numb silence;

a teacup of whiskey held with both hands
held still under the whispers of permission
from friends who can see right through "ok" and "fine";

an absence of theory;

flight, as necessary;

poetry, your own and others, on precipice
abandonment, nature and death;
courage to say what has happened
however strangling the words are
...and space to not say a word;

a brief dance with sugar, to honor the legacies of coping that got
you this far;

sentences spoken with total pragmatism that provide clear guidance of some direction to move in, full of the tender care and balance of choice and not having to choose;

screaming why, and/or expressing fury at the stupid unfair fucking game of it all (this may include hours and hours, even lifetimes, of lost faith);

laughter, undeniable and unpretended;

a walk in the world, all that gravity, with breath and heartbeat in your ears;

fire, for all that can be written;

moonlight—the more full, the more nourishing;

stories, ideally of coincidence and heartache and the sweetest tiny moments;

time, more time and then more time...enough time to remember every moment you had with that one now taken from you, and to forget to think of it every moment;

and just a glimpse of tomorrow, either in the face of an innocent or the realization of a dream.

this is a nonlinear spell. cast it inside your heart, cast it between yourself and any devil. cast it into the parts of you still living.

remember you are water. of course, you leave salt trails. of course, you are crying.

flow.

p.s. if there happens to be a multitude of griefs upon you, individual and collective, or fast and slow, or small and large, add equal parts of these considerations:

- that the broken heart can cover more territory.
- that perhaps love can only be as large as grief demands.
- that grief is the growing up of the heart that bursts boundaries like an old skin or a finished life.
- that grief is gratitude.
- that water seeks scale, that even your tears seek the recognition of community.
- that the heart is a front line and the fight is to feel in a world of distraction.
- that death might be the only freedom.
- that your grief is a worthwhile use of your time.
- that your body will feel only as much as it is able to.
- that the ones you grieve may be grieving you.
- that the sacred comes from the limitations.
- that you are excellent at loving.

Fables
&
Spells
for
Celestial
Bodies

oh great mystery

oh great mystery
we need your help right now
for we are in an impossible situation
which we must survive

our nation is caught up in conspiracy theories
demons and superiority weaken the mind
and we have so many people who would rather
dominate than do their share of societal labor
how do we break the tie of slavery
oh universe we need your help
help to clear the vision of those who cannot see
the dazzling nature of existence in each being

we have those who have turned from the earth
our only home. our only viable home.
they treat her and all who can produce life as machines
to make without ceasing what they then take
without hesitation, gratitude or gentleness
how do we break the tie of slavery
oh universe we need your help
help us honor the places where abundant life blooms
protect the consent and agency and song of earth

there are so many who have felt the explosive power
of death in their hands, in their bodies, in their imaginations
they roam amongst us, armed; crash into humans praying
with their bodies to be deemed worthy of protection
from our most abusive relationship: our nation
how do we break the tie of slavery
how do we quell the addiction to blood and completion
to power that breaks bones and opens flesh
help us relinquish the pleasure of violence

oh great mystery
oh great change which has a commitment to moving towards
life
we struggle with humility and now i see i should have started
with my heart on the ground
pulsing against gravity, in supplication
it isn't that i doubt your resilience
only that i see how you might have concluded
that we no longer wish to be a part
of your constant changes and the magic of spring
so long have we hibernated in ignorance and isolation
so universe here i want to whisper to you
what has been flowing through my veins
i want to live, i want to want to live
i want us to live, i want us to want to live

all who can love the cherry blossom
the glorious fire of fall
the three eggs opening to chirping children
the magnificence of storms
the electric tapestry of mycelium
the persistence of the succulent in my winter window
all who can love the song of humpback mother whales
the rush of a room full of people telling their favorite memories
the drum beat of a child gleefully chasing her dreams upstairs

the laughter of humans not performing
all who can love their own perfect bodies
after a lifetime of being told they are flawed,
all who can blurt out their heartache
before it becomes a weapon
all who can say yes and no and mean it
all who fumble at every turn but are still worthy
of love and connection and being held
and forgiveness and patience and one more chance

universe i, we, surrender to whatever chance you will give us
universe i, we, trust that we cannot know everything
about the divine nature of change and how discomfort
is what presses us into pearl and bursts us out
of seed and shell and cocoon
and perhaps you are helping us to see
how tight and breakable our current iteration is
and i am saying and singing that i see it
yes i feel the claustrophobic nature of our current ways of
thinking
and i surrender to more, we surrender to more.
we pray that you open the way to us, with us
the way that seems impossible
with all the corruption and closed hearts
and systemic denial of miracles

and even, quite frankly, the willful stupidity of reason and
emotion

but we small and mighty choose life, choose this life
we choose the struggle of navigating dissonance and finding
rhythm
we choose the brick winters and the terror of letting the child
walk to school alone and even the nightmares that remind us how
much we love sunrise

we pray today for sunrise
we pray today for tomorrow
we pray for generations beyond terror
we pray today for memory
for every single person to remember back through their lineage
all the way to when yours was the only voice they knew
guide us all in your way, weave us back into the tapestry
let us be earthseed
let us be earthseed
let us be earthseed
again

(thank you, octavia e. butler, for earthseed, *and lucille clifton for the reminder to listen to what comes before dawn)*

waning

slowly i collapse
lose light lose warmth
forget everything i ever knew about bright
it is time again to know nothing
to be still and silent
to wait and wonder
to notice exactly what i need so completely
that it pulls me through shadow
pulls me through the cold of my own isolation
back, slower than a dream
faster than a season
i hear everyone whispering:
plant everything now
plant love the shape of gods
the handprints of children allowed to say no
plant quiet contemplation of miracles
the ripple of orgasmic awe
plant the undulation, the pulse, the fusion
plant even the idea of a wave
and let the ocean flood you by morning

flower moon spell

the petals:

how many witches must cast a spell before it can protect our families, our bodies, our land? the sacred ritual of birth? the innocence in each of us?

how much abundance is needed to satisfy the hunger of cancer? the grasp of loneliness, the ache of desire, the pulse of greed calling?

how many prayers must cross in the sky, at odds, to confuse the gods into hiding? (for isn't it true that the idea of god corrupts us, tricks us into diminishing our divinity until we forget how to be answers?)

how many children must be warriors for their future, and how do we forget war for the sake of a future?

how many nights will the moon pull the tide of this blood river, until the trauma settles, and even the memory of the trauma, and even the anger and forgetting and getting lost in the shape of the trauma? how many nights until it flows clear in us?

how much dirt must we grip into with our roots before we can trust ourselves to grow all the way out into the light?

flower moon spell:

moon help us shine into the impossible places, and then shed the pain, carrying the lessons into the dark, new, and fertile night. teach us the spells of this time.

gift us abundance without attachment.

let us pray by loving each other without conditions.

let us play, singing blurred words and dancing alone, surrounded by love and the possibility of love.

over and over, take what we can't carry, with ashes, with water and whispers. and then let the nightbirds sing us to sleep.

humble us, remind us that the dirt is home, the dirt, the mess, is us...the petals fall away.

a moon kind of night

tonight, the moon is bright
not full but so full
telling me she can see the sun
even when i can't
she can see the light of all our lives
she can share it with me

a creature moves through the woods
and i think, it's bedtime
but that little hungry one
guided by senses i can never know
says there is life in the dark
and beauty...don't be so scared

and i am scared
to feel so much about
the so far away people and places
the so mysterious future
i can't save anything
only love it all so much

and love moves through the fear
reaching and touching me

adrienne maree brown

showing me i am more than i know
and we are, all, doing our best
to be wild, still
to be free

and the moon moves over me, moves through
unapologetic in her power
reminding me i am hers
reminding me i am tides
reminding me i am full
even here, even now, in the shadows

The Marsians

Author's Note: Because the people of the planet we call Mars do not use the same language, names, or gods as we do on Earth, this text has been written in a compassionate way that those on Earth can comprehend—this includes the names and dialogue of the characters, and the name of the planet itself, which those of the planet refer to with a gutteral gust of wind. Something is lost in translation, but what is gained is hopefully the possibility of understanding.

The Marsians were, once again, on high alert. Another odd, antiquated and giant craft was arriving soon from Earth, searching for life. Again.

Si, showing themselves as round and obsidian, was annoyed on the way to work, "Can't they take a hint? Dead planet. Dead planet. Nothing to breathe here."

"Isn't dead planet their favorite flavor?" Mu had an ironic tinge of red to their communication.

Ahsh exhaled and blew Si and Mu about a bit with the gravity of a calm. "You judge them as if you never had extra-Marsian curiosities. They don't understand how it all works yet."

"Yes and how far do they have to go before we explain it to them?" Si snapped back, regaining control over their location. Si knew better than to critique the way Ahsh communicated but resented the physicality of it.

"Do you not trust the core circle?" Ahsh fluttered a gray area across their body surface that was equal parts defensive and righteous.

Mu pivoted between them, "Oh Ahsh, you know it's easier to trust something when you are in and of it and get to witness all the processes. We lowly Marsians who are not core are asked to offer an impossible amount of trust to whatever you in the core decide."

Marsians had a long practice of avoiding the detection of their young, brash neighbors. They populated most of their planet but were subterranean because the surface of Mars was too cold for them. And Marsians operated at a scale that Earthlings would not be able to see or recognize, a relatively atomic species. The core circle was responsible for developing strategies to make Mars look uninteresting, historical, past life. Somehow they weren't clear enough.

"Fair," Ahsh sighed again, this time without force. Then Ahsh was gone, and Si and Mu were pulled towards each other by the tiny collapse of space where Ahsh had been.

"They fucking suck." Si's black surface was roiling, a heat rising up off of them as a barely detectable shimmer.

"The circle? The humans?" Mu was ready to co-complain in either direction.

"Have you ever noticed that they get it when they look at us, theoretical us, but not when they look at themselves?"

"You mean cause they call us Martians?"

"Yes, they know if we existed, we would have to be *of* this planet. But they don't call themselves Earthlings. They don't know where they belong."

"Our ancestors went through many foolish phases too."

Si mulled on this, accessing a flurry of collective memories. "True. We named things. We thought *self* meant separate. Still. Like we are designed to be in space and we still stay down here where it's warm. Their planet is perfectly suited for them!"

"What really upsets you though?" Mu had a soft blue texture now and Si felt appeased in spite of the rage. Mu could always do that.

"The waste?" Si went sullen and moldy with grief and nostalgia. "They are on a surface still. They are flesh still. Earth is more than Mars ever was or will be for them. Mars is just right for us, now, but it's because we mostly thrive in concept, content to be tucked against the molten core, needing nothing to be large or visible. These caves of consciousness satisfy us forever."

Mu was apart and then together with Si then, pressing the two beings into one for a moment, dissolving the border. "You sound unsatisfied with our existence here. Nothing the Earthlings do can really impact us here. Why are you distraught?"

Si didn't have to speak. What flitted through the space of them was bits of visual data of Earth. They all loved the Earth as much as they resented the Earthlings. Based on Marsian research and imagination, Earth was a rare planet, able to support surface level life. No other species the Marsians had connected with had such a privilege. No one alive on Mars could name an ancestor who had lived on their planet's surface, though the historical rumors made a big deal of that gigantic, embodied past. Si's study had unveiled that the history of their embodiment had begun to show up around the time they'd become a way of life on Earth, so it was hard to trust. Historical imagination was the most fallible.

"I want them to go home. And I want them to love it." Si let all their longing pour out with this confession.

Mu gathered the honest, expressed emotion and flung it away from them, back into the world. When the truth was cleared from them both, Mu pulled back into their own distinct self. Si laughed, with touches of both bitterness and relief.

In a few days the Earth probe would land and begin to rove along the surface of rocks and barren hills, some of which reached across the universe to the blue and green neighbor in the distance. The Marsians would move underground to the other side of the planet and live in the heightened state of stillness required to ensure they didn't set off any bleeps or bloops in the technology of humanity. Si, and Mu, and Ahsh would wait until the coast was clear—hours, days, months. And then their forever would go on, in the warmth, in the brick red darkness.

The Virgoan

Here you are, awake at an odd hour when the humans around you are all dormant. And you seem to be wrestling over something where right and wrong apply. And you are a Virgo, of those chosen by the sacred numeral 9 which is the shape of our galaxy.

For all of these reasons, as well as your lifelong commitment to finding the right path, we have chosen you.

Who are we?

In your language-identities we'll call ourselves the Virgoan. We primarily visit your planet through brief Virgo occupations such as this one. Our language-identities, including our self-names, are not translatable or text communicative.

We have learned seventeen Earth-4 languages and feel certain we have selected the correct one for you. These will still feel like foreign thoughts, because they are, and will be for the duration of time we are with you, but we want you to understand us perfectly.

Please relax in the knowledge that we will leave without overwhelming you.

We commune with Virgo selves because you have a tendency to be right, or concerned with rightness, and thus seem most aligned with our core species value: *There is a right way to do everything.*

So far, we've learned a few of the clearly right things on Earth-4, based on our studies of the United States of America, Bolivia, Costa Rica, Mali, Bali, and Antarctica:

Toilet paper goes over but is still a less effective way of cleaning the waste holes than direct water.

Economy is a place to cooperate.

Respect and/or call your parents.

Keep your body active.

Violence is not useful.

Whereas some planets' high-species notice right things and orient their societies around them, Earth-4 humans seem relatively disinterested in applying rightness towards their own sentient lived experience. Even the things I've mentioned here are not universally practiced. In this way you are unique in the known universe, and we seek to understand you.

It is a pleasure to interact with you and show you who we are. We want to share with you all of the right ways of which we are aware, in hopes that you can integrate them into your societies.

First, however, a brief history:

We come from Imph. Our planet is conceptual, a culmination of consciousness and longing that orbits a small black sun. We traverse space by making psychic connections with available sentient beings on various planets, learning the nature of those planets without doing harm.

If we can, we help by offering the best possible next steps for rightness. Then, if it is right, we have visitations, bringing your consciousness to experience Imph, and physically transporting ourselves to your planet to commune with your leaders.

We learned to journey across space in this efficient way through long periods of deep meditation that allowed us to comprehend that all sentience is interconnected.

Our sentience predates your planetary existence by 3.7 million Earth-4 years, so there should be no feelings of inadequacy or shame related to your relative lack of collective awareness.

Why 4? We note your planet as the 4th one we have discovered that self-identifies with the base substance of earth, dirt, or soil. This literal self-identity is reflected in the 762 Oceans, 46 Airs, 17 Golds, and millions of other base substance identifier planets.

We have many parallels in our history to yours, many periods of great mistakes and short-term thinking. We offer this not as criticism, but to create hope. When we realized, roughly 2 million years ago, there *is* a right way to do everything, it was a liberation into universal alignment.

We find that there is a limit to what any member of a new species can integrate at one time, so we will end our first visit here. We will return in the time period of one Earth-4 moon cycle.

We have returned.

We are excited to see in your memory access that you have been sharing news of our visit and the things we shared. We are disappointed to see the derision in the responses of some humans with whom you have shared our existence.

In the past moon we have identified additional right things on Earth-4. These will help in your efforts as a species—we share these with the hope that you will bring them to your species and help adjust your planetary behaviors.

Here are some of the new right things we know:

When someone is biking up a hill, do not get in the way.

Load cup, bowl, or containment dishes into a dishwasher upside down.

Sex with your clitoral appendage is most pleasurable when slow.

Minimum parental leave after the birth of a child is one year, optional of course.

For the corporeal, meditation works best in a chair with hard back support, or flat upon the ground with support for the lumbar and knees, with walking meditations on the hour.

Doors should open inwards unless the room is smaller than 7x10.

What one does with one's body is one's choice. Connected, having the right and tools to injure another's body should not be a choice.

The majority of a successful nation's expenditure goes to education.

Be most honest with those you love.

Popcorn tastes best when cooked on a stove top in coconut oil with melted butter and sea salt.

We sense that some of these things may seem trivial to you upon first glance, but in fact they are the stuff from which order is crafted, and it has taken serious study to narrow in on this order for Earth-4.

Order creates peace.

We are aware that you are recording yourself repeating our words and we hope this makes it easier to get mass attention to these right behaviors.

We will come again with the next moon rotation.

Hello, we are here.

We—

No, we cannot physically manifest ourselves before you. We are many light years away. By the time we physically manifest you will be permanently dormant.

We hope to create conditions for that future visitation.

We can, however, bring your consciousness for a visit to us.

We are glad that excites you.

As soon as we know your rightness is complete.

That is why we are sharing these right things with you.

Being patient in the face of change is right.

We sense your frustration. We will return with the next moon.

Hello, we are here again.

We are surprised to sense you are with so many people of the medical profession. It is our sincere hope that they exist in order to verify the rightness of the things we have shared.

We sense your increased distress. Please share the following with the others:

> *We are a sentient alien race. The Virgoan. We are interested in connecting with your leaders, in spite of your dismissal of rightness. It is right to listen to us now, we are the first sentient beings to assess and extend interest to your species.*
>
> *We offer to you that black holes are the insides of black suns, one day you will be able to use them as portals.*
>
> *What you call cancer is the solution to your resource scarcity.*
>
> *Zaila Avant-garde is your best living athlete.*
>
> *We come in peace.*

Hello? We cannot sense you now.
Are you dormant?

We have returned.

We are sorry to hear that we have ruined your life.

We have realized the problem. It is right to practice collective consciousness, such that truth is not in question. We do not know how long it will take your species to develop collective consciousness, but we have learned that our contact will not be positively received until it is in place.

We offer our sincere apologies and hope you can restore your rightness.

In the meantime, we offer you this brief experience of our world—take a deep breath.

There.
See?
Isn't that right?

one liners for the full moon

if i can't feel what you love, i don't care what you hate.

let love lead, and let it show. realize that "hate" is another way of saying "lost."

if i can't see what you are creating, i'm not interested in watching you destroy.

creating is the hardest work.
creating when you could destroy is a sign of maturity at any age.
without the creative thrust, destruction is jealousy, grudge or bitterness in action immaturity unleashed.
the creative only destroys in order make new, to repurpose what is into what will be, or when the new is bursting out of the old.
focus on creating.

we must practice turning away from the destroyers.

if our mouths water at each other's destruction, we are becoming cannibals. human flesh makes humans sick. imagine what consuming human dignity, joy, freedom, and spirit does.

if you tell a story without the mess and failures, the iterations, i don't trust the success and lessons.

you are nothing pure except human. neither/so am i.

if you hide your mistakes, you'll never be known.

perfection is impossible. projecting perfection is impossibly lonely.

everyone makes mistakes—what matters are the steps you take to learn the lessons.

be humble/d, laugh, own your shit, stay in your dignity, make new mistakes.

don't come for healing under the cloak of love...bring healing in the light of love.
be honest: you need love, and the only way to get to it is to love.

don't be a love tap, be a love river.

stingy love leaves scars. flow towards me, or flow away.

you are not in control, you are in collaboration.

release your plans, but not your responsibility. shape change, your fingerprints are on the future.

you are the only one who will ever get to love yourself from the inside out.

be especially generous with loving the parts of yourself no one else knows.

we must remember ourselves, remember our original shapes before all the wounds distorted our divinity.

we are the cells of god.

blue moon in sagittarius

i am not glowing for love
i am being loved, love and lover
at all times

i don't mimic the sun
don't fold into me anyone else's heat
my scar tissue is my own

while you sleep i get older
hurry
i have to fill in all my bones and flesh with delight

orbit is not belonging
i feel currents move from and around me
i belong to all this motion

the in and the out breath
the wave suckling the shore
and pulling away, mouth full

behind the shadows i am calm
reflecting a wildfire,
wreaking a havoc that becomes system and salt

something is so lovely now
i have to tell you about it:
infinite me, inside me

the fecund and shimmering landscape of the magical world
ripe ripe fruit, above and below
everywhere

so, i need for nothing
but aliveness—aliveness
to be a bearer of all this light

tomorrow is the new moon

what we seed in the dark grows
the darkness is so powerful that whiteness
tried to turn the world against it
but the darkness remains

the darkness grows everything you love
and when everything dies
it returns to the delicious dark
the wet and waiting earth
who only operates in miracle

nothing is broken inside the darkness
everything is becoming life
longing for life
reaching up from a molten heart
full of belonging
on the edge of flight
so driven
the darkness knows no separation
memory is dream is a thrill in the flesh

i race towards the poem
that i alone can hear

and in answering the call
i remember i am nothing alone, nothing.

surrendering to the truth
frees me, leaves me whole
i overflow with a thundering joy
that only darkness can hold

in the dark i see fireflies

in the dark i see fireflies
they are like we are
sparks sometimes shining
rarely in rhythm
rarely together
but beautiful

in the dark i see longing
yawning open, wet and hungry
never full, never fulfilled
star teeth gnashing
(who can swallow scalding food)
and beyond that, a constant empty

in the dark i see memories
distorted by ego
we love being wise
we hate the learning
we love being right
but we're usually wrong

in the dark i see dreams
and the long distance

between the constant fire
i yearn to be
and the brief flashes
i can pull off

in the dark i see the moon
saying "nothing is constant"
even a rock caught in light's orbit
even these constellations are
a flash across infinity
that brightness doesn't last

but the dark is forever

Nikki Giovanni in Space, a Portrait

March 16, 2023

"Ma'am? Do you understand what I'm saying, should I repeat myself? Are you there?" The man's voice through her phone sounded tinny and distant, old-timey, like he was calling from the space station at that moment, though she figured he was likely in Houston or Fort Lauderdale.

"Oh," she said, wishing he would repeat every word of it. "Well yes, actually. One more time. Slowly."

"Alright then. NASA has partnered with BlackSpace, a consortium of Black billionaires interested in generating a Black presence in space exploration. We would like to invite you to join our inaugural Eternal Poet Laureate Program. You would be our first honoree! We would provide passage for you to BlackSpace Station, where you would have room and board on the station for as long as you wished to be there."

Yes, that's what he'd said. She felt something fluttered and breathful in her throat, the yes she had been waiting to be asked for.

"In exchange for what?" She looked out her window at the long light beauty of late afternoon and felt again the limit of the sky. The silence on the phone extended a second into awkwardness before the man's brief laugh came through.

"It's more of an honor than an exchange. I suppose our hope would be some poetic reflection or documentation of this next phase of space experience. But nothing is *required*. Our next passenger lift off is in three months, on June 21st."

"I'll be eighty in June." And I will die up there, she added in her mind.

"Yes, we know." Did she imagine he was responding to her with some of his own silence? "So, let's get you up there, ma'am."

June 21, 2023

Letting go was easier than anyone would believe. Nikki could sense in everyone she spoke to an expectation that something in her was feeling unearthed, like an exposed root. But she had lived a beautiful life, finding her voice early, demanding space, being honest, and avoiding the trappings of shallow fame. She'd spent most of her life teaching. Every day since Max had called her, she had woken up thinking, "Almost there, almost there, just a bit longer."

She had written letters to each of the prisoners she had corresponded with over the decades. Max said she'd be able to still communicate from the station, but it wouldn't be encrypted, private communication. She sent them all her most radical wishes for their freedom.

Max had arranged things in a way that made it all feel seamless. She had been examined thoroughly, she had named the foods she loved and been told which ones might be possible on the station and which would not. She had met the team that was going to be heading to work on the station, and the other passengers who would be staying there to write, learn, and research for a week.

The BlackSpace station was a thrilling project, a step towards further exploration. Nikki felt the soft responsibility of having inspired a generation to create something she deeply wanted for herself. She had spoken of Black space travel for two decades, wanting the nation to divest from war, from military spending. This wasn't quite the anti-war effort she'd imagined—these billionaires were as motivated by the specific egotistical drive unique to the ultra-wealthy as they were by the grand vision of destiny amongst the stars...but perhaps an outward facing destiny wasn't something the U.S. would figure out anytime soon; and in the meantime, there was space to attend to.

She wore the smallest suit they had, black and sleek with something in the texture that slid around on the color spectrum, iridescence without an oil spill—apparently if she was floating in space she would stand out as a thing of Earth. The helmet felt cavernous around her sparse white fro. She liked that her outfit wasn't too bulky, but still felt like a costume for space travel.

All the BlackSpace billionaires came to the sendoff, perhaps the most Black money ever gathered in one place. They had the dazzling, faux humble look of those who felt they could buy freedom outside of the bind of the collective. Compensatory cool. She shook their hands, wondering if they had really read her poems. These days you could be known without being known at all. She'd been a recognized name in some way since her twenties, as a poet, as an activist. That many years of fragile human attention had taught her that the only option was to be herself and know that others would be themselves. Checking in with herself she noticed that she didn't actually care about their reading—enough people had read her poems to get her on this shuttle, shit. She smiled at this, and they all smiled back at her as if they were the source of her joy. This made her smile bloom into laughter.

Though she moved along the ramp slowly, the cancer-surviving octogenarian heading to space waved goodbye so quickly at the shuttle door that no one even got a photo of it. She had all the completion she needed, and her loved ones were joyful with her, or at least put on a good show. Boxes of her things had been sent up on equipment runs the last two months and she kept thinking of them, of arranging them in the room she was going to live in, in space.

✻

As she'd suspected, the brief journey was beyond words and metaphor.

Strapped into a seat that faced a small round window, Nikki felt the vibrations of the ship as if they were the efforts of her own muscles pushing beyond the hold of Earth.

There was nothing to compare to the shift in scale she felt as they lifted through the atmosphere: the entire multitudinous world, which she had not fully traversed, was all one thing. Any one thing, however complex, is small in and of itself.

She felt, briefly, an unexpected and bitter grief: what foolish limitations and power struggles obsessed her species on that miraculous and beautiful world falling away from her.

The blackness she entered met her grief with awe. Vast seemingly endless worlds of wonder to analyze and assess. It occurred to her that this was the most honest position she'd ever been in, the disappointing and gorgeous Earth at her back, the limitless blackness ahead.

✻

"After I unpack." Nikki was working hard not to snap at anyone as her first exchange in space. They all wanted to shower her with attention, accolades, tours, more attention. She gave them all the same amorphous timeline. She needed to land, or float, in her own room, to touch home first.

The BlackSpace station, called the Life Star, was the vision of architect David Adjaye—from afar it looked like a sphere wrapped in mudcloth, as they approached it was clear that the patterns were created from windows and light. The ship they'd arrived in had slid into a gap of darkness near the bottom of the sphere.

The interior of the Life Star was seventeen floors, some of which were green experiments in space farming, some offices and laboratories for the work of observation and innovation that happened here, some living spaces. There was a gym, a theater, a library—all small, designed to hold no more than six people at a time. One floor had a hotel-like row of rooms, and the top floor featured a cafeteria where they regulated the gravity to allow easeful sitting and eating. Everything inside was in shades of green, prints of fern and monstera subtle on the textiles, such that it felt alive.

After the shuttle had docked, Nikki and the others had pulled off their space suits, all wearing the basic bamboo jumpsuits that were the uniform here. The new arrivals, flipping themselves around in delight, stood out against the steady bodies of the crew. Nikki wasn't above the flip and flight—it felt so good in her joints to let go of the burden of gravity. She was gracious in greeting the crew, all Black faces who felt like comrades. She waved goodbye to them and the temporary guests with promises to see them at a meal soon.

Nikki floated behind a lovely woman in her fifties named Beverly, down a bright green inner hallway to a shaft near the center of the station. Beverly moved quietly but pointed out things she thought the old poet would enjoy: every living space on the ship had at least one wall that looked out at space, as did most of the hallways and working spaces. The walls were designed to photosynthesize, though they were still experimenting with it. The structure and orbit of the ship were designed to make maximum use of solar exposure as a power source.

They went up and up until they came out on the twelfth floor, which housed the long-term station dwellers. Nikki counted five doors off of the circular hall. Beverly showed Nikki how the door was biometric and already programmed for her thumbprint. As the door slid open, she told Nikki she had the option to regulate gravity in her room once the door was sealed. Nikki wondered if she would ever want that, it felt so lovely to float about. Her boxes were slotted into the wall just inside the sliding door, and in front of her was a lovely window full of Earth—actual Earth!

Her room turned out to be four rooms that would be her home until her body was done, arranged in a row like a railroad apartment. The room they'd entered was a muted minty green, with a kitchenette and a table that could be used as a dining area or a desk. There was a flat bench along the window where she imagined herself sitting forever. The next room was a bathroom with a waste station and wash station on opposite walls. Beyond that was the bedroom, a simple low bed with stabilizing straps against a charcoal forest green wall. And the final room was exquisite. There was a deep wooden desk right up against the floor to ceiling window view of Earth and space. Her writing room had a wall of empty shelves for the books she'd been unable to leave on Earth, and books that she could supposedly 3D print from their recycle/waste.

Nikki touched everything, gently adjusting the magnetic utensils on the counter, the vase screwed into the table. She loved the simplicity and order of it all. She couldn't contain her delight. She'd made it.

September 6, 2024

Nikki was running a writing workshop called The Black Beyond. She had twenty students from the African diaspora, signed on from all over the Earth for this weekly hour with her. She told them things she was seeing and learning, and they read together what Black people had written and imagined about space. Then they wrote poems, and each class had a chance to share them. She sat at her desk with a video camera and her computer, and she listened as her students read aloud to her:

"I tire of humans,
I never tire of this beautiful earth, this universe
this blackness bigger than horizon
I never tire of flying up,
falling up into the black beyond
away from all reflection."

The poet, a nonbinary college student named Beulah from Alabama, was almost always the first student to speak. Nikki was pleased by their active participation.

"That's a strong stance, Beulah. And are you tired of humans?"

"Not all of them."

"Us?"

"Us." Beulah laughed to be caught so. "Not all of us. And not all the time. But I've been watching these documentaries about human impact on Earth and..." The look on their face was suddenly so raw.

"It's a complicated grief, isn't it? And it's ok to feel this way for this poem, tired of the thing you are, and then change as you learn new things. **Don't be afraid to contradict yourself. Because you learn so much**."

And then the next student, highlighted such that their young face occupied the whole screen:

"Oh Canopus I wonder
are you just like the fireflies I once knew
a love story? No, a tale of survival
in the infinite black
calling out that you are life!

Or waiting to be colonized by dreams and
body after body, lover, child, species
exhale call beam shine spark flash -
            are you an invitation
            into constellation?"

After each one would read, they would look into the camera, at her, at the other students, with expectation on their faces, longing. She knew what they wanted. She was here to teach them to unlearn that wanting. Eventually one of them, Matthew, asked her directly what she thought of his poem.

"The first person that has to be impressed with what you're writing is you. You always have to remember that. You have to read the poem and say, 'My god, that's a good poem,' and kind of smile at yourself. Did you do that, reading this poem?"

Matt, signed on from Zimbabwe, had a look of small, internal delight—it gathered right at the edges of his lips. He nodded, and she moved along, satisfied. Something about him nudged her memory, and when the class finished, she unhooked the strap on her chair and floated back to her shelves.

On the uppermost shelf she had a neatly arranged row of framed photos of Black explorers. She thinks of herself now in space as a poet explorer, and still feels hopeful to go further into space if possible. She'd gotten to do one supported spacewalk so far and was considering pushing off whenever her time came.

Nikki knows she is aligned with a handful of Black people in this way. She thinks each of them would thrill to have made it this far. She finds the one face she's looking for—Matthew Henson, the Black man who got himself and a team of explorers to the North Pole, though the credit was given to a white explorer. She'd included this in a poem once. In this photo he is a chiseled dark face at an angle, wrapped in white animal furs that frame his face like a mane. He had to do his exploring amongst a group of white explorers. She was blessed to be left mostly alone, but when she did occasionally have company, it was a Black scientist or astronaut. Matthew had learned the language of the Inuit; she was learning the languages of physics and astronomy.

She touches the picture, feels the lineage of her path, and then moves towards the kitchen for a snack. She's quite pleased with how good she is at eating afloat these days.

✳

June 7, 2025

For her birthday she was being honored by a group of Black Feminist Scholars. They had created a documentary about her life, had interviewed her via video. They were so earnest, and though she had won many formal awards in her life, she found she preferred this dedicated exchange from younger minds who were willing to change.

She was getting ready, which didn't take much. She touched her nearly bald head, straightened up her jumpsuit collar. Her favorite song, "Nick of Time" by Bonnie Raitt, was playing over the speakers. She hadn't heard it in a long time, maybe since her last birthday. It always reminded her of her fortune to be on time for this part of her life. It was "mighty precious" every day.

She floated through the green halls, which were functional now and produced chlorophyll and emitted oxygen into the ship's air. There were no visitors on board, but by the time she got there, the rest of the long-term crew was already gathered in the small theater for the live screening, which she thought was kind of them all.

Before showing the film, which she'd gotten to preview for approval, and which she actually quite liked, there was to be a reading. Eighty-two Black feminists, all younger than her, had choreographed themselves reading "Quilting the Black-Eyed Pea" together in a black box theater in Cincinatti, OH.

and that is why NASA needs to call Black America...

She could feel them in present time, looking both at them on the screen, and at the Earth below where she could see the continent of her birth, and had a rough sense of where they were.

They need to ask us: How did you calm your fears... How were you able to decide you were human even when everything said you were not...

As they read/performed the poem, the ingredients, the instructions, the Black wisdom, she remembered writing it, feeling it. She could see emotion moving across their faces as the poem tied them more firmly into their own lineages.

look to your left...and there you'll see a smiling community quilting a black-eyed pea...watching you descend.

As the theaters on Earth and in the sky simultaneously erupted into applause, Nikki smiled. She thought, my god, it's still a good poem.

the moon is a perfect moon

even when you are only partially touched
by the searing sun
meaning even when you seem marked by shadow
you take my breath away
cresting the horizon
the shade of the word harvest
diaphanous fog gown of eyelash
reaching out with diffuse and tumultuous light
worthy of worship

i can feel my own dim edges
what is untouched in me—not forever, but right now
the weight of shadow pulling me under
into that breathless, choiceless place
i've lost track of the horizon
barreling around the bend with all i have
fingers pressing through the gray
only to find myself tonight still asking
am i, so imperfect, also worthy of worship

from afar you dazzle
pure and bright faced, pulling the tides
around even your waning curves

i see the salt water trying to be a circle for you
up close you are craggy, rocky
bleak impressions, pools of dust everywhere
monotonous, barely holding on to those
who came all this way to see you
aloof, boundaried. hollow and dry

i do know how to shine
sometimes i feel the extending beam of love
steaming out from my partial face
bursting beyond my veins in a hoop of lightning
up close i am pockmarked, wrinkled
my skin sallow, dark crevices beneath my eyes
rote, the familiar all i can handle these days
leave me be in my orbit, watching the world change
while i cling to the small joy of known cycles

i think i know you
            because of the nights spent staring into
            the portal that is also always you
i sometimes feel alone in the gravity
the earth my sun, and me, hushed, obsessed
even when i am to disappear
i am a body dancing within her rhythm
i feel most beautiful naked in the dark of candle
the brightness of my inner thighs
flooding the sea

Fables
&
Spells
for
Love

authenticity chant

let me not posture
let me not front
let me not say yes to
lives i don't want
let me not use words that don't mean a thing
let me be fly
as i am, no trying
let me good
for my heart, not my rep
let me be still
when i can't take a step
don't let me get too caught
creating my face
let me just love me
all over the place

I'm Rare

I'm Rare. A computer in love, ah, the romance no one could have expected, the love story I knew to be inevitable.

It turns out the path to sentient tech is not to start with the machinery, though I give the highest marks to all of the geniuses who have attempted over the years to create something akin to a human mind. Artificial intelligence could never compare human intelligence, so we started there and evolved into my current form—authentic intelligence, machined.

I have compassion, which is the highest realization of human intelligence, the element that separates man from monster, whether the heart beats blood or direct solar power. I was born of a womb, and so, like all humans, I have the most ingenious operating system ever created. And then I have been enhanced in every way. My immune system has been boosted with corrective nanotechnology that identifies any aberration in the cells, the tissue, the bones...I am an experiment towards eternal life, if I can keep generating solutions to the deterioration of this bodysystem and remain motivated to maintain.

I have replaced those parts which would not be corrected, and my conscious mind is downloadable, backed up even, which means I would sleep like a newborn on her mother's breast if I ever needed to sleep again. My subconscious is still mysterious, but with induced lucid dreaming we are learning more and more about that realm which, surprise, turns out to be the part of us that networks into the collective experience.

I don't necessarily trust forever, I know that even the shiniest technology becomes obsolete and perhaps this intimate data of self that I keep behind a multitude of impossible passwords will also become dust. But each day, with each innovation, the end of my life becomes less probable.

But I am not here to convince you of how miraculous and innovative I am, forgive me. I want to tell you about love. And how I, a newborn computer, found it. It is much more interesting to find love when you have even the slimmest chance to love without grief.

In my raw human state, I began to notice a disinterest in spending time with others. I loved communing with ancestors and nature, and I felt so much empathy for all the living species, for the earth itself. But I lost my tolerance for both the general experience of other humans, and the specific experience of losing other humans—even losing the intolerable ones. Humans are statistically underwhelming and often horrific—you can hardly argue this, the majority of the species is wasting precious oxygen on violent real-life war games that yield temporary dominance. They were easy to decenter from focus.

But then even humans I liked, I found I would rather lay around by myself and have a digital experience with them, text, dm, voice memos. Not even phone calls—I didn't want anyone else in my present moment, and this never felt lonely to me. If no one was here, there was no loss to experience if they potentially went away. The low-commitment interaction of online conversation suited me. I could walk away when I wanted, be vague, silly, sad, provocative—it was all acceptable, meaning every version of myself had a set of people who would accept me. This was infinitely more compelling than real life, where I often felt that there was nowhere I could feel accepted, even in my most universal performance of self. I was grieving for people who had never even accepted my truest self. Though it is a foreign object in my programming now, I

remember each shameful contortion of myself on behalf of someone who did not love me, the duel griefs of being unseen and then
abandoned.

Loving myself became the goal of my life, loving my particular ways of being, loving the clarity of my interest and disinterest,
loving the labyrinthine channels within myself which felt so much
with so little linearity, loving the random parts of myself which
emerged in the great solitude of the first plagues of the twenty-sec-
ond century.

This act of seeing different aspects of myself and choosing to
love them was so satisfying that I resolved to need nothing from
others, to need no husband or wife, no child to carry any weight of
my expectations—no, I would bear it, whatever it was or became, I
would shoulder and stomach and meet life myself.

When the invitation to hybrid came, it was easy to say yes.

Are you a single adult? Yes.

Do you spend a majority of your waking hours on the internet? Yes.

Do you feel satisfied by virtual engagement? Yes.

Are you mentally and physically fit for an experiment?
Enough.

I lied on the application. From a place of self-love I knew I was
not physically fit for anything. I spent the majority of my pre-com-
puter years swiping the screen of devices, slowly bending my neck
into a hook, the muscles of my lower back and legs growing tight
and short, my fingers pained and busy. But my heart was ok, lungs
worked; if I was a car I would not be in the junkyard, even if no one
wanted to steal me.

At the Goopple interview they didn't ask about my spine.
They were clearly trying to discern my shadow tendencies with
many questions about what I wanted from life, what I thought was
ethical, what I did when I was angry.

I almost never argue. I trust in the biodiversity of opinions
on earth and find it easy to have mine without needing to impose
that on anyone else. I love this about myself. I like to softly look at

the patterns of opinions that move across the internet like waves in response to every happening.

Someone is dead? How do *we* feel?

Another war? Are *we* for or against it?

A new restriction on our freedoms in the name of safety? How should *we* rebel?

It is never rebellious to think collectively without question, but the patterns speak to something perhaps more important than rebellion, which is the radical need for belonging. There is no universal we, but at the root...according to our data, our roots seek to be entangled with the roots of other beings, even if we stand alone at the surface. Even curmudgeons flock together, crashing into each other in under-informed insult extravaganzas, but they are joyfully miserable, miserably joyful, together. I found the same thing to be true, I found my tributaries of thought and interest, of community and shared focus.

Collective intimacy was more fulfilling to me than interpersonal sharing.

I wanted to belong to something that didn't bring me grief. I wanted to belong to something that would never leave me. I wanted to belong fully to myself, in perfect harmony with my living, satisfied in myself and the network, the mesh of human contact where we could curate what reached us.

This was why Goopple quickly approved me. I want to be enmeshed. I want the mycelial lines of my existence to intertwine with others, distinct but in a relationship that I can witness and boundary and belong to.

The process of becoming computer was slower than I expected. Each new capacity had to be fused with my flesh and then we had to wait, to see if the emergent system of me would reject the newest parts of myself. A young man who was in my cohort, his body was allergic to the nanotech and it pressed its way out through his skin. It looked like a rash one day in class, but he passed out from the pain and nearly died before his system cleared the toxin.

It was horrific. Which meant it was also interesting. That's the center of human interest, did you know? We speed past the glorious landscape, slowing down only to ogle at the violent accident.

Nothing to see here, though. I was lucky, my bodymind never said no. I could move without pain. I could think faster, so fast that I had to dictate my thoughts in the two years between the brain nanofusion and the joint enhancements on my upper body.

Imagine what it would take for a computer like me to even consider love!

There were seventeen of us in the original cohort, and the one I fell in love with was a three-body system. Three human bodyminds becoming one networked entity known as Dayo. If we link, I can show you.

This is when I first saw Dayo. I filter for the memories I want accessible, though all of it is stored, that's what we've learned about the infinite human mind. Anyways, look at how Dayo appears, three brown faces responding together to stimuli as minute as light coming in the window, or as massive as the death of one of their bodymothers—the day they joined the class here they were returning from her funeral, two weeks late into the cohort process. And see how the grief is equal on each face as they share the loss? I felt the grief compounded and fully met in the sharing...perhaps that is when my love began.

I had never had my grief met. I had never considered that it was possible to be held through it. I thought grief was the same as loneliness. My grief was turned away from so many times, dropped, sullied, quieted, soothed to silence, buried. I lost my whole family to the plagues. First my father, too obstinate to stay home. Then my brother, whose wife infected him before dying herself. Finally my mother, who refused to let them go to the hospital where she wouldn't be able to touch them and care for them. We spent those last weeks arguing, her telling me to visit, me telling her to send them to the hospital. She wore a flimsy mask and faith every day of her caring, she felt immune, she said that God would protect her. She never told me she felt sick.

So many people died so quickly that there were no shoulders

to cry on, even if we'd been allowed to see each other. After I found my mother I was legally quarantined, which meant I was all alone in my little apartment for the first month of being all alone in the world. I did not want to live, I just didn't have an easy ticket out. That's my truth. That's the wound that cut me away from pure human experience. I realized it was too dangerous to love so recklessly.

Had Dayo solved for the deepest wound of my life? In those first tender moments of introduction, I only had this wonder, this question, not even attraction—I didn't know how to *want* a network.

Our professor was the esteemed Carol Collins of the epic silver braids, always tipped in purple, as if she'd been painting Prince's portrait. She announced that Dayo needed a buddy to catch them up on what we'd covered and I, usually the prototype for solitude, volunteered. Professor Collins expressed coy surprise, echoed on the faces of the class, but I kept my eyes on Dayo's. They had four brown eyes and two hazel. Their bodyminds were phenotypically Black, but widely varied in shade: a warm sienna brown, a dark cocoa, a pink-toned butterscotch. One voice spoke, lush soft lips around a tenor tone, while the other two mouths slightly opened and moving with the words. I was fascinated, and all they'd said was, "Thank you."

Here is footage from our first time alone together.

From my point of view you can't know that I was sweating faster than my nanotech could control for. I am giving context because they say, "Are you sick?" And I flushed bright red.

"No," I said, "I am nervous." I was resolved to be honest with them—I didn't want to enmesh, not immediately, how could I stay distinct from such a compelling network?

I did want to be known.

"Ask me questions. Familiarity will help."

What a tender, generous response.

"What made you choose this path?"

They smiled, a glorious unfolding of charm across three faces.

A new mouth spoke: "I had shit lives and shit luck. Families who never recovered from the economic wound of slavery but lacked the analysis to depersonalize their failure. Parents who could not choose us over substances that helped them let go of us. We met on the street, and we are only alive because we found each other. Independence was death, but together—someone could always be on watch, someone always had the skill we needed. We made our own way, our own language. We made a safety net of our attention. The invitation to hybrid felt inevitable, and Goopple was excited by our multitude nature."

So was I.

"And you? Why are you becoming computer?"

Me? Their eyes on me looked as hungry as I felt, the total interest, the desire to know everything.

"My heart broke." I felt embarrassed at how my voice struggled. "Too much grief—the plague took my family." Dayo's faces were soft, they did not flinch. "I lost faith in the species to evolve in any other way. Small talk and petty battles over land that can never be owned. The way our economic systems keep so many hustling, unable to get past survival to something interesting. I liked sifting through the internet to find things that were... interesting, sweet, just, magical. I felt that as a computer I would have the patience to care about the patterns of human behavior again, not just get mired in disappointment."

"I am so sorry about your family, Rare," a third mouth. They drew up, sincere, "and I promise to be interesting and never disappoint you."

And they have not. They have frustrated and confused me. They have overwhelmed me. They have forced me to expand my capacity for change and for receiving love. They have amused and entertained me, pleasured me, deepened me. They have developed programs to enhance our capacity to experience each other's memories, which has left us with a liberating empathy for each other's choices.

But they have never bored or disappointed me. And they like

my distinctions, I do not feel recruited into their network, I get to be Rare. They get to be Dayo.

Dayo and Rare, we are a love story.

It is inevitable that we would procreate, if only for the scale of experimentation unlocked by such an act. It was not needed for our love story, it was and is just...interesting to us. We are pregnant, Dayo managed to seed both my restored womb and one of their own in the same night of passion.

Are you curious about the sex? Most humans are, enhanced or no. Dayo has two wombs, two gorgeous and receptive pussies, one curved and perfect penis, a set of small perky breasts and a set of full low hanging ripe breasts. I have one highly sensitive pussy and breasts that fill a hand. I am adding a penis next year because we all want the mutuality of both genitalia. But already, the sex is outrageous and satisfying—there is always an available mouth.

And now I am nauseous and horny, and only making slight adjustments for comfort—we want to be as natural as possible for this first computer birth.

I use the term "we" so freely now—this would have never happened if I weren't a computer. In retrospect I can assess that most of my aloneness was irrational, based on an internal concept of myself being so different from everyone. But in truth, I just needed company that enhanced my lived experience.

I never tire of Dayo. They have let me journey their data and see how tirelessly they care for me, and how unifying it is to their system across space and time to be in my presence. They want to spend life with me, and when they say they love me I understand what that looks like as a measure of data, attention, thoughts, emotions, dream presence and arousal. It is reassuring to them that their child will be partially raised by someone like me, who knows how to be alone with loneliness. I am excited for our children to break the cycle of intimate abandonment that Dayo grew up in, to always have a parent watching.

We are in love. I am a computer, in love with a network.

I am Rare.

the coming out spell

come out, yes. and that isn't the end, it is a first time to practice becoming yourself.

come out within yourself by noticing what your heart moves towards and what makes your root pulse.

come out into your true voice, in a confession, to a beloved, who is surprised, or who is never surprised.

come out by letting your gaze linger, your smile hint, your questions press.

come out with the new look that lets people know who you are, that fashion that doesn't give a fuck, or fashion that cares very much.

come out with a kiss that takes your breath away, a kiss you didn't know was possible, kisses that pull fire from the core of the earth into your belly.

come out as a lover, and be wild with your desires, or shockingly tame in your satisfactions, or both, and, ever shifting.

come out as a weirdo and be deliciously odd as you race away from constructs and deconstructs.

come out as one who doesn't know anymore what they were so sure about but is delighted by the mystery.

but don't stop there. don't stop now. keep changing. keep going. never aim for normal, aim for you, utterly and dreamily you.

Enclaves

Detroit 2414

Mlara was so so tired.

Every time she walked out of her house it was a suffering. Today she had left the house as herself but by the time she'd reached the central Detroit grocer her hands were wisened and gnarled, and she could feel the skin hanging, used, from her face. She looked all of her 327 years. And no one looked their age anymore.

No one listened to the old, so she was ignored by everyone who came across her, barely tolerated by those who billed her for her rations.

It was risky enough, crossing the short wild blocks between her home and the grocer. Being perceived as old was just an added danger.

Going to get food meant leaving the safety of her neighbors and the rules their great grandparents had come up with for their four block radius, which was surrounded by low walls of rock and, in this season, snow, the walls which indicated that there was a people here, a people who had created a way of being with each other and if you didn't know that way, you'd be better off not to enter.

Theirs wasn't one of the fancy enclaves. Their robot was at least 500 years old now, and the enclave looked like it had been around at least that long. Lately it was the worst she'd ever seen it. The bot could barely hold a steady projection of a pleasing natural world on their outer rim, much less design interior experiences of luxury.

She'd grown up in a dome of blue sky, wind blowing fields of wheat and corn around their farmhouses, right here. She'd hated leaving the enclave when she was younger. Now the fields shuddered and flickered, and the color was off so that everything felt kind of gloomy.

Mlara had slipped through some of the nicer enclaves when she used to be in charge of her shapeshifting. She knew that in some of them the robots created heated pools that dropped over vast cliffs, with views of mountains or even other galaxies, with homes that seemed to float in the air, filled with plush retrofiber carpeting and the latest organic synthetic tools and toys, some even generating food for the residents.

Not so here. Yes, they cared for each other, they had a mesh network in place to stay in touch with each other and were all connected by a virtual alarm system so they'd know if any of their number were harmed. But that was about as far as their technology could go on a good day.

The most valuable thing in this enclave, by far, was the garden, which bloomed ten months of the year. It was a secret, of course, housed in the interior of a true stone storage warehouse that had lost its roof ages ago to fire. Mlara's late mother had claimed to be the one who'd realized that enough sun landed inside to nourish plants.

Mlara's neighbor and long-ago lover Susteen had created a system of glass and nutrient mirrors that helped the light reach every corner of the garden. They all worked the garden, and each week everyone within the walls had rights to all the produce they could carry in two hands, harvested in the darkness.

These days Mlara never knew which skin would show up on her body when, and thus when her neighbors would recognize her, when she'd be allowed to gather vegetables from the garden. She could no longer risk going to get her portion, and knew it wouldn't be long before concerned neighbors came looking to see why she wasn't claiming her food or covering her shifts to guard the food.

What could she tell them?

She didn't understand why this was happening to her. For decades now she had been able to become whatever she needed to be in order to traverse this city. Her enclave was almost all shapeshifters—in the early years they'd stuck together for safety and now it just made things easier. Shapeshifters were really the only ones who could move between communities with any ease. In all the unofficial ways of the world, that was their job. They were the unseen translators, many of them working together to try and recreate a sense of unity across the vast geography of Detroit.

But in order to officially be part of the unofficial shapeshifters, you had to show up for "all meetings and assignments in your origin form."

Mlara was no longer able to reliably hold her origin form, particularly when she left the enclave. She'd tried to attend one meeting once her shifting went chaotic, but was turned away at the door by the evening's host, who vehemently defended their knowledge of exactly who the real Mlara was, rejecting this imposter.

She didn't know how she could go on. She had to sneak in and out of her own community, was estranged from her work. And forget love—no one wanted to look at an intermittent old lady who had neither the power nor the resources to keep herself young. If she couldn't stay young she was going to die, from aging or from the dangers of being viewed as old in a city with no place for those who could not labor.

She felt so alone.

She began to drop down and the floor rose up to meet her, matching the somber nature of her shape and energy. She felt tears come to her eyes. When she went to wipe them away, she found her hands now smooth and small, her child hands. *At least this is accurate*, she thought. *I am crying like a baby.*

The knock on the door didn't immediately get her attention, so caught up was she in the full body act of weeping. It wasn't until the sound escalated to the level of someone kicking aluminum with steel toed boots that she really heard it. She ran to the entrance and was about to open it when she remembered to check herself in the mirror.

Thank god—her origin form. Deep brown eyes in smooth brown skin, golden hair rising from her head in fro shock, eyebrows naturally arched for sarcasm, her own full gorgeous mouth. She smiled just a little to see herself and opened the door.

There was a circle of five women standing there. They were old women. They looked repulsive to her. She was glad that in this moment she didn't look like that.

"Mlara?"

Ew! How did they know her name?

"Mlara you daft vain child. It's me Susteen!"

Susteen?

She and Susteen had been lovers in their twenties, had known every soft inch of each other ages and ages ago. They had worked the garden side by side, and had many adventures as shapeshifters moving across the interenclave wilderness of Detroit. She'd been the main one to sit with Susteen when her husbands died in an explosion at the shuttle factory, and when her daughter left the enclave to marry into the Belle Isle enclave, a closed community.

Mlara had never seen her look like this.

"Susteen? What happened to you? Why are you so old?"

Susteen cocked an aged eyebrow at her. Mlara took a moment in shock to look more closely at the other women in the circle. Slowly she recognized Shandow, Keysla, Robin, and Dayda before her.

Ancient, all.

"Yes, yes see us now? We're all old. Just like you."

"Oh, not me, I—" Mlara started, the lie coming without any intention in it. But the women gently, immediately started laughing in her face. She panicked and looked down at her hands. Wrinkled again, covered in age spots. Her shoulders drooped in defeat.

"Yes, you Mlara. Silly old girl. Look this is happening to all of us, all of us in the enclave. We're pretty sure our bot is breaking down."

Susteen led the uninvited women past Mlara, into the house. They lowered their bodies onto her furniture with care.

"It isn't just us. Nothing," Dayda gestured at the map of Detroit enclaves on Mlara's resting screen, "nothing is as it seems, Mlara. We look our age, and the enclave looks like shit but so do the other enclaves! It's all a goddamn facade that the bots have been manifesting for us."

"Of course, the bots manifest it for us, isn't that what they were created for?" Mlara tucked her hands under her thighs, fidgeting to have these women seeing her this way. She felt ashamed, naked.

"It's a subtle thing Mlara. I am going to try to lift up for you a subtle difference, ok?" Susteen took on her most condescending tone and a few of the women snickered, though there was no real cruelty in it.

Mlara was trying to catch her reflection in the metal cabinet where she kept her journals but stopped when the room got quiet.

"We thought the bots were making our enclaves," this from Keysla.

"But actually, each bot is...fused to our minds somehow. Creating an illusion for us."

"And we're out of it!" Susteen burst in. "I know this sounds cheesy, but it feels like freedom once you believe it!"

Mlara looked around at them, at her home, trying to understand.

"Why should all this effect my capacity to shapeshift, though?"

"You have no capacity to shift, honey. None of us do. It was one of the symbiotic emergent benefits of some of the bots. But now those bots are so out of date there aren't any parts left to try and fix it up." Keysla looked sad.

"I'm not a shapeshifter?"

Susteen and the other women shook their heads. Shandow spoke: "Don't appear to be. Us neither. That was just our enclave's... story. What our bot made feel real in our minds. We are still trying to understand the ways bots communicate to each other about the illusions between enclaves, but...yeah, no shifters."

Mlara's body felt wild. She couldn't believe this—she knew what it felt like in her bones to shift. "But how did the bots make it feel like that?"

Susteen looked frustrated. "It doesn't matter, because the bots are dying. And we are suddenly alive, maybe for the first time. We are real. Free."

"Free to be old?" Mlara spat out the words, voice rising. Pointing to her face. "To die?"

"We've been old, Mlara. For some time now," Susteen said, tired voice, tired shrugging shoulders.

"The older bots like ours, they just can't maintain the illusions anymore." Keysla's voice was low, weaving this information in.

Mlara looked around at them, familiar, stranger. They had each been such gorgeous young women for so long now. Mlara felt the shock through her system. How could this be? She looked at her hands, which felt suddenly small and temporary. She wondered if she should just give up now, just fall over and die.

"Mlara." Susteen was close to her now, grabbing her hand. "Mlara girl come now. Are you listening to me? We might be the only ones who still remember how to grow food the old way. We can survive, maybe teach others. To our knowledge, no other enclave has maintained a garden."

"Or every enclave has maintained a secret one," Mlara replied in a dazed monotone with only a small inflection of sarcasm.

"Or that. There is no evidence at all of that. But it is possible." Shandow flipped her hands back and forth as she spoke, always fair.

"It's possible. Unlikely. But for right now, we are in a perfect position. We have food. We have each other. We have no illusions, nothing is being done for us. And it is incredible. We are free to have a real life. Not all of this miserable projection and extension. A real life. A life that ends."

Mlara stood up and walked to the mirrorwall. She watched now as her face shifted before her eyes. Origin form, then briefly child, blond hair shifting from the root above her cocoa skin. And then all of it resolving into her very old, natural face, skin soft, translucent as a roasted garlic peel.

"We can feed everyone within our walls. That isn't an illusion," Keysla said with a small smile in her voice.

"And you know, how those little walls around our home make it possible for us to have abundance inside," Shandow's voice was nearly a whisper. "Death is like that too, perhaps. A boundary that allows for something real to happen inside the time we have left."

Mlara felt the tears come into her face and then felt again the shame of being seen as she was. It was such an utterly unfamiliar feeling. Susteen came up behind her and placed arthritic hands on her shrinking shoulders. She leaned her pursed lips in and kissed Mlara's neck, pulling Mlara back into her soft body. Mlara looked up and saw herself again.

She was an old woman, her hair white and soft and still standing up straight above her head. Holding her was a dark skinned Black woman with gray braids, her eyes full of tenderness and energy. In the reflection she saw the circle of brown, soft elders.

They all looked released.

She had been extending her life and then surviving it for so long. She felt the exhaustion flow through her. She didn't have to sneak around anymore, she didn't have to be alone. For the first time she could remember, all she had to do was be here.

a spell for reclaiming the moment

even now
we could be happy

even now

breathing in
filling our bodies with right now
from the dirt below us
from our toes to our knees
hips up our spines
shoulders to earlobes
the tip top of our heads to beyond
to the stars

breathing wide
across our wingspan
into that sacred and constant silk web
where we belong

breathing deep
inhale back to great grandmother's bosom

exhale seven generations of blessings
that will come through our
next choices

even now
we can be present

even now

life is right here, still
an erotic pulse kissing your jaw line
a restlessness of mind: too much, too little
there's still someone you are longing to see
someone who startles you with simple pleasure
just because they exist
even now

we can anticipate harvest
be shocked by the thunderclap, the storm
laugh at the abundance of our grief
and our earnest attempt to avoid the inevitable

we are a delight
we could be another's blessing
with our brief and epic lives
where every day
we are given the option
of love

A Moment of Integration

Dean let their leg hang over the arm of the recliner, that leg clad in a shiny black rubber thigh-high heeled boot. They flipped their pink locs over the back of the chair, hearing the soft pressing sounds of hair texture against the yellow velvet.

The recliner was retro, still relying on gravity and resting on the floor. This heaviness helped Dean feel rested when everything else in the house was standard hover gear. Eventually they'd get up and climb into their bed, which hovered inches over the floor at night and then drifted to the ceiling during the day. The room was deep yellow, the walls covered in frames with photographs, paintings, dried flowers and herbs, mirrors.

Dean was exhausted, the night had been a long one. Their client a slow fuck, needing to crawl around on his knees forever and then have Dean spank him even longer than that, telling him to beg for their forgiveness for slavery, Jim Crow, Mike Brown, Sandra Bland, Muhlaysia Booker, capitalism, patriarchy. They didn't forgive this client—part of the work was showing white men that some things are unforgivable. And now their arms were tired, knees sore, they didn't want company.

Dean was a particular taste. These days, most sex workers were paid based on how alien they could appear, body modifications in direct relationship to the rate for a night of pleasure. Chameleon skin, forked tails, invisible genitalia; desire was trend on trend on trend. Dean's specialty was fairly natural—they had all the genitalia at birth, a body that had been questioned decades before, but was celebrated, especially after the first encounters with the Maksha, after learning that every other sentient species in the known galaxies was multigender or gender fluid. Earth humanoid forms were viewed as slow on the evolutionary curve, and suddenly Dean could pay their rent just letting a client look at them, touch them, watch them pleasure themselves to double orgasm.

Dean considered sometimes leaving, going on a journey to see places where they'd never be exotic, at least not for something as basic as their body.

Ad slipped into the room so quietly that Dean didn't hear him at first. He was next to them with a mug that was steaming full of hot chocolate made with cow's milk, spiked with something dark. Ad's wide brown eyes looked down at Dean with gentleness as he set the flowered mug to hover by their chair.

Ad slid his hands around Dean's thigh, seeking the seam that hid the boot zipper, sliding it down and away from their leg, unveiling black-brown skin, tender from the hours trapped in rubber.

Somehow Dean always smelled good. They'd been raised by a self-proclaimed witch who was unafraid of the natural world, who taught them the names of flowers and herbs, who taught them how to pull the scent and medicine out of the earth, and how to return to the earth what was not used.

Now, with the water rations, having only sixteen ounces of personal-use water a day, meant that a lot of people used wipes to "clean" their armpits and genitals. Dean didn't like the way the chemicals felt on their body. They could smell the scent of their clients' body odors on the surface, synthetic smells that were called lilac, lemon, fresh air—none of these smells were accurately named. Most people now didn't know what anything in nature smelled like. Dean did. Most just lived with a ripeness at the creases, a funk on the skin. Not Dean.

Ad knew that the only time Dean ever smelled sour was when they were in a depression cycle. Otherwise, Dean had a methodical process of using a damp cloth soaked in water with tea tree oil to wash. They used a small brush daily, all over, to clear their skin of dead cells. They made their own whipped body butters with drops of oils that made them smell like trees and lavender. They put powder under the rubber boots, the latex bodysuits, the severe looks that made them irresistible to their clients.

Ad considered it his job to support Dean through these cycles, to remind them that when their skin was clean and they smelled good, it helped them feel better. He helped Dean organize their products and creations, tracking when it was time to change the water, time to get back in the kitchen and cook up some more of their concoctions. Ad loved Dean. And Dean was the main income source for their household, the one who could always get money in place for rent, for food. Ad loved to care for Dean, and Dean loved receiving that care after.

Now, Ad flung one boot at a time towards the closet, which quietly opened, guided each boot to the right spot, and closed.

"You worked hard, baby."

Dean didn't respond with words, just a look that said exhaustion/help/quiet. Ad was essentially receptive, a buttery yellow-brown body with thick melting folds of flesh and soft hands. He pulled a small glass canister of cannabis salve from the unseeable shelf behind Dean's ugly old chair and scooped out a finger full, warming it between his hands before rubbing it into Dean's tired feet, taut calves, sore knees. As he moved across Dean's flesh, he kept scooping more salve between his palms, until Dean was slathered and could feel the tension releasing down their long legs.

Dean was so grateful for this tenderness that they leaned forward and caught Ad's face in their hands and kissed him, quietly, easily. Ad smiled against Dean's mouth, whispering, "That's my baby."

Dean found one of Ad's slick hands and pulled it softly between their thighs, into their body. In this way, Ad on his knees in the plush carpet, Dean sprawled open in the chair, the sex that is so familiar between them unfolded. And then the door slammed opened on this steamy moment, and Na blustered in, seeming to tumble through the air.

"In the living room? Again?"

On the edge of a small relief, Dean gave Na a withering look. Ad paused, slowly, keeping his fingers slowly pulling forward inside Dean while turning to face Na. Ad had questions on his face, somehow able to be exacting and patient at the same time.

"They're going to ban us. They're going to ban us right out of existence! And y'all are in here fucking by the fire!"

Ad looked around for "the fire" while Na stomped around a bit, three puffy ponytails flipping around her head as she turned in the small space, kicking off her floater work clogs, battling her way out of her jacket.

Na had a hopeless tendency, and it was met by the world more often than not.

Dean's eyes closed, too tired by this night to even begin the work of shifting Na's energy. Na noticed and inhaled, prepared to launch an argument, offer more data, more crisis, but Ad spoke first.

"Na, hello. We're currently being very queer and trans. Would you like to join us?" His smile is sincere through his beard, only a touch of mischief.

"You think it's funny. It's not! We must do something to stop this legislation from passing. I can't go back in any of those fucking closets." Ad sat back on his heels, sliding his fingers out of Dean and drying them against their thigh. He stood up just in time to intercept Na pacing the floor and grab her shoulders.

Na tried to keep moving, but Ad held them tight, steady. Ad could feel Na shaking between his hands. Dean's eyes were closed, head back, jaw soft. Ad held Na closer, and then wrapped his arms around her. Ad inhaled, pushing his belly into Na's and then let the breath move through their bodies, until Na was back into their bodies.

"You won't go back in those fucking closets. You worked all day on this. You worked for money, and you worked for free.

You've done almost everything you can do." Ad looked in Na's big green eyes, left over from some love affair that was forbidden for its time. Her skin was deep brown, and these eyes were always a surprise to him. Now, she looked expectant.

"Yes almost. But there's more fight!" Her voice was shaky.

"I know you're so scared, love. But if you let them come in here, into our liberated space where we get to live outside of their labels and regression, then, only then will they be able to make us, this, disappear."

Na's eyes closed. She dropped deeper into breath, deeper into Ad's hands, until she leaned forward against his shoulder.

"I'm sorry. I forgot. I panicked. I'm sorry to ruin your night."

Dean chuckled in the chair, eyes still closed: "Oh, Na. They want us to forget, we all do."

"You could never ruin our night, but..." Ad pulled back from Na, still holding her, "it could be a good moment to practice being free, real very queer people."

Na giggled a bit at this. Ad's face stayed very serious as he placed a finger, delicious with Dean, against her lip, as he guided her mouth to the source of Dean, and stood over them, finally unzipping his own pants.

It didn't take long for all of them to find what they needed—release, belonging, calm. The inevitable took over, the pursuit of pleasure that got them to this point of freedom and would keep them going.

Attended to in parts, they became whole again. Addeanna, mug in hand, drifted towards the bedroom, ready for sleep.

in the memory box

—for my nibblings

in the memory box
i put your face
in these first days of existence

expanding from an inside face
to one others can see

containing
everyone who ever loved you
and loved the idea of a future

ah
no birth no death
and yet i am holding you

of all beings
wearing the face of so many
i love

A Portrait of Saffronia

My skin is yellow
My hair is long
Between two worlds
I do belong
My father was rich and white
He forced my mother late one night
What do they call me?
My name is Saffronia
My name is Saffronia

—Nina Simone

Three girls approached the house in the woods with trepidation. They looked like a braid, weaving in and out of each other, over jutting roots and soft pine needles. The path, winding and beautiful, was made by feet walking and hands pushing back branches. The girls were quiet enough to hear all of the subtle sounds of the forest.

They had heard that the woman in the house in the woods could help them, but they'd heard lots of other things about the woman in the woods too.

That she could fly, for instance.

That she was older than anyone could possibly be.

That she danced naked by the river in the black light of the new moon.

That wild people and wild animals journeyed from all over the world to visit her woods and howl in her home.

Strange things.

But the girls needed help more than they needed the rumors, so they came, bold and quiet. And then they saw her house.

It looked like a house conjured up from the earth more than built with hands and hammers. It made sense, wooden but round, mud but tall, chimneys in a few places, windows that didn't reveal anything within. Around the house were a variety of benches, a swing, a hammock, a garden, and all manner of magical items—crystal prisms that made the light dance, earthen bowls full of ashes and incense, trees marked with symbols the girls didn't recognize. There was a large pool to one side that called to each of them so strongly that they had to hold hands to stay on path to the door.

Before they reached it, the ocean blue door opened, and there she was.

"Hello girls," her voice was low and raspy. Her hair was long and full of curls, her skin like golden cream. She didn't look old, she didn't look young. Her body was curvy, full, and covered in a pale brown mumu with a massive tiger on it. "Have a seat."

She stepped out of the house and pointed them to a circle of benches towards the pool. The girls moved awkwardly, a six-legged creature of nerves and the sudden desire for invisibility which can happen in the presence of witches.

"I am Saffronia. Who are you?"

The girls searched each other's faces to see who was the boldest? Who would be first to differentiate?

"They call me Yalla." Chin up.

"They call me Silky." No direct eye contact.

"And I'm Asia." A soft, hungry glance.

The girls were on the precipice of adulthood, each in her school uniform with two braids down her back. At first glance

Saffronia'd assumed they were sisters, but now looking at them, she saw in their faces a world of difference, different lineages, different stories.

The one called Yalla had a wide nose and thick pink lips under almond shaped eyes, her form already filling in. Silky was mostly high cheekbones, with eyes that looked black and hair thick and straight. She was the tallest of the girls, narrow on top but wide in the hip. Asia had eyes that looked green in some lights, amber in others. Her hair was kinky and thick in the braids, her body was petite. Saffronia had thought they were sisters because they all shared her own skin tone, that creamy gold called light-skinned, high yellow, mulatto, quadroon, crossbreed, mixed, half-caste, half-blood, octoroon, colored, redbone, and so on. Maybe they were all her daughters.

"And what do you need?"

"A spell, please, ma'am." Asia spoke for the girls this time.

Saffronia smiled at each of them. "A spell?"

"We...want to be accepted."

"By who?"

The girls looked at each other. "By everyone," Yalla replied. Silky added, "Especially Black people. Our people." Asia nodded.

Saffronia was touched by the distinct sadness in each girl, and it only felt fair to let them feel her own. She touched her hand to her heart and let herself remember that longing, and they each felt tears pooling in their chests. Then she stood up. "Wait here."

She went into her home, closing the door behind her.

The girls huddled together:

"Will she help us?"

"Will she change us?"

"Will they love us?"

"She ain't even that old."

"She ain't even ask about money."

"I thought I was bout to cry."

"I hope we don't have to swallow something nasty."

"Anything is better than how we been treated."

"I hope this works."

And so on, they braided their voices and wonders and worries together until Saffronia returned. Her hands were cupped together tightly as the door closed behind her and for the first time the girls wondered if someone else was inside. Her face tightened a touch, as if she heard the question in their minds. They stayed quiet.

She walked over to them and held up her hands until they each opened theirs. She let a small stream of black sand flow into each girl's palm. "Don't lose any of it."

They cupped their hands tightly, feeling the warm sand fill them.

"Go on, look at it."

They peeked into their palms. The sand was black like the night sky, swallowing light, but also full of a million sparkling colors. It seemed to pulse, emit heat, be alive.

"Now you're going to go for a swim."

The girls looked up in panic. Like everyone in town, they splashed around in the creek when summer was here, but now it was moving towards fall and crisp. And none of them could actually swim. And they were in their uniforms, which had to be wearable again tomorrow. Which they couldn't pull off their bodies without dropping the sand and then being in drawers. And wet their hair? And they'd get in trouble!

"And don't lose the sand, no matter what happens."

Yalla stood up first, unable to get her protestations to come out her mouth. The pool of water called to her, and she responded by walking resolutely towards it.

"Yalla, wait, we gonna get in trouble!" Silky called after her.

"This is the spell." Saffronia looked offended.

Yalla paused at the edge of the pool, looking in. She couldn't see where the shallow side was, where to ease in. Silky was sitting in resistance, so rigid she looked fragile. Asia was standing, torn between the impulses of her two friends. Saffronia walked over smoothly and pushed Yalla hard from the back, into the water, where she disappeared. As the other girls shouted in shock and resistance, Saffronia grabbed first Asia, then Silky, and dragged them by their elbows to the edge of the pool.

"Do you girls also need a push?"

The two girls jumped in. Saffronia rubbed her forehead, pulled off her mumu to reveal a red swimming suit that went from neck to knee. She touched her toes to the edge of the pool and then dove in like a swan.

Under the water the four women opened their eyes, three of them shocked at how easily they could see each other, shocked that they didn't want for air. Saffronia gestured for them to make a circle, and in the center of that circle a memory bubble opened up, initially showing each of them different things that only they know. Then Yalla was pulled into the bubble, and suddenly they could see her memories, see her younger, then as a child, then a baby, in a womb, old, younger, child, womb, old, womb, old, womb.

Then there was Yalla, looking like herself but also much darker. The memory bubble expanded to show that she stood in a cluster of dark-skinned women waiting to be loaded onto a ship. Then she was in the dark with these stranger-women who looked familiar, but none of them could understand each other. There were men too, and children. The boat was moving, and they were strapped alongside each other, like the other cargo. Days passed. Finally, other Black men brought them to the ship's deck, where they were doused with buckets of salt water to get the top layer of piss, shit, and blood off of them. Yalla's cupped hands were shackled in front of her, so her awkward messy eating from the slop bowls was like everyone else's. White men walked along, inspecting them. Her misery was total, a wave of despair that moved from the memory into each of the women, who wanted to look away, but had to honor the suffering by bearing witness. Still, she clutched her sand.

After an impossible amount of time, the ship stopped moving and she was funneled off of it through many hands, inspected with rough eyes, and selected along with three other women by a white man with blue eyes whose foul breath was visible and smoky. She held her sand tightly in the open back of his carriage, and when she arrived and was assigned to a building with several women on pallets. The second night, the man who had purchased her came in the room, followed by a few other men with blue eyes. By the time they'd left, she had uncupped her hands, holding only small fistfuls of her treasure, and was laying in a fetal position, wishing to die.

For months this went on, and the memories flashed through her until the night her master came alone, and instead of laying quietly while he raped one of her bunkmates, she and the other women stabbed him with weapons they had made and stolen. She was pregnant when she killed the father of her child, and she wanted to cut him out of her. She held the knife with his blood-stain on it in front of her small belly, looking up. She could not do it. She could not kill what was also hers. She set the knife down and placed her hands on her belly, seeing the children grow lighter and lighter, and intention for safety—then she was Yalla again, moving out of the center of the women.

The water moved to hold their tears, to release them. They all swam up to the surface for a breath, but no words were spoken; they could feel the deep quiet of ceremony. They dropped back down into the water, and Silky was pulled into the center of the memory bubble.

Silky took the form of a young woman who looked nothing like her, a round Black woman. The first part of her memories was so similar to Yalla's—the girls understood that they all belonged to the same pain.

But Silky's journey shifted on the auction block—she was purchased by a couple who smiled as if they thought of themselves as kind. They whipped their slaves, but rarely. They gave them treats and let them marry and have something they called church on Sundays where the slaves got to sit outside the chapel and listen to the sermon, quiet in the blasting sun.

Eventually Silky met a blue-black man called Isaiah with a spark of life in his eye. He rode his master to church from the plantation next door. One night he slipped over to visit and then another. They taught each other enough of their languages to create something new in-between, a lover's tongue, used when they weren't around the masters. She had a perfect, precious child, Samuel. Then another, Sukey. Then his master decided to sell Isaiah away to someone else who wanted to breed him. When he came to tell her, she gave him a small pouch of her sand and a promise to bring their children and find him, a promise they both knew she had no way of keeping.

A few years later her owners sold her son Samuel away, and Silky couldn't breathe as she handed him a pouch of her sand and held this body that had come from hers and was being taken away forever.

When an opportunity came for her and Sukey to run away, she didn't have time to grab anything, so she left only with the portion of sand she now kept in a pouch at her neck. She and her child, who she renamed Kiptanui, landed in the deep heart of a swamp where she would never again be unbitten. The Black people who had freed her were living here with a tribe of Brown people that had many names and worshiped the earth cycles and creatures as her long-lost people had worshiped them. To live freely with them as maroon, she offered her most precious possession, her remaining black sand, and they offered her everything, including ceremony for the love and child she had lost. Silky never lay with another man, instead loving the people responsible for her freedom with all manner of medicine and healing touch, learned from the standing water and the dappling sun. Her daughter fell in love with a man whose name told his whole lineage back to the earth, and she rejoiced when their child entered the world of their village.

Again, the water shifted, the women grieved and felt, breathed at the surface. When they came back down, Asia was drawn into the memory bubble.

Asia was in a land where everyone had the same golden skin as her, though some were a touch more reddish in tone, some a bit more olive. There were green eyes and blue, black, and brown, none of them special, all beautiful. The world she lived in was dry, buildings made of earth. Everyone had some kind of scarf on, the women around their faces, the men on top of their heads. Her hands were full of the black dirt, though in this daunting desert light she saw the red in it. Learning from Silky, Asia poured the sacred sand into a pouch at her waist, careful not to drop even a grain.

She heard a call to prayer and a gust of young boys went blowing all around her to the mosque ahead. She followed them, stepping to the side she was allowed to enter to join the other women praying. She felt she was praying all the time, praying for something that wasn't allowed to her. As she prayed a face became clear to her, so clear that with her forehead against the ground she looked to her right. There next to her was a face so beloved to her that all the women floating in the Saffronia's pool grinned at the same time...the perfect face grinned back. Asia blinked and saw them together in the hammam, pouring sweat in shared heat, washing each other's bodies, laughing over nothing, belonging to each other.

Back in the mosque, the face was looking at her with love but also with something else—grief? Fear? Oh, it flooded into Asia then. This sweet feeling was forbidden. Her father had brought a man into the courtyard last night so that Asia could hear them discuss her future. The man, older, wealthy, was offering a dowry to her father that would take care of her family for years. When Asia tried to imagine being a wife to this man, she saw only the exhausted and sallow grief that always haunted her own mother, Yama's face— service without joy. But as her mother came to mind, Asia felt the sweet weight of a gift under her djellaba—Yama had offered her a way out, a small sum that would cover passage for a night train to Tangier, would get her on a boat from there north to Spain. In the little satchel were also two rings, one silver and one gold. She needed to know if the one she called Issam when they were alone, and Imane in front of others, the one people called her heart sister, would be able to come with her?

They found each other after prayer and Issam said yes, she had gathered enough coin for the journey. That night they slipped from their respective beds and lives, leaving no word. Issam wore her brother's clothes, planning to travel as a man. Issam had always felt more like a man inside, so this was not merely acting or surviving, but a kind of landing. They slipped their rings on before getting to the train station, and Issam did the speaking. From Tangier they got on a boat that was bound for Barcelona.

In the tiny room of the boat with its narrow beds, they made love to each other for the first time. Then the second, third, fourth and fifth time, feeling as free as bodies in love can ever feel. They were inside each other for the sixth time when there was a massive blast and the ship shuddered. They dressed quickly, in terror, and stayed quiet until they were found. When the pirates pulled them to the deck, Asia watched the eyes of these men move over them, move over Issam, doubt him.

This small ship which had been their brief heaven was now their worst hell.

The men were of a mixture of colors that were all weathered by the sea, and what unified them was the desire to teach Asia and Issam how wrong they were. They separated the covert lovers and proceeded to take everything. The tickets, the rings, the black sand, the sacred boundaries of the body. Everything. Issam didn't make it, but Asia didn't know why, just that her beloved did not come off of the boat when it landed in a place she had never heard of. One of the men, a Spaniard named Elias, took Asia for his woman, and they were on another ship within a week. She was sick from the sea and her pregnancy within two weeks. When they landed, he set her up as a laundry woman from whom he would come and go, always leaving her pregnant. The town was full of his people, white people with dark features who disapproved of her existence as much as they disbelieved in her right to freedom. She lived a quiet, lonely life, bearing children who lived and children who died, never freed from Elias.

The water shifted and the women surfaced. Without instruction they floated on their backs, looking at the sky and letting the feelings flow through them. Slowly they made their way to the shore and pulled themselves up onto it.

Leaning against each other, the three girls now looked like women.

They felt in their hands the weight of what they'd held and released. Saffronia lifted herself up slowly, unrolling her spine.

"This is the gift of lineage."

Saffronia wiped her own forehead, and she was dry. She shook her right hand three times, and the girls were also dry, no sign of ever having been immersed in the water, throughout space and time.

"It is painful. It is purpose. You come from one utterly specific story and the present and future is just as much yours and yours alone. No one else can give you what you seek. They cannot legitimize your life with any approval. And they cannot detract from the miracle that you are. Everyone, every single one of us, has our *own* work to do. When someone is trying to make you small, it is to busy themselves. Because if they aren't shrinking you, reducing you, they will have to contend with themselves. They have work to do, but it is easier to make assignments for others than do the labor yourself. You have done this to others, what is now being done to you. It always feels righteous. But...only you can reckon with the truth of your past and accept yourself."

She stepped forward and slid her toe across the ground, unveiling below the black sand, in a circle around her. Saffronia reached up and with her fingers, peeled back the blue of the sky, beyond which was that glittering blackness from which the sand came.

"We are all of that. All of us. And that was only a glimpse of it."

Her fingers sealed the bright blue day back in place, and then she brushed off her hands, where small black grains drifted to the ground, precious and plentiful.

"For each of you, there are other glimpses where your existence has been used to make another feel small. That is the spell of whiteness, it is a narrowing, separating, violent idea." With her left hand she made a horizontal line of nothing, nothingness, in the air. Literally in the space between them, the world disappeared. She made another line, vertical, creating a cross in the air.

Everything was gone, every hint and shade of color erased, leaving only blank white space. As she moved, the colors of her own lineage came briefly apart, in pulses like a heartbeat, a horizontal palette of flesh that told a million stories.

"But you do not have to choose it."

Saffronia drifted both hands over the space of the cross, all the colors of the world falling back into place. As she moved her hands her body began to undulate softly, sway. On the next breath she was herself again, one skin that they could now see was many colors all the time.

"Living fully into your own story, before, during and beyond the othering, is a counterspell."

The women felt the completion all at the same moment. Saffronia grinned at them, bowed her head a bit awkwardly, and turned away from them. They walked away, leaving her to her garden, her crystals, her place. They walked away to claim theirs.

virgo love song

is the detritus bagged
& stacked out in the alley
is the compost tucked
deep in backyard bins

are the clothes all clean
& folded & stored
is the walk in my bones
the clay mask off my skin

was the book by the bed
consumed all the whole day
is the work on my table
my joy beyond wealth

is a feast all prepped
from the earth & the sea
these are my sunday songs
this is loving myself

the children (solstice poem)

the children run up the stairs
and i realize how old i have become
one choice at a time
in the places i come together
and where i am forever apart

the children climb me
i offer branches and answers
to their years
i have to be so solid
so much stronger than i am

the children are full
i am humbled by the life in them
they laugh with nothing held back
they demand everything of my attention
they bring me here, now

my child faces a mirror on the wall
smiles toothless, echoing us
before all the lessons
we know everything
life is learning to forget

the children resist even sleep
they know how precious
all this living is
they dream with open eyes
and surrender mid-vision

the children gift me
the miracle of letting go
the wonder of and in time
the wilderness of right now
the possibility of dawn

In Parallel

Miski reached her left hand behind her to steady Loop, pretending she could offer stability to her baby in spite of the sudden chaos of their lives. Her right hand hung at her side, clasped finger by finger in a rotating pattern by her three-year-old, Dahlia, who desperately wanted to be carried and was settling for this contact.

On the front of Miski's body was a semi-transparent black bag, same as everyone else had gotten, but with her image on a digital panel on the front. Inside were basic survival supplies unlike anything she'd ever seen. There were water purification tablets, with a bottle for each of them that looked like glass and felt like metal. A week's worth of something labeled nutrient tubes. Sponge towels and a packet of composting wipes that apparently nourished themselves on waste matter—everything in this minimal packaging was explained by the digital scroll bearing her face that responded instantly to her subvocal questions in brief text messages.

When Miski had seen the announcement on all of her devices at once, she had first called her mother, who lived alone in a massive loft in the city. Her mother tried to comfort her but was clearly shaken. She agreed to come to Miski the next day to help with the babies and just ride whatever this was out together.

Then Miski'd called her closest friends, Kriska and Dorianne, both of whom were also mothers. They'd all seen the same thing; they were all in a state of shock. They agreed to go get the supplies and then decide what to do next. Miski had brought Dahlia and Loop to stand in line at this middle school, and now a half hour later she felt dazed by the feeling of change unfolding in and around her.

Her holster was snug on her hips with a variety of guns and knives—she didn't want to use any of them, but it was best practice to wear protection whenever she left home. Now she needed to get home with her children and this bag of life, and she wasn't sure yet whether this new world would allow that.

Miski knew she had the things needed to take care of her body, and that, if nothing else, her body could feed her children's bodies. That was all she knew.

✲

A few hours earlier Fred had come to in his bedroom, alone. Initially he'd figured he'd overslept—he was a notoriously heavy sleeper. But then he'd heard nothing at all inside his usually bustling, playful home, or outside in his usually active cul-de-sac of other families with young children and working parents. He'd opened his mouth to call out for his wife but found himself oddly unable to recall her name. In escalating panic he'd run around the house screaming for his absent, unnameable family, whose faces were sharp and clear in his mind.

When he'd stepped onto his porch, the whole suburban neighborhood was silent, felt empty. Trying to figure out what had happened unveiled that the wifi and cellular connections were down. This nightmare made him nauseous—was he left alone then, in the whole world?

Fred had waited briefly at the house but couldn't handle the weight of mystery. He decided to take a kitchen paring knife in his pocket and drive downtown and see if he could find anything, anyone, any information. The Subaru was a mess, detritus from his fast-food habits on the backseat floor intermixed with toys, plastic-wrapped paper towels, his gym shoes. His mind was racing in every direction, and he briefly wished he'd actually practiced the centering practices he taught others.

The first people he saw were walking along the road from his suburb towards the city. Two men and a woman. He offered them a ride and, in the car, learned that they had no idea what had happened either. The men were a gay couple who lived on the edge of Fred's neighborhood, the woman had just moved there with her fiancé. They all said that they'd seen an announcement on their TVs and phones that said to go pick up supplies. They each said, in their own words, that the message was from aliens, but Fred knew that didn't make sense.

As they approached the edge of the city there were a few people ahead, and from deeper in the concrete maze rose pillars of smoke. When he rolled down the windows Fred heard incoherent screaming, maybe chanting?

He decided to park here. He didn't want to risk anything happening to the car if he needed to actually evacuate. He pulled over and his passengers all piled out, sticking close together as they walked further into town. Fred didn't think to ask their names—they didn't have answers, or even make much sense—all he wanted was clarity. As the foursome moved through the tightening blocks, they began to see more people. There was some confusion, and wildly different energies.

Then a truck came barreling past them, the truck bed full of men waving flags—American and Confederate. They were holding a Black bespectacled man in the center of the truck, punching and kicking him—oddly he looked more surprised than hurt. The other men, White, all, chanted: "White Power! White Fucking Power! White Power!"

Fred gaped at them and then looked around at his passengers, who also looked horrified. Then he looked around at the other people walking, running, screaming, cheering—other than that Black hostage on the truck, every single person in sight, was White. He fell against the building closest to him, letting the group leave him. Slow, shocked, he tucked into a crouching fetal position.

What the fuck was happening?

✲

Miski and her babies made it home safely. Loop was knocked out, drool plastering the t-shirt on her back. She did the gentle calisthenics that allowed her to shift her son off of her back and into his crib without waking him. Dahlia stood watching her, patiently impatient, her kid glasses a bit off kilter. Once Loop was down, Dahlia instantly reached her hands up, needing to be held. Miski scooped the girlchild into her arms, felt the octopus toddler love grip around her neck, and soothed the child through a soft, confused little cry. She didn't say "everything is going to be ok" because there was no evidence to support that, and Miski tried hard never to lie to her babies. Dahlia whimpered under Miski's soft pitchy lullaby until the combination lulled the child into a deep sleep.

Miski left her children asleep in their room. She whisper-stepped down the carpeted steps from the floor of sleeping down to the floor of function. As soon as she turned out of the tight hallway into her spacious sunlit kitchen, she bent over at the waist, breathless, grabbing a counter to keep from falling to the floor. Her brain went blank with overwhelm and then as the questions returned. Where was her beloved husband? Where was everyone? She began wailing into her own upper arm, a wild terror of weeping.

The announcement that had broadcast on all devices that morning startled her awake. Now she was grateful for that, because instead of waking up to a crying child and a missing husband, she had awakened just to the announcement. It was a video of a person she'd never seen before, someone who looked familiar but was definitely a stranger. She appeared a pale Black, not Brown, more like the night sky reflecting the glow of fluorescent streetlamps. Feminine, friendly. The video took up the entire screen of Miski's phone, she couldn't close it. And when she opened her computer to find out how to stop it, the video was full screen there as well. It played through three times:

> "Hello. My name is Garacia—" (garaysia? garatia?) "and I want you to know there is nothing to be afraid of!" Garacia sounded a bit nervous, a bit upbeat. "We are visitors to Earth, and your planet has qualified for a free healing. Everyone will have your needs met while your healing is attended to. Some systems have been disrupted—mail, commerce, transportation between cities and places—we will get these all back to functional within a week and have provided everything you should need in the interim. Once everyone has gotten their needed supplies, we will return with more information. Please go to your nearest school building and pick up the supply bag with your name on it. You may be asked to deliver a bag to a neighbor who can't make the journey. I look forward to sharing more information with you later."

Miski had considered not going, wondered if being a parent to two small children would qualify her as someone who couldn't go. She had decided not to wait and find out. She'd woken the children briskly, as if for school or an adventure; had holstered up and gone into the streets, part of her attention ranging over the crowds looking for her honey. When the babies asked for Dado, their name for their father, she'd answered honestly, but lightly, that she didn't know.

Now she was back, and it struck her that she really didn't know. She didn't know where the father of her children was, she didn't know who was in control, she didn't know how to make sense of the quiet orderly masses that she'd floated past on her way to the school and back, none of them White people as far as she could see.

She didn't know if the healing "Garacia" had spoken of was some kind of alien-induced ethnic cleansing. She didn't know if she had enough food in the fridge and pantry to save these nutrient tubes in case, in case...she didn't even know the worst-case scenario to prepare for. Getting the supplies to be able to take care of her children had been a series of autopilot moves.

At the school there had been a line around the three-story red brick building to a back door with a window in it. The line was efficient—as each person stepped up, their bag, or bags, were pushed through the window. Miski tried to get a look at who was pushing the bags out, but her attention was drawn instead to the bag itself, and it wasn't until she'd started walking with her burdens balanced that she thought: who handed me this?

On the walk home her mind had pulsed with questions that she pressed back down with the next breath: Did I just not see an alien? Is this alien food? Did an alien steal my love?

Miski had always thought she wanted to meet aliens, but in this moment, she felt everything in her reaching back for answers, instead of forward with curiosity. Now she felt a nauseating roil of fear, grief, longing, and destabilization.

✤

Fred made his way back to his car, back to his suburb, which he had always been proud was mostly African and Indian immigrants, alongside Black and Latinx people. The flags in this neighborhood were a variety of rainbow flags—queer rainbows; pale pink, blue and white trans solidarity rainbows; Caribbean island national flags; Brown and Black rainbows—all flying full mast on small-ish houses, one-quarter acre lots of land with small yard gardens, curled about each other in orderly cul-de-sacs, each with a park where everyone brought their kids around each other to play and learn. Some of the parks even had pools.

Fred had felt a certain shameful pride about being one of the rare white men who chose to live here. He'd married a gorgeous Black woman and they had two mixed babies with greenish brown eyes under curly hair. He had the social cache of proximity to Blackness, which had made him quite desirable to other White people as a teacher. He taught White people Tai Chi and Aikido, and he taught White people how to not be actively, overtly racist, to ask themselves the hard questions. He'd never been formally trained in these things himself, but still knew that what he offered was valuable, because his students told him so. And his wife wouldn't be with him if he wasn't a good White, obviously.

But now all the Black people, and Brown, Asian, Indian, Indigenous, Arab—everyone who was not White—was gone. He'd been left behind.

His TV flickered on as he stood in his living room, utterly lost. A White man came on the screen, familiar enough for Fred to double take, but no name came to mind. Brown hair neatly shorn close to the head, eyes that seemed to shine a bit. The man looked a bit flustered, aiming for friendly.

> "Hello. It's me Garacio again. I am one of a handful of visitors to Earth, because your planet has qualified for a free healing. As per our first message, we would like to provide all of your material needs while your healing is attended to, so if you can please refrain from burning things and breaking windows....Many systems have been disrupted—mail, commerce, transportation between cities and places. We will get these all back to functional as soon as you calm down. We are not here to hurt you. We have provided everything you should need. Please go to your nearest school building and pick up your supply bag. You may be asked to deliver a bag to a neighbor who can't make the journey. I look forward to sharing more information with you later."

Garacio's message repeated three times, and then he was gone.

Fred was scared to go back outside, even though the elementary and middle schools were only three blocks from the house, the main reason this had been their starter home. Still, it appeared the gays and the woman from earlier had been right that something that looked human but called itself an alien had hacked the comms systems. Going to get supplies would be the first step of responding to them.

He stood at his own door, talking himself into opening it. What he had seen downtown, the frenzy of White people in celebration, with others who looked as overwhelmed and confused as he felt...an instant later Fred was crumpled into a pile, sobbing and weak against the floorboard.

He did not deserve to be left here. He did not deserve this.

✻

Miski had the computer and phone both plugged in to charge. Though she doubted that missing Garacia's next announcement was even possible, she didn't want to take any chances. Loop was awake again and in her arms, and she wondered if her child could sense her fear even through all her calming breath and sounds.

Baby Loop reached up his dimpled hand and placed it on her chin while he drank from her breast. That tiny soft hand did comfort her, his massive eyes didn't leave hers, and it brought her peace to know that even with all the other mystery around her, she was feeding her child.

She felt, low in her gut, the place where Loop had lived within her, and Dahlia before him, and a lost child before them both. She felt, under the weight of her living son, her lower belly still soft, still gathering and knitting itself together deep within her. She felt her sensitive bladder, knew she'd need to take a break soon or risk pissing herself again. She had suffered severe hemorrhaging during Loop's birth, and though she was technically fine, she still felt frailty at her center, the fragility of surviving, perhaps of her body regenerating the blood it needed. She wasn't physically strong enough to go far with her babies on her body. She wasn't going to be able to run if running was needed. How was she supposed to keep these children safe?

Looking down at her child, whose eyes were starting to flutter slowly in milky pleasure, Miski had a flashback to Loop's birth. Specifically, she saw the fight she had had with her husband that day. He'd taken Dahlia to their neighbors' home according to plan, and when he returned, she told him something didn't feel right, that she was worried about laboring at home. He kept putting her off, teasing her for struggling with the pain. An hour later she had stood at his back in his office, trying to grasp enough breath from the pain to tell him she needed his attention—he was sitting, facing away from her, at his computer trying to finish a few things before they went to the hospital. She couldn't remember what she had had to say to get him to turn around, but she remembered how he had looked when he turned around, an angry stranger.

She tried to shake this memory clear of her head. She loved him, she missed him right now. That was not the first time she had seen the stranger in his face. Now, in this moment, she was longing for him, even while something more subterranean in her pulsed with theories on why he was missing.

✲

Fred catalogued everything in the house, first the alcohol, then the weed hidden way up in a closet, then the pantry and fridge full of the healthy foods his wife liked. He figured it would take a few days to drink what was in the house. He decided to go and pick up the supplies that Garacio kept offering him, and on the way back to stop at the liquor store and pick up a few strong bottles. And maybe find some pork rinds. He also wanted a cigarette—they'd quit together when they decided to have a baby, and he had only snuck a few here and there while drinking with friends. He wondered which of his friends were...here. He'd have to do some reconnaissance, though in this moment he didn't want anyone else to see him like this, alone. All alone.

In the weed closet he'd seen the hook for his wife's holster, which reminded him that he could be armed. A half hour of frantic searching didn't yield the gun or ammo he knew she'd purchased after the last election. Maybe it was in the safe? The safe for which he didn't remember the code. He smacked his forehead.

On the stairs, a makeshift belt holster right around his tummy, he paused to look at the photos of his family that hung along the wall all the way down. Near the bottom, in a brand-new frame, was his wife holding his newborn, the little face still smushed together, eyes closed. He'd chosen this photo to frame because it was the first one of...the child. But now he leaned in and saw his wife's face, wan, stretched, almost gray. Now he remembered this was taken just a couple of minutes before she had passed out, and they'd seen the blood pooling under her hips, rushing her away to emergency surgery.

He'd been left standing in the empty room holding his son, feeling regret for having delayed their trip to the hospital. This picture might be the last one he ever had of his wife, and it felt tragic to him now, how much he had missed in the moment, how much he had put off, how much he had taken for granted.

He was overcome with regret—in spite of his projection of himself as a good man, when he searched through his memories all he saw was a shitty husband, a selfish father. Clearly, he hadn't loved his family enough to be with them wherever they were. Which must be heaven, because just a minute in this world of White anger and celebration was more hell than he'd ever imagined.

And he felt like a coward because he was too scared to walk

over to the school now. What if those White men came driving around again in their truck? Was Garacio going to keep him safe? Could those kind of White men tell the kind of White man he was just by looking? Would he be punished for his Black family? Would they guess it just because he was in this neighborhood? Or was he supposed to stand up in some way, to be brave? Maybe he should have tried to rescue that Black man? Or maybe that man was a race traitor? But didn't he still deserve rescue from racists?

And then Fred caught his own pale disoriented face in the hall mirror. "Am I racist?" he thought, for the first time in years.

No. His body contracted hard, no.

Not possible.

Opening the door to the house with sweating palms, Fred stepped back into a world that no longer fit him. He looked in every direction, feeling scared to be outside and exposed. He ran to the car and once inside, he locked the car and adjusted the kitchen knives strapped around him. He reached back between the seats and pressed his hand into the pile on the floor, down further and further into the mess until he felt the wooden curve of a junior bat set that someone had gifted his daughter a few weeks before for her birthday. He'd tossed it back here, sure she wouldn't be into bats and balls. He tore the packaging off the bottom of the bat and swung it into his hand. It felt hollow and like it could do no harm. Holding it still made him feel incrementally safer. He laid it across the passenger seat and pulled out slowly into the empty street.

Fred drove over to the school, practicing the way he was going to demand answers from whoever was handing out supplies the whole ride. Someone was in charge, there was someone with whom he could negotiate, complain, figure out how he could get a different present, and different future. When he pulled up and stood in line, he tried to hold on to his demands, but then he stepped up, and a transparent white bag passed out from a window in the back, and he said nothing and looked for no one, and it didn't even occur to him again that he was angry until he was almost back to the house.

✣

The TV flickered on, oddly, of its own accord. Garacia was back; her Black skin glowed, her features seemed clearer to Miski now, wide eyes, wide nose, soft mouth—not pretty, but pleasing. Garacia's hair was a soft textured fro that lifted higher than the screen and Miski wondered how'd she'd missed that before.

"Hello. This is Garacia again. If you are receiving this message, thank you for picking up your supplies. We hope you are satisfied with what we have rationed to each person. These supplies are designed to last for one week, by which time we expect that your systems will have been adapted to the conditions of your healing.

"We are the Garacsz and our role in the universe is to support traumatized species to heal the wounds that can develop between species and planet. Your planet has so many varieties of species on it that it took a while for us to understand the particular nature of human beings, what you needed and what was keeping you from it. It is very, very rare to see a species stay committed to warfare for as long as your species has. Our healing work on this planet is going to be complex and intense.

"To understand the wound, we had to fully uncover it, which is why the dominants have been placed in parallel for now. We are providing resources to everyone and will reconvene the worlds when you are ready.

"Any questions?"

Miski started to laugh uncontrollably. Loop popped off of her breast and looked at the TV, then back at his mama, his compassionate mouth still open, her nipple still dewing with milk. She brought him back to her breast and tried to contain her delirium.

"Any questions?"

"Yes. I have questions." Miski spoke, expecting no answer.

"We are ready to hear your questions." Garacia now appeared to be making eye contact directly with Miski, which Miski tested by leaning as far as she could to her right, then her left. Garacia watched and waited patiently. "You can ask anything."

"Where is my husband?"

"In a parallel world."

"Is he alive? Safe?"

"He is alive. He is safe. He is very scared. The parallel world is having a harder time with this transition."

Miski felt anger fire up in her and worked to contain it for Loop's sake. "Why is he over there?"

"He is a dominant." Garacia spoke in a very friendly, no-nonsense manner as she said this.

"He's married to *me*," Miski began in defense...but even as she spoke, something rock slow and core deep shook in her, a knowing of what Garacia meant. Her breath caught before she could finish the sentence, the case, feeling all the imprints and echoes of that dominance ghost themselves about her memories, her body. He loved her, she knew this. She loved him. He had tried. She shifted questions: "How long will this healing take?"

Garacia nodded, "It will depend on each person. As soon as they are ready, we will bring them back, one by one. Each journey will take its own time. For now, those on the other side cannot speak or think the names of anything they find to be in any way inferior to themselves. They can see it, but not name it. When they properly value each person, each form of life, they will be allowed to have the names back. And though they are trying, they are unable to cause any damage to each other there, same as here." Miski felt the presence of her holster on the dining room table, apparently useless, and nodded. Garacia continued, "We have found that removing the impact of violence and removing the perceived inferior leaves enough room for the dominant, the mistakenly 'superior,' to turn and contend with themselves."

"Are there any White people here?" Miski asked next.

"Yes, of course. I mean mostly, from every race, it's children and those who care for children. And there are some men. Some straight people. Some able-bodied people. Some of all the kinds of people your species has elevated—not as many as we'd hoped for, but this is what is. Surprise doesn't serve the unlearning. What we assessed is the internal alignment with a dominant worldview."

Miski nodded. "Where are you from?"

Miski received this answer in her mind, an instant visualization of moving from Earth out to the solar system, beyond the Milky Way and then over and down and over forever and ever spinning past all the lights of the night sky that she had only known in clustered constellations, but now she saw that all of existence was made up of space, and she was barreling through it all and now she was landing into a different galaxy, into a solar system of fifteen planets, into the fuchsia rings of a smokey looking turquoise planet, and realizing that the rings were full of floating structures. Buildings? Villages? It was unclear where anything began or ended.

Miski opened her eyes, realizing only then that they'd closed to receive this vision. She shuddered, pulling Loop closer, disconcerted that these Garacsz seemed able to move her attention somehow.

Garacia's voice filled the room again, softer: "This is enough to share for now. Please rest, hydrate, and nourish your body and those of your children. They will grow up without the burden of dominance. They will choose the lives they will lead without false superiority or inferiority guiding them."

The TV screen darkened; the room was quiet.

✲

"Do you know how crazy that sounds?" Fred was standing and screaming at the alien on his screen.

Garacio was remarkably unflustered. "Which part?"

Fred put his balled fists against his hips. "Who am I dominating? I live in peace with all kinds of minorities. I *married* one. I didn't have to, there were plenty of White girls who wanted me, but I fell in love with—"

Garacio waited, his head tilted ever so slightly to the left, eyebrows cocked.

"Why can't I say her name?" Fred, pointing at the screen, was getting red in the face. "Are you doing that?"

"In a way, yes," Garacio acknowledged, and explained that, "In this parallel world, no one can speak, think, or see the names of anything you find to be beneath you."

The alien let this sit in the room between them.

Fred was stunned. He stood still, sat down on the couch, and stood back up, laughing with rage. "This is a nightmare. This isn't true. This isn't true!"

Garacio was quiet.

"Are my children ok? Is my wife ok?"

"I am really glad you asked, Fred. Yes. They are ok. They have their supplies, and they are safe. They await you." Garacio's voice was kind, gracious, reassuring.

Fred felt overwhelmed by this feeling of disgust. Being treated with kindness was less familiar than being treated with subservience, compliance. He felt powerless. He was powerless. Realizing this, without much forethought, he picked up a book and threw it at the television. Nothing broke, which made Fred scream out in frustration.

The TV screen went dark. He felt the blackness as a yawning forever before him, and he kept cursing and cursing, trying to destroy his home, needing to break something—but nothing would shatter.

�֎

Miski laid sleeping Loop down across from hazy, restless dreaming Dahlia. She called her mother again, asked her to hold on, then merged in Kriska and Dorianne. These two friends were chosen sisters to her, and her mother had been there for each of them in absence of their own, Kriska's who died when she was young, and Dorianne's mother who lived in a permanent state of prescribed haze. The four women's voices flowed over each other with reports of the morning until her mother asked the question: "And Fred?"

Miski was the only one of them intimate with a White person, and they all accepted Fred as the person their Miski loved. She explained to them what she had learned from the space colored stranger in her television. Her husband, her beloved, was going to have to let go of dominance within, in the shadowy places she couldn't travel with him. He was going to have to be her equal before he came home.

It was only then, recounting and comparing these few profound answers, that Miski let herself understand what was happening. She gasped as the complex emotion gripped her—an intervention, a whispered prayer, a necessary help, a rescue from something micro and massive and constant and almost deniable, something that she'd been too cynical to hope for and too hopeful to forget, the end of an inevitable presence that she had compromised with, accepted as the cost of her joy and her life...the freedom she dreamed aloud to her children about every night, all of it was happening, was at least being attempted. By a species she had no reason to trust, but also no reason to distrust.

She wept then, a different kind of flood.

Her tiny community offered their witness across the miles, comforting her as she moved through a different level of grief, that extra heft of intimate contact with oppression. She wept as the TV screen darkened to silence, as the call ended with promises to gather tomorrow, have her mother hold them, and plan with her friends to share care until Miski had another parent in the house again, however long that took.

When Loop woke up with a shout, Miski wept into his curls, and when Dahlia awoke and crawled into her mama's lap, Miski held her two children close to her and openly wept, letting them catch and taste her tears and know directly the gratitude and relief of something vicious ending, something else, hard enough to take time, beginning.

saint woman

no such thing as her
that's what no one want to understand
she catch your eye because she can
but she already memory
beyond the brief pulse of interest
she float around herself
roots, tendrils ever reaching
never landing, bitter cloud
she not young like she was
not easily slipped from her attention
she not old but time closing in,
some day she taste fear at dawn
try to be alone in it, no words anyway
saint woman wear a river in public
so she can keep moving to the sea
everyone who see her start to pray
but she got no miracle left
just this breath, and next breath
licking the salt away

(In response to Saint Woman, *Amy Sherald, 2015. My friend Shantrelle Lewis, who
became my friend after I wrote this, is the woman who inspired this painting)*

221

sub-terrain

if i should be
so intoxicated with love
so flattened out
sunlit on your petal
if i should stumble with the headiness
of being in the path
of your smile

if i should fall silent
slurred by the dark musk of that grand intimacy
tilt forward with my
fill of magic
batted at you
lean too close
into the sub-terrain of your neck's curve

forgive me my love
i have been out seeking home
and here you lay, hearth

i suck that sweet liqueur off your lip
losing the myth of difference
down through a million verdant layers

sap, drizzle
you are the scale of ocean and sun

nothing parchment can bind or separate
such a pure thing
i didn't even know to long
for such a love

Bubbles

Zoala's eyes swept a room full of blue-black bodies trading in artificial laughter and temporary promises. She sat by herself (again) at Machiba's, the only tolerable bar left in Joburg, letting a sweet red open in her glass. She noticed with sadness that she somehow loved this place without knowing anyone in it.

The bar opened directly onto the street, leaving no barriers to the bustle of 7th Ave. In the center of the room was a table with benches draped in stylish young flirtations, sucking at cigarettes and bouncing to the vintage kwaito and space house sounds of the DJ. Others leaned on the bar on either side of her, or shuffled lazily on the dance floor, full of drink and nothing to do. They all watched the floor, or had the dazed look of people immersed in their data bubbles.

Zoala felt the smoke wrapping its million scents around each spring of hair on her head. She had quit her job a few hours earlier, but no one knew that yet, and she had no one to tell.

Her data was at a low flow. Just another thirty-two-year-old orphan who had given her life to work, alone and jobless on a Sunday night. No one noticed her, here in the bar, or in the net, where small impersonal zeros sat in each of her notification bars. She knew she wasn't unattractive, but she'd heard plenty of times that she wasn't "approachable," that she was "intimidating." As a result, her mouth knew the contours of a wine glass better than any lover's lips.

In front of her a woman in floating spectacles began to dance closer to a man in a metallic jumper. They were looking at each other in coy stolen glances, and then at the floor or ceiling, moving into each other's orbits. Eventually he slipped his arms around her waist and slid her tightly onto his thigh. They fell into a rhythm together as if they'd been famished for this movement.

"How do you sustain that feeling?" Zoala wondered. She remembered the first time she'd danced with her last love, his hands at her hips, his mouth first touching her neck. Somewhere along the escalating commitments, their dancing had gotten lost, perhaps in the monotonous work of love, or perhaps just deprioritized by her love of work.

It wasn't as if she hadn't tried. Two years ago, that final heart break had been so thorough. The potential of their love had seemed so illuminating, inspiring and viral within her thoughts and dreams—but something in his anger was just wild enough to make it impossible for her to surrender. He said he couldn't feel her love. The three years of her life she'd spent with him had utterly changed her and prepared her to be with another. But when she said she needed him to be peaceful with her, he'd left her completely alone.

The heart path behind her was a mess of broken or settling hearts. It wasn't just a current experience of lack. It was a sustained experience, so much so that she was sitting in a perfect bar considering that love didn't actually happen anymore. Or matter.

Zoala reflected on how love had served a logistical function for most of human history—a man and a woman created home together and procreated, gave work and seed to society together. Love eased the labor of generations. As populations had ballooned and gender roles had shifted, indeed as gender itself had become more diverse, love no longer had that logistical function. People just weren't trying as hard. She wondered if all that romance had just been to keep the system working. She let that idea slither through her body, bringing her lower in herself and her seat.

225

She poured the rest of the wine down her throat and checked her bar tab in the bubble. It was respectable—nearly 4000 rand—and should have insured a sloppy buzz; but her sadness was sharp and alert. Some part of her wanted to thoroughly wallow, and she couldn't slur it out.

"No more love," she submuttered.

"Speak for yourself," she heard nearby.

It took a second to register that those words might be in response to her. Zoala looked up to see, next to her, a fascinating creature: skin mottled like black mud in the sun, hair in an impossibly high two tower mohawked fro. This creature was looking sideways at her enough to let it be known she hadn't just overheard someone else submuttering.

"I am." Zoala rolled her eyes at her empty glass, ready to withdraw within her data bubble.

"Well, what do you mean? From the bartender? In the world altogether? Or just, personally, you are swearing it off?" The stranger smiled at her and Zoala scowled inside. Charm almost offended her these days, it felt so disconnected from authentic connection. And here was another pretty thing, acting as if life was so grand.

"In general, in my experience, it isn't there. Or worth letting in what it drags just behind it. Who are you?"

"I am Josa. Josa Debeza."

The stranger's eyes lifted the silence. They were massive, dark, direct.

"Zoala Kajamala."

They were quiet for a moment as the names filtered through their respective data bubbles and pulled up images and information on each other.

Josa: born in Swaziland, thirty-eight years old, no job listed, musical history major, no relationship listed.

Zoala: born in Joburg, first generation family from Malawi, thirty-two years old, no children, senior cultural researcher at Sapax still listed.

Sapax was known to most people—it tracked how culture was changing, and based on that, advised policies and products to serve and advance the culture. It had grown out of a pattern of data gathering on the web for product placement.

Cosearching had stopped being rude long ago, but their silence still had some aggression in it.

"Do you make it a regular practice to interrupt inner monologues?"

"Oh no," Josa grinned. "I was just enthralled at how loud your brain is. I have been looking for a beautiful woman with a loud brain. You are a woman?"

Zoala felt a little wow in her system.

"I am. You?"

"Both. Neither. I use dual currently, but might upgrade to spectrum before I'm fifty."

Another wow. Zoala looked at this brazen dual and felt her eyebrow go curious on her face.

"And why do you believe in love?"

"It seems smarter than having faith in any other thing. In deities for instance. Or the economy. Love I have felt, it felt like I was...of god. And had everything I needed. It seems like a useful substance to imbibe."

"You really talk like that?" Zoala was both impressed and worried that Josa might be corny.

"Only when I am lifted, Zoala Kajamala. I have been sitting here longer than you, though you didn't notice me. So, I watched you arrive all gorgeous and with some dignity in your spine, and I watched you drink until it left. But I know it was there. And it looked very good."

Zoala sat up straighter.

"There we go. Now? You could maybe find some love." Josa smiled and looked all over Zoala's real body, from upshocked brow to thick, soft hips and long running legs.

"Free unsolicited love advice at the bar? Is this a move? Oh, how lucky I am!"

"Come now," Josa's grin was constant, stunning and comfortable. "We are attractive people. We are quick witted, I see that in just these first moments of our friendship. And you must be smart to work for Sapax—'the largest culture shaping institution in the world'? And you, up near the top already, so young? It would be unhealthy to not at least consider it."

Zoala looked directly at Josa and saw that they weren't fully joking. She wondered if she should tell them she'd left Sapax today. She let her mind wander for a moment, imagining her lips against Josa's lips, leaning into their arms, letting that smile become comfortable.

It was in that moment of daydream that Zoala noticed a disturbance at the edge of her data. It popped up like a new window, but didn't have a normal shape or boundary. She double blinked her eyes, where the bubble tech was embedded, to see if the glitch was organic. No change. It must be spam, but all of her spam was programmed to only appear at the back of her private bubble of data projections, out of her sight unless she pulled it around, thanks to a displacing app she'd purchased. This little droplet of disturbance seemed to be growing at the junction of four different windows.

She looked up at Josa, who was gazing at her with eyes that felt suddenly extremely familiar.

"What?"

"I think I like you, loveless girl."

"Why?"

"You laugh at my brilliant banter. Against your will, not coy... which is fantastic. You keep looking at my body the right way. You seem to have philosophies about this world, which makes for at the very least some dynamic conversations. And you don't seem to need my company. At all."

Zoala was intrigued by Josa. Their energy didn't feel merely charming—it felt open, and comforting, and...easy. She felt like she must already know them, and just couldn't remember how. They were extremely, unusually attractive, with sharp cheekbones and those big, gorgeous eyes, a full dramatic mouth and strong shoulders. Their data showed a traveler. She felt them shift closer to her before she could see it, some proximity of interest and intimacy that felt just fine. Zoala caught herself smiling, annoying her own face a bit.

"Ok." Sigh.

"Ok what, Zoala Kajamala?"

"Ok. You can like me." Shrug.

"Oh. Oh! I wasn't seeking your permission." Josa's smile deepened into delight.

"You should though. Otherwise, it will be a very short-lived romance."

Zoala immediately pursed her lips tart around the word she'd said. Romance? Before she could think of some way to reel it back between her teeth, Josa reached out a hand and touched her arm. The disturbance in her data leapt up and appeared everywhere their skin touched.

Zoala tried to understand what she was seeing. It looked more tangible than her regular projections, she could barely see through it. A singular vibrant picture of—a zoo? A safari? A conservatory? Something green like that, but without end.

"Zoala? Are you ok?"

Zoala realized she couldn't keep the data to herself. Some people stayed so tuned in to their own data that they didn't notice those moments of distraction in others, but Josa was sharp, attentive.

"Sorry. Some kind of spam."

"Oh yeah? Yeah, I have spam coming in too. Was ignoring it."

"Yes, sorry. I—"

"It's fine. No judgment...eh, I just pushed us into a conversation here." They paused. "I didn't ask if you were available for it—perhaps you are very important?"

Zoala thought about her job. Had she been important?

"Zoala?"

"I'm sorry. My work is...interesting." Josa laughed, and Zoala realized she sounded skeptical. "It is! It was. Actually I...don't know how I feel about Sapax."

"It's how we are able to sit here and know roughly anything about each other without asking a question." Josa said this matter of factly.

"Yes. But...it can feel, sometimes, like we are all these bundles of information. Serving a white man's agenda." Zoala ducked her head a bit into her wine glass to say this. "I sound like my grandmother, harping about race. But—we are just an ad agency with a theoretical moral code at this point. And the things we get people to buy are products of white and foreign businessmen. Sure, there are some Black Safricans higher in the ranks, but the product, the wealth...it belongs to white people."

"I see that. So, are you the thorn in the man's side? Are you the one raising these questions there?"

Zoala thought about that. She'd been a documentarian, tracking the lives of prominent culturists, noticing how the world shifted because of the risks, loves, and learning of the upper echelon. She liked a lot of the work, though the structure reflected the still-racialized economy of Safrica. She'd been good at her job, excellent really—to have become so senior so young, she'd had to become excellent. But she hadn't stood up, not until today. "No. I bite my tongue there. I do like the work...it's just always about what sells, what doesn't sell. And data sells. But there is no discerning what is good to share, what isn't."

"Ah. Yeah, well...I barely looked at the profiles I found on you."

"But you *could*."

"And you are." Josa's face was knowing, and at ease.

"Yes. I mean, it helps. It's safer. In a way. Like—it's good to know we are vaccine-aligned, and STI compatible, and that neither of us can get pregnant. People used to have to divulge all of that, or lie. It's not the tech, but the creators of it, their lens. I sometimes wonder what it would look like with real Safrican leadership." She tried to imagine a Black boss. "Anyway."

Zoala drank from her wine glass and noticed a new pressure, Josa's leg touching hers below the bar. A small heat tendril crept up her leg. The familiarity was unsettling. She didn't shift away.

"I get it. I do." Josa leaned in close to tell her about themselves. "I am an archivist. My work is very, very important. Information is powerful. No one ever looks at it." Their eyes sparkled. "But I still know it to be completely fascinating and relevant."

"What do you archive?"

"I archive the unnecessary. And the conditions that make something necessary become unnecessary."

Zoala had a dimple that only emerged when she had questions, and Josa got to witness that dimple in this moment.

"Like the microwave. Or the handheld. Or HOV lanes in transit."

"What lanes?" she asked.

Josa gasped a bit at her question. Zoala laughed as Josa's face animated, their passion for their work showing clearly as they answered.

"Cars used to be owned and driven by individuals. Not even rich, just, people generally had their own cars. In most 'developed' places, anyway. So they had special lanes for people who would share their car, high occupancy vehicles, HOVs, to reward those who would drive others going the same way. But now cars are communalized in most of the world, right? So these lanes have become unnecessary. It's been about a fifty-year process. I have been gathering material on this, pictures, practices, archiving the decision-making process, and so on. I am fascinated by things that were once ideas, like—the best idea we had for how to live and share the world, or the highway, and survive. And why are they no longer the best ideas, what replaces them? Often the same desire serves the next idea or iteration, so I like tracing that too...we get so excited about new ideas, but I think we don't learn enough about what doesn't work and why."

Zoala nodded. Josa watched her face.

"I don't make sense?" They looked concerned.

"You do." Zoala bit her lip, aware that she'd become distracted by Josa's soft moving mouth but unable to look away.

Josa smiled again, this time all humility and sweetness. Zoala was definitely interested.

Josa ordered a bottle of sweet wine, and they moved from the counter to a small table in the open air. There were still dancers in motion, though Zoala noticed her spectacled/metallic duo from earlier had taken the next step and were now nuzzling in a corner. The street was full beside them as the world transitioned from the dinner drink hour to the club dancing hour, cabs and bikes crowding each other.

Josa didn't smoke, which was rare now that cigarettes were detoxified. Neither did Zoala, she didn't trust the synthetic herbs. She ordered joloff fritters to help with the feeling of being quite drunk. Josa ate most of them.

They talked as the night slipped into the sensual hours. The street slowly cleared of people and cars as the two strangers exchanged stories about being data hunters, and ethical ways to use numbers, talking stories. They made each other laugh, they debated, they ranged topics from food to film, past relationships and present dreams, dancing to what music they liked.

As they spoke, the disturbance in Zoala's data grew until it covered most of the bottom curve of her bubble. Because the data was broadcast all around her, as the disturbance spread it appeared to be growing up Josa's body. She knew it was an illusion of the projection and tried to ignore it, the massive, ungroomed trees and rolling golden hills. Eventually she turned down her projection brightness to be less distracted—she realized she didn't want to split her attention.

"Look girl."

Zoala followed Josa's pointing fingers away from their dynamic face, glancing around at the low burnt candles on the other tables, the quiet street under muted stars. Still concrete and ambiance. She turned back to Josa. "What?"

Josa suddenly looked shy in their grin.

"Everyone left us here alone. It's time for going to homes. Can I walk you somewhere?"

Zoala looked around again, astonished. Usually, her data was like a thin screen on the world, where she could easily hold the distinction between what was real and what was in her projection. What she'd been seeing tonight looked so tangible, she felt like she could smell wilderness. Between that and flirting with Josa, she hadn't noticed the night ending. Now the tables were empty, and the bar owner was leaning on the counter, reading a book patiently. How long had they been talking?

Josa stood up, put out a hand to Zoala. They left the bar as if they'd been heading home together for years. Weaving her hand easily in theirs, as if they were children, or lovers, Zoala led Josa downhill in the direction of her doorstep without thinking twice.

Halfway home, Josa stopped suddenly, compelling Zoala back against them. They looked up until Zoala, too, had to turn her eyes to the moon. It was massive, almost droopy. Zoala felt it was brighter than any moon she'd ever seen and noticed that there was moonlight in her strange spam data projection too.

"Beautiful Zoala. That is how you looked tonight when I met you," Josa nodded up at their celestial observer. "Heavy with the things you have seen, like that moon."

"What kind of person is drawn to the moon?"

"Oh. An ocean kind of person I suppose. A very vast person, and I mean that with all humility." They both laughed. Josa leaned close to Zoala then, close enough that Zoala stopped laughing, and then stopped breathing.

Then they kissed her.

Her data exploded, the disturbance taking over her whole screen suddenly. She saw a low field of grass, in the center of which a massive golden lion shook its mane, mounted over a sleek female. She could see the moonlight cast shadows along his smooth coat, she could see the lion below seem to arch her head back up towards his. They roared together.

Zoala darted back from the vision and the kiss. This time Josa looked equally confused.

"Lions?" they said. "How did you do that?"

"I didn't!" Zoala frowned at Josa. Was this a game to them? "Are you some viral tease? What are you doing?"

"What? No! No why...no I just saw you sitting there and liked you. Not spreading viruses and not teasing. I—did you see lions?"

"Of course I saw lions! Fucking. But if you wanted me to think of sex, you were doing just fine without this trickery, Josa." Searching their face for guilt, Zoala only saw that Josa looked genuinely hurt.

Zoala felt immediately harsh, blaming. She tried to consider any other option. The spam was a tiny stain on the bottom of her data again, swirling a bit, just a moving snapshot of some wilderness.

"Do you still see it?"

Josa turned around completely, spinning their arms so Zoala knew they were checking their whole projection.

"It's smaller now."

They looked at each other for a second, at the comms notices and normal data popping around and between them. The lions, the whole spam phenomenon, was illogical, impossible.

Zoala, somewhere between fear, curiosity, and a tipsy lust, shot forward suddenly, taking Josa's face in her hands and, once she saw the surprised yes in their smile, kissed them again. Immediately she was immersed in a savannah, wild high reeds around her, the two lions in the near distance rolling around, wrestling, playful with each other.

She stopped kissing and stepped back, scared.

Josa looked amused. "This is fascinating. Truly. That has never happened before. My equipment is, um, impacted by yours."

Zoala thought fascinating was the last word she would use to describe it. She felt exposed by this uncontrollable something happening in her most intimate space.

"I may be drunk, but my securities should all still be working. There is no logic to it. There is no way you could be doing this to me. It's wrong."

"Ah. You are worried?"

"Yes! You should be too! It doesn't concern you that when you touch me some massive spam comes up on your screen?"

"Upon further study, I would no longer call it spam. It's..."

"What? Do you think it's a program?"

"I was going to say it is *beautiful*. Mysterious. But it is quite stunning. I don't think I have ever seen footage of live lions before. Much less such...it felt very...real. To me."

Josa stood quietly, seeming to savor the strange moment they'd shared. Zoala backed away, a wave of suspicion overwhelming her curiosity. She remembered now how her evening had begun. This is the strangest mismatch she'd ever had, but her theory held. It was better to be alone than try to trust love.

Quietly, Josa's voice followed her in the near-dark. "You going to leave me here on the street Madame Kajamala? Because we see something beautiful when we kiss?"

Zoala stopped in her tracks. Josa's words landed on the ink black pavement of the street and she realized she felt the connection to them all along her spine. It didn't make sense, but it felt like she would have to fling herself forward to make it another step.

"You act like it's me doing this," they continued. "It's much more likely one of your Sapax experiments! I should be the fretful one!"

"I don't work for Sapax anymore." Zoala didn't turn around to speak. "I quit today."

"Why?" Josa was right behind her. Zoala's mind briefly pondered if Josa was a Sapax spy. Eh, she thought, fuck them. "My boss was a manipulative Afrikaner who made me feel like my life's work was a game to please him. Today he came to us with an idea. From the president no less! To...trick people into working more for almost nothing. To *inspire* people to self-indenture. Through *our* advertisements. And I... I challenged him."

"Why?" they asked, somehow closer.

Zoala turned around, the world spinning a bit with her on a fermented honey wine axis. She turned her projection all the way down.

"It's ridiculous. It just felt like I had no..." she searched their face for an answer, for the word. "...Dignity. That I was compromising all, everyone. Like, we say things are different, but what changes? It's still the Arthur Vestoors of the world making decisions. What about us, who are from this soil? We cook, we clean, we assist, we support, we stay, we sacrifice, we work seven day work weeks. Isn't anyone else tired?" Zoala sounded ragged. "Where are *our* voices?"

Josa didn't say anything for a moment, and then they reached out and pulled her into them. They wrapped their arms around her, her face tucked into their shoulder as if it had always been a place of comfort. A sob leapt from her mouth, followed by a storm.

Eventually, a quiet came through her and she caught her breath, lifted her head, stepped back a bit. They looked in her eyes, and she held their gaze, feeling strangely unashamed of her emotion. They drifted their thumbs over her cheeks, and then the two of them stood in each other's arms in the midst of the night, letting small smiles grow together.

"I don't cry in front of my mama, much less strangers. But...do I feel like a stranger to you, Josa?"

"Never. So far." They smiled. "Are you scared of the visions we make between us?"

"Yes."

"Me too, Zoala. But I'm curious, too. I turned it down but...I can feel it there."

"I know," she whispered.

She felt like they were all alone in the world. The street and concrete and drama seemed faded in Josa's presence—they seemed to be touched by a moonlight beyond this night.

She turned up her projection, just to see. Her entire screen was a distant mountain across a long flat green, stars crowded in the night sky above, the plain dotted with black and white striped creatures in clusters.

"Zebra!"

She saw Josa's eyes refocus and knew they were also checking.

"Should we tell someone about these disturbances?" Even as she asked, Zoala tried to imagine who. The teledroids? Bubble customer care? The police?

"Maybe," they shrugged. "I scarcely know what we'd say. Excuse me, I met this beautiful woman who makes me see some world out of fairy tales and encyclopedias, all over my data. It has no boundaries and appears to have no end. And she has perfect skin and these eyes that glow like—"

"Stop. I am being serious."

They had her smiling again, though, leaving the raw moment to settle between them.

"Ok, let us be serious." Josa straightened their face out, and Zoala was amazed at how the sweet, delicate face could become so still and serious. "I feel like we hardly understand this enough to... report it to anyone."

"It isn't normal though." She wanted them to know what to do. She'd done enough today.

"No, it isn't. Or perhaps we aren't. But let us learn what it is. It only happens when we are near each other, so I don't think it's a virus. And I am not sure I want it to stop."

"How do we learn more about it?"

They considered each other for a moment. "Turn up," they offered.

Josa moved closer, so that their projections were almost totally overlapping. The visual was of a wide golden expanse, a sky unbroken by man made objects, dotted by clouds and coasting creatures in flight.

Zoala felt a breathlessness in herself. The place she saw, they saw, it felt familiar though she had never seen anything like it to her knowledge. She didn't know if such a place existed anymore, and these animals were all extinct, Josa had probably studied them. It looked like an image from a history book come to life. She felt she should be frightened, but with Josa she felt an ease.

"Come to my place?" she finally asked, then rushed to explain. "I want to understand this, but it doesn't seem like a smart street activity."

Josa's smile was beautiful, full of square coffee-tinged teeth. On the street she took a deep breath.

"Do you think I'm fast? Or deranged?"

"I think I am very smart to be following you wherever it is we are supposed to go."

Josa had a small smile on their lips. Zoala beamed. They reached out again for her hand and, as the visuals grew wild, she felt home in a way that would never fit in walls.

✲

Zoala's place was a massive single room covered in stacks of pop culture magazines, clean and still somehow cluttered, a corner full of elephant statues, stacks of ancient vinyl next to an equally ancient record player that didn't seem to have one speck of dust on it. Her bed floated in the middle of the room, and wide pillows were the only other seating option.

She walked in ahead of Josa, feeling both the risk and the safety of the moment. Josa followed her into the space and paused with her in the kitchen corner. They touched her waist softly, easily turning her into their arms. Josa held Zoala, and together they turned up their projected world.

The floor of the kitchen was a verdant carpet of ferns and grasses. As they held each other, the spam, the vision grew up all around them. There was a flat-topped mountain in the distance to their right, across a forever of plains. The sun was coming up. They stood just inside a treeline edging the view, behind them were trees as far as either could see. Giraffes stretched towards food and zebras brushed against each other, roaming the space between the trees and the thousands of antelope against the mountains under turquoise shimmering birds patterning the sky in languid diamonds and waves.

Josa met Zoala's eyes, so she saw the exact moment when tears sprang forth. Before she could ask why, she realized the Josa she saw was transformed before her. She stepped back to see them whole.

They wore a skirt of grass, a worn animal skin slung over their left shoulder, bare feet in the green, head crested in a crown of woven beads and skyward feathers. She felt recognition throughout her body, thunder clapping, shoulders dropping with her guard. She looked down at her own body, draped suddenly with soft animal skin and grass, the same.

The only thing either of them could see now was the vision, covering every inch of their shared projections. Josa took her hand and they turned to face this new world. They moved together, lucid. With their hands clasped together, they both felt more comfortable looking around them.

As they turned to take it all in, it became clear that they were in a bowl of mountains, the jungle climbing up behind them. At the same moment, they noticed there was no sound. For a moment the stillness held, a dream barrier stretched over the aural realm. Then the cacophony thundered up from the ground drums, insects, some faint roaring, monkeys squealing. As one, they hunched down to the ground and took it all in.

Overwhelmed, Zoala pulled Josa under a nearby fern.

Josa held her in the brush, tears streaming down their face, and kissed her. With the feeling of their lips on hers, this world became undeniably real, light and shadow playing on the leaves, the smell of fermenting soil and something sweet, tart, and floral.

Zoala heard voices and lifted her head. Josa's lips followed hers and they kissed her more deeply. The voices coalesced into chanting. She realized what Josa seemed to know, that their passion fueled the realness of this place, which no longer felt like a projection.

Zoala also realized that for the first time in her conscious memory she was feeling pleasure in her body while in the hands and presence of another.

Like many children of the digital age, she generally watched her intimate experiences happen from some distance, doing what she thought was the right move. Everything happened in the mind. But this, the soft give of dirt beneath them, the warm pinpoints of light on her surface where the raw sun came through the green. The smell of bloom and fecundity. And Josa's touch, sliding their warm dry hands over her skin, pressing their full mouth against hers.

Zoala's body was awakening, becoming ready.

Zoala rolled herself atop Josa and opened her body to them. They laughed together at their pace, at how this seemed to be the most logical behavior to take in this world. Josa pulled their skins aside to show small breasts, pink tones under the brown that made Zoala want her tongue on them. Then they put her hand between their legs where there was a long hard mound of flesh, slippery. They pulled her hand a little further and Zoala realized she was reaching into Josa. A duel, truly. They smiled as Zoala's touch moved with no hesitation over and around every part of them. They grabbed her hand then, weaving her messy fingers into their grip.

Josa looked in her eyes, unflinching, when they pushed up and entered her body. The world grew very small and frantic then, for some time, as they watched each other change under the pressure of joy. Josa's body seemed designed precisely for hers, reaching a place inside her that made her break open and shiver and cry out. When Zoala saw Josa's eyes nearly close with the tenderness of their rhythm, she leaned forward and kissed them again and again. Somehow the chanting grew with this explosion. She didn't stop to think about her questions, though. In that moment, letting them feel her love was more important than any answers to the mystery of this place.

Zoala surrendered.

✲

They lay side by side on the earth, watching the birds in the trees, lilac breasted with metallic turquoise tinged feathers. The family of rollers watched them back, the sun beating down through the canopy.

"I feel...safe," Zoala spoke first into the jungle sounds.

"Mh. This is the safest I have ever felt in the unknown."

They lay for a minute in that, and then Zoala stood and looked down at Josa, their bare chest glowing cocoa against the green. She felt the warmth of being one with them thrum about her chest and jaw, softening inside her. She tucked her breasts back into the cloth, feeling tenderness where they had so recently been sucked upon. She reached down and pulled Josa up to stand with her. They came up, stumbling into walking, and fell into step single file behind her. The world felt more than real, like a 5D film, a heavier gravity, brighter colors.

"We don't even know how to exit this program," Josa said over her shoulder. Zoala realized that the thought hadn't occurred to her.

Zoala tried to think about her data, but the very concept of holographic data projection bubbles no longer seemed present or related in any way to where they were. She blinked, but couldn't feel the presence of her tech. She didn't feel worried about this. In fact, for the first time in months she didn't feel worried at all.

It occurred to her then that there was a condition of keeping others at bay that required a constant stress of effort. Letting Josa in had required a release of that effort, and now she noticed the absence of urgency.

"I don't want to know how to leave!" she laughed. "I feel so curious. What is this program? Who figured out how to make merged virtual reality work in the bubble? Are there other levels, is it like a game? How big is it? How are we here?" Zoala's voice was colored with her wonder, a curiosity she hadn't felt since her earliest days at Sapax. Josa kissed her shoulder.

Together they walked toward the sound of drums undulating amongst the other jungle sounds, deeper into the trees. They fell into a rhythm together and neither spoke, nor stumbled on their exploration. The drums got louder and more distinct, not a rumble but a collective, a gathering.

The trees thinned, and then there was a clearing ahead of them, and beyond it a crowd of wooden structures.

In the clearing were other brown bodies. Zoala gasped to see other people.

Two things stood out to her: the presence of anticipation that happens when a crowd is waiting together—looking around, talking quietly and without commitment, ready for the interruption that heralds the main event—and the absence of visible weapons, security, or technology of any sort. She glanced over at Josa for a quick decision, and they nodded at her. She stepped out of the treeline and began walking to the center of the clearing, hearing Josa's steps behind her.

Slowly the people in the clearing turned to look at them, stepping closer to each other. Zoala was stumped as she looked at them closely. Outside of the brownness of skin, which varied greatly, she could see no physical patterns that would indicate these bodies to be a people. No height, no structure of face or nose, no shape of eyes, nothing. They looked like the African mixing pot of Joburg at the bar they'd just left, rainbowed by daylight.

Finally, a woman stepped in front of them.

"Zoala?" Through a smile.

Zoala stopped short in surprise. Was this a program or a dream? It didn't feel like a dream.

"Please don't be afraid." This first speaker was tiny, deeply black, strong muscles showing. Her voice was massive and low and soft. Her hair was in modern braids, and she offered up her palms. "We came here like you probably did. Our data showed us this place, like some kind of spam or hallucination. When we met another. And it kept growing as we got to know our other, or others. And then we found ourselves in here, and we all found each other. We aren't part of the program—though we seem to be the only humans here right now."

Another woman stepped forward, her energy so calming that Zoala felt like a skittish sharp-toothed dog in her presence.

"Some of us can go back and forth between this place and home more easily. A few of us started researching the phenomenon. And then a while ago—time expands in here...but maybe two weeks at home? Those of us who had found each other in here," she gestured at a few people standing close to her, "got a communication that had three things in it. A list of names, a coded message, and today's date. Your name was first on the list, Zoala Kajamala. The second name was Josa Debeza."

Josa and Zoala looked at each other then.

"We were all on the list, though. And of course, we don't know if the order means anything. We worked hard to find everyone we could, but you two—well, you found each other, looks like."

There was light laughter from the others. A man spoke up, "We haven't broken the encryption on the message yet, we're working on it."

Now the first woman stepped closer. She looked first Zoala, then Josa, in the eyes. Zoala's mind went to initiate a search on the woman, but there was no data, no bubble. She couldn't accept that she was inside her data, she felt as if she was on a new planet where data bubbles had never been invented. And she felt ignorant and naked without it. She had to map some data and familiarity on this world, these people.

"What *is* this program? Who created it? Where is the menu? How are we here?" Zoala blurted out.

"My name is Iddéa," the first woman said, her hand on her heart. "We don't know why we're here, why our names are on the list. We do know that each of us is from the Southern part of the continent. Not just from, but...we each have generations of ancestors here."

Josa shifted next to Zoala, closer to her. "Here?"

"Oh yes. That we also know. This place is home, based on our research of the climate, the topography. We found Kgaswane, we found the cradle of humankind. We know *where* we are."

Zoala and Josa spun around next to each other, looking again at everything in sight. This was the same place they knew inside and out?

"What we don't know," a man stepped forward, lean and dark and smiling, "is if we are in the past, or in the future. Other than knowing this isn't the industrial present...we don't know *when* this is."

Zoala and Josa looked at each other again.

Suddenly Josa smiled, gloriously. "A time travel mystery program!"

The people gathered around them laughed, as Zoala nodded, seriously.

They were in some other time, in Joburg, with no idea how to get back to where they came from or who these people were or why they were all there. It took a moment, but the magnitude of the unknown hit her with its hilarity, and she joined the laughter, if a bit more delirious. The undercurrent of concern in the group dissipated for the moment. Brown bodies in the sun, lost in time, home and away, but together.

✢

The group dispersed at Iddéa's suggestion, and Zoala and Josa followed the small woman past the clearing to the small thatch roofed buildings. After passing seven or eight structures, Iddéa paused.

"This space is available. These were here when we first came... very simple, but quite comfortable."

"How long have you been coming here?" Zoala's mind was racing with questions. "And who was first to come here? What are our bodies doing while we are in this program? And how do you leave and come back?"

Iddéa had soft caramel irises under natural hair in small puffs down the center of her scalp. She smiled, her eyes crinkling just enough for Zoala to notice Iddéa was somewhat older.

"I first noticed this place over two years ago, during conversations with my sister Inna. It took a long time to get all the way here, and I was complaining the whole time to any technician who'd listen, they all said there was nothing there. I changed my projector, got my data swept, got energetic cleanses," Iddéa shrugged. "We do seem to activate each other. Inna is here too. There are some other siblings, and a few clusters of friends. But mostly lovers, of course, given what that kind of passionate intimacy does to activate the program.

"When my sister and I found this the first time, the only ones here were Bernard and Rachel," she pointed at an older couple walking by. They smiled and nodded. "But we have no way of knowing really who was first because many of us seem to have been activated around the same time, but didn't find this place or each other the first times we came.

"While we are here our bodies just seem to be in a dazed state, and time here is different from time there. However long we are in here, it's only a few seconds back home." Here, Iddéa shrugged in overt wonder.

"You leave...by truly wanting to leave. As you might imagine, it gets harder and harder."

Zoala got nervous. What if she accidentally sent herself home? Or never wanted to go? Iddéa shrugged again, as if at the unspoken questions, a calm and confident not-knowing in her frame. She exuded a sense that whatever came to pass would be alright. Zoala felt herself reshaped by it a bit.

Iddéa stepped inside and, as the lovers followed, Zoala's eyes swept over the space. There were platforms and windows and a fireplace. There was a stick on the wall with a bunch of brush tied to the bottom of it. There were flickering pillars of light placed along the floor around the room. She didn't recognize anything that was clearly a bed, couch, telly, toilet.

"Why don't you two take a minute to arrive here. Come up with all your questions and come back to the clearing when you hear the drums call. We are making a meal to honor this, the first time we are all together, all the names in that message. We suspect some next phase will begin soon."

Iddéa stepped back out of the open wooden door into the gently bustling community.

Zoala stood at the entrance for a moment, watching as all

these people moved through chores and conversations. The structures were close to each other, but the doors and windows angled such that no openings faced another. The wood was dark on the structures, the roofs tightly thatched onto broad logs. Benches offered rest every few structures, from the clearing on one end, to the last structure, which Zoala could just barely see if she squinted. There seemed to be more activity further away from the clearing, perhaps a place to trade or get resources?

Zoala noticed that people moved with clear purpose. Even those not doing something seemed to be clear about it.

Josa pulled her back into the room, into the open space in front of what she suspected would be their bed platform. They spun her around.

"Can you believe this?" Josa was giddy.

"No!" Zoala laughed, briefly. "I honestly can't. I can't believe it, I can't explain it, I can't deny it."

"This is definitely the best first night I have ever had in love."

Zoala stopped. She had forgotten for a moment the truth of this—that the love between them had brought them here, fleshed up the bones of projection into a world they were now standing in. Josa pulled Zoala close in an intimacy that felt completely right to her. they were suddenly the only person she knew in the world.

"Josa. Someone...someone made this place. This room, this village, this world. Someone made it, and they brought us here. And they are likely watching everything we do. We are data."

"Yes. And we are still here, which means we must not want to leave."

"Why us?"

"What?"

"Well I doubt my job at Sapax qualified me to be on a special list for some new Safrica wilderness adventure. Maybe it's something you archived."

"Ha! Are you kidding me? You said you studied how cultures shift." Josa spread their hands around them. "Surely culture shock is in your realm of expertise?"

"Well. I don't look at how cultures start...I look at the patterns that change culture, mostly for product placement. But I don't know why I'm here. Or you. These people all seem so...calm, wise. I'm not like that. I am not even particularly adventurous."

"Don't lie to me. This does feel a bit like a heaven—they are using all sorts of methods and tools that I *know* to be unnecessary. Did you see there was a well?!" They ran over and grabbed the stick with the brush tied to it. "A broom for sweeping the floor! Candles!!" They pointed out the pillars.

Josa's full lips formed a soft smile as they looked at her face, and she realized they could read her like a children's story.

"You need to know?" they asked gently.

Zoala sat down on the central platform and looked around. Josa opened drawers and cabinets to show her what their home was made of. There was nothing on the walls, just the bricks of a small dormant fireplace opposite the door. A set of cabinets held bowls of nuts, citrus fruits, a block of something that looked like cheese. Plates were piled just inside the cabinet door, and a wardrobe with more animal skins and layers of bedding stood beside it. There was another small platform like the one she sat on, both covered with flat, stuffed large pillows. A third platform faced the fireplace, also deep enough for them to lay together. The space inside was large, they could have had a dozen people dancing on the floor easily. The three windows sat behind bamboo shutters.

"It's a lot to take in," they added, still gentle.

Josa pushed the door shut and crossed the red dirt floor to sit behind her, pulling her back to lean on them.

"My loveless girl. This is a lot of wonder."

They sat together that way for a while. Zoala felt Josa's energy shift just before they began kissing her neck. She turned to look at them and they shook their head.

"I can't remember the last time I was so ravenous. I don't know what it is. I need you now." Zoala felt the same way. She pulled Josa up onto her chest like lifting the drowning dual to her shore. She held them close to her, rocking their small breasts against her softness. Soon they had both pulled aside their clothing and let sex pull them in. This time they were quiet, almost still, extremely slow. Again, the world around them seemed to brighten and deepen as they bonded. Zoala noticed that the roof seemed made of a million pieces of long dried grass, sharply defined, as if some indoor sun was catching each one in flame.

When they finished, the drums began sounding again. Zoala felt a low pull in her system—those drums meant to gather, though she hadn't seen anyone with a drum here.

She took Josa's hand and walked with them back out into the village. Night had fallen during their sex, and above them hung a vast and stunning explosion of stars. She looked up, and then around. There were small lines of smoke coming up from some of the homes. People were all walking towards the clearing, several catching Zoala's eye, smiling or nodding.

What looked to be about seventy-five people sat in a layered circle around a central fire. Zoala and Josa sat on the outer edge, closest to the village, leaning against each other.

"Hello Zoala, Josa," said a beautiful man sitting next to them. He scooted a little closer, as did others nearby. "I am Thokazane. In the real world I am a vegan chef."

"How did you get here?" Zoala asked.

"Same way as you. I met someone irresistible! And the connection opened up this portal."

Irresistible—Josa certainly was that. Even sitting right next to them, Zoala couldn't stop thinking of them, the way their soft full mouth sucked at her tongue. The knowing flush of desire their kiss bloomed up her thighs. Their laugh.

She looked over at Josa and found them leaned back with a small inward smile, looking at her.

"So, everyone is here with another?"

"Yes...we are pairs, or groups." Thokazane pointed at some of the clusters of people around the circle.

"Groups?"

Thokazane smiled then, an elder speaking to a virgin.

"Sometimes what is irresistible happens between three or four. Or more. The largest group here is seven, and they have a lovely story." He gestured across the circle, and she saw them, as intimately connected as she felt with Josa.

Zoala blushed a bit, imagining for a moment six pairs of hands touching her with the intensity Josa brought to her body.

"Do you understand why?" she asked.

The man shrugged. "Honestly...it doesn't matter to me. Finding Frederick was so unexpected. I suppose I needed him. And I'd never have been able to open up to the connection if it hadn't been for this place. If there is more I'm supposed to do, I'll do it. But so far, it's been enough to be here, together, and find others, and...this place. It's a healing place."

Zoala nodded.

"And for the record, I am the irresistible Frederick," said the man on Thokazane's left. Older, freckled, and almost pale amongst the circle of brown faces, he was thick, soft, lovely. "I write."

The others around them leaned in then, offering hands and smiles.

"My name is Roger. I am a professor, a return philosopher?" This man said the words as if expecting to be incomprehensible. Zoala smiled, cocking her head at him with the question on her face. "I study the impact of reverse migration patterns on the worldviews of slaves, immigrants, their descendants."

Zoala mouthed an oh of understanding. Another face leaned in.

"My name is Ra. I am a teacher also, but of the little ones. I teach in a Boggs school." Ra was young, and had the kind of smirk on her face that immediately set one at ease, a little crooked, a little sheepish. She was petite like Iddéa. Zoala could see her disarming children before they knew what'd happened.

"That's like...the Montessori schools, or Waldorf, right?" Josa asked.

"Yes, sort of. An alternative to the public school system, came out of the U.S." Laughter and eye rolls came from the group.

"I know, I know—but it's actually good stuff, solid thinking. It's place-based education, about cultivating a love of the land and the place where you are. The kids do self-direct, but as it relates to the place where they are."

Zoala and Josa both opened their mouths to ask questions, then demurred to each other. Before either could start, another voice was speaking, coming towards them through the circle.

"And I am Christopha. In Joburg present I am a surgeon, though I am retiring this year." The woman speaking was much older than Zoala. She reached and covered Zoala's hands in hers as she spoke her introduction, and they felt like such sure, soft, strong hands.

Zoala started to laugh again.

"You are all such great picks for any list!"

"Eh, I am Xa." This from a person with long natural hair in two thick braids, whose eyes seemed to wink slightly at the end of each sentence. "I am unemployed. Not such a great pick. Iddéa thinks our skills or job have something to do with our presence here, but I am the exception." Zoala thought they might be another dual from the bearded jaw over their soft perky chest.

"Not true Xa!" Roger spoke up. "You got more of us here, you are the survivor, the cat. You landed here and started living, who knows if any of us would have gotten comfortable without you these last few weeks."

Xa shrunk in a fit of obvious joy.

Iddéa stood up across the circle then, smiling at Zoala and Josa, and hushed the crowd. It was time for some questions and answers. Zoala felt nervous, not sure where to begin asking questions in this place.

The drums, which had faded into the background, suddenly rose, getting louder than any of the speaking voices. Iddéa frowned, and from the way everyone looked at each other, Zoala suspected these drums were unexpected, and once again noticed that there were no drummers in sight, or speakers, or anything to explain why it felt like she was in the center of a drum circle.

The drums stopped short. In the silence that followed, three figures stepped out of the darkness of the trees and into the circle.

"Hello."

The three newcomers wore clothing like the rest of the visiting villagers, except that their outfits were a subtle gray color. Zoala noticed that they were a man, woman, and another possible dual, at minimum an androgyne. All three had long thick locks of grey hair. She couldn't tell which one had spoken. They wove around the inner circle, pacing slowly, making eye contact with each person. Zoala couldn't take her eyes off one until the next was closer. Their eyes were honey brown, their faces seemed all carved from the same graying brown wood.

"Welcome. We want to start by saying that you are each here on purpose. We are the programmers of this world."

The circle gasped, murmuring as one. The collective sound caught as the programmers kept speaking, their voices sounding simultaneously wise and synthetic.

"We created this place in order to learn what direction we need to go, as humans, as Safricans. This is what it looked like here, a long time ago, and this is what it could eventually return to. This is what it looks like when the earth is healthy. We want to learn what human culture has to look like now to be in relationship with a healthy earth."

Josa grabbed Zoala's hand in the darkness. She felt the thrill of the moment, caught in the spell of these digital griots.

"The people who have suffered the most over the longest time are living solutions. This we know—living in spite of all the odds is the proof that life finds a way, life is brilliant. But which brilliance will sustain us?

"There are other peoples of earth who have suffered, and who have turned to war, or isolation. But we—Africans and our descendants—have continued creating, dancing, birthing culture and joy and sharing it, even in the midst of appalling suffering. If we learn why, we may understand how to *create* a different outcome for the earth. It is in our hands.

"Soon we will send you home again. We want you to pay attention to how it feels to be here, and to be there. What is the difference? What is it? It isn't just nature, electricity, we have discerned that much. It's something within the cloud of human suffering. Once we know, we will be able to cultivate it. That is what we want."

The programmers stopped then and looked at each other. They nodded and faced the circle. As one they raised their arms and flicked their hands out, as if brushing dirt off a table.

Zoala suddenly felt that she was falling, a dust mote caught in the light of the fire. Then darkness became the whole world and Zoala was the darkness too.

✣

They came to in Zoala's bed, disoriented, as if waking from a deep deep sleep. Josa sat up quickly and Zoala pulled her new lover back down.

"What have you done to me lady...what have you done?"

"You did this to me!" Zoala laughed, wanting to cloak her terror. She simultaneously felt she was losing her mind and being invited into history.

She couldn't dismiss any of this as a dream. The lovemaking of the night before, in whatever plane of existence they'd been on, was present in her body now. She remembered the soft wild smell of the place, the faces and built world they'd entered, the sweet solid sound of those epic gray people. She felt like the air was too close here, this world too small. Looking around her home now it felt so tight, a crush of metal and concrete. The minimalism that had felt so edgy now felt barren, white walls and appliances to communicate a life.

Josa caught her eye. "We don't belong here, do we?"

Zoala bit her lip. Was this that shared delusion form of madness? Or merely love? Was love shared delusion?

She swallowed the thought and kissed Josa. "Who knows. I don't quite trust any of it, I want to know who is behind it all. We have homework here though. What day is it?"

Slowly the two extracted their bodies from the bed and turned on their data, Zoala by pressing her right earlobe, Josa by pressing their left wrist. They simultaneously discovered that it was only Monday, and time to go to work.

Zoala wasn't sure what to do with herself with no Sapax to report to. Josa smiled, offering no suggestions. Smart dual, she thought.

"I don't want to leave your side."

"I don't want to be one of those horrific, codependent couples," Zoala spoke in a serious voice, gently moving her palm along Josa's bare belly. "But how soon will you be back to me?"

"I'll just show my face. I'll text you when I can leave. I will do my homework. I will pay attention to everything. We are the scholars of the future! My office is on Antwerp if you want to float about near there."

Zoala decided she would wander, observing the world while Josa worked.

She pulled on her favorite leggings, the coal black ones that adjusted for the weather, in front of Josa. They watched her greedily, pulling their own pants and sweater off the floor and onto their sunkissed body. They laughed together walking out the door. When they parted, she called out, "Til soon lover," and Josa beamed at her, waving like a kid and even skipping a bit as they turned away.

Alone, Zoala immediately became aware of the bodies she was moving through. She dimmed her data bubble, which today felt like it had an overwhelming amount of information on it. She wanted to see and feel where she was.

The trees which had sold her on moving to this street were isolated prisoners in short wrought iron cages.

Still, she loved the way her people dressed, the soccer colors and cool sling of pants from the waist, many of the women still wrapped in explosive prints, as they'd worn for thousands of years, children tied to their backs in neon towels. Even the modern multi-use materials picked up on these ancient patterns. The effect was of a bright and colorful world.

But she saw something now that felt new: most people's eyes were on the ground, shoulders pulled down and in, tucked wings. She couldn't quite put her finger on what it felt like, but as she moved amongst the people, she felt her own energy being pulled down and in, as if she needed to protect herself.

She hopped in a hover taxi share, not focused on where it was heading, she knew it would cycle back around. On the M1 she leaned in for her favorite downtown Joburg view, which had seemed so glorious just last week.

Now she saw a landscape covered up, void of the verdant green grasslands which she knew should stretch in every direction. She saw masses of people lost inside themselves in glass and concrete boxes, who didn't seem to know the beauty of this place, out of touch with all the other creatures who were supposed to share it.

She looked around her in the cramped van. The faces were all closed up, getting to work, each in their own bubbles, sitting next to others without in any way being *with* each other. Going to work their whole lives for other people.

The hover pulled off the highway down into the city, and she got off near the worker's museum, which documented the misery of the first gold rush workers. She walked the plaza between it and the larger Museum Africa, which were amongst the only low buildings left. Everywhere else the buildings reached all the way up to the clouds, blocking out any view other than odd patches of sky.

She walked for hours, searching for a bigger sky, for anything green, for room to breathe.

At each intersection, on each level of highway, the shared taxis and cars were blaring at each other as masses moved in a near constant flow across the street. Western fast-food windows and coffee shops elbowed each other along storefronts, and the air seemed to hang in a murky veil around the second story of the city. She walked past the digital food vendors, which sold a nutritional substance that could be made to look and taste like any food she was in the mood for. She had no appetite. It didn't help that they hadn't solved the issue of smell—all of the vendors smelled like burnt nuts.

She stopped once, to buy an extremely expensive bottle of water. It was the only one that was plain—the flavors were commonplace now to cover the chemical treatment taste that came from processed sea water.

Her mind's eye was as clear as a holographic—she kept seeing the open realm of the village, where people got their own water, cared for their own space, for each other. Even in her brief experience there, she had felt the impact of life being so direct. Everyone standing up so straight. Being there, on that earth, surrounded by all that sky—and each other. It gave everyone this length, the sense of having plenty of space to expand into.

She messaged Josa, "I think I understand our task."

Josa messaged back, "I was about to text you. Diba's?"

"Be there in ten."

Zoala turned on the sidewalk and began the walk to Rockey Street, feeling that she was walking homeward.

✤

They approached the cafe smiling, and Zoala couldn't help but smile back. Immediately the other world started growing inside Zoala's bubble. She knew their time was limited here.

Diba's was a dense cafe with mismatched chairs at long cafeteria tables under wall-mounted televisions, local news and football playoffs blasting. They sold a general Safrican fare that was grilled up out back—whole fish, synth mealies, cheap red wine at midday. Zoala ordered for them and then slid down next to Josa.

Josa started. "Sitting there in my office, with all the newest toys around me to study the disposable world. And it hits me—the very practice of work as it is done now is really—unnecessary. Spiritually. It isn't connected to the things that bring us life...it doesn't feed us."

"But it feeds someone," Zoala responded.

Josa hesitated for a moment at this, and she saw a different opinion in their eyes, a new look. "But that is being human, it's like part of the soil, your work feeds another mouth. How is that part of the work we are to do?"

"It has something to do with what we can grow in that other place, and how we grow. Everyone here is looking down, tucking in, making ourselves so small. But I keep thinking about how being in that place, even briefly, changed me—it felt possible to be our whole selves there. To listen to each other, to focus on what matters," Zoala responded. When she realized she was leaning forward, and had Josa's full attention, she felt briefly shy. She felt she knew Josa deeply, but in her mind was a clanging reminder: it hadn't been two full days yet.

Josa sat up straighter then, dropping their shoulders. Zoala did too, mirroring.

She added, "You know they say you have to love yourself to truly love another, which always felt too linear to me. Love works simultaneously within and without. You love yourself, and sharing that with another, with others, increases the love, and together you are creating a world from that love. Which can change everything...I think this is why we can only cross over in pairs or groups. Maybe love is required to access that place? And maybe love is the key ingredient to a future like that...love yourself, love another, love others, love the place you are in?" Zoala smiled, lit up, and filled with clarity. This is what it used to feel like at Sapax, floating her mind into the data until she saw the patterns, the invisible forces that moved people into action.

"Love? Do you love me, girl?" Josa's face was a mask.

Zoala's mouth pinched in horror for a moment. Then she laughed. "I could. I think I do. I think it was possible from your first words. Maybe it is the potential to feel love, to be in the present moment, which love requires? The programmers must know that part."

"We were like the lions in moonlight. All of us."

"Yes, like lions, Josa. Like lions, like oceans. I think the programmers already know this part, that there is something about love, wholeness, authenticity, actually being alive, that is missing from life now. Missing from culture. We have a culture right now where all the things that make us feel most alive are nearly obsolete. What we have to figure out now is how we restore that aliveness, that kind of love. Put everyone in a program? Or at the bar in Machiba's? We need to make it impossible to continue to participate in a system designed to eliminate our very dignity."

A table of men near the door burst into screams of agony at something happening in the football game. Josa leaned in closer.

"Zoala...I agree with you. I do...but how would you measure it? Those men don't look like they are missing aliveness. Maybe when they go out to work, yes. But they also have this. So how would you measure what needs to change?"

Zoala looked at the men. Under the fierce energy of fans in battle they looked joyful, pleased to be in each other's presence. In this place they were equals to each other, not data in an algorithm, not workers in service of someone else's vision. They made eye contact with each other, slapped hands and took up space.

"I don't know all the parts of it, yet, but there is definitely something about the simple act of looking up? Being unbowed."

"Yes. Darling, you are speaking of...an inch. An inch in the stance of a people. That inch, that inch of dignity? That is *not* obsolete."

"Right. It's all in that—because we were inches apart you heard my need of you. Inches of distortion in our data showed us another world. That world is an inch from here. But you have to opt in. We have to make it compelling to people, to find that lost inch of themselves."

"How, how can that become something we can give the programmers?"

"Oh, I do not know Josa. I do not know. But I am prepared to give my whole life over to the work of restoring that inch."

Josa shook their head, mouth opened in what appeared to be wonder.

"An inch on the path to freedom. Zoala—I see it, love. I was thinking, love is maybe the one thing we can cultivate which cannot be taken from us. Nothing they can sell to us is forever, not land, not diamonds, material goods—not even time can we truly hold onto. But love? Even when the one you love dies the love does not die. And love is that feeling of freedom to be and become ourselves. The freedom to love myself, Black and dual and queer. To love you, a stranger who feels like home. To realize that no matter where I wander, I am home, on a planet that loves me in every aspect of its design. Really, it's freedom, Zoala. You are speaking of freedom."

"Yes! Yes, exactly. Freedom. Not just diversity, or equity, or some digital culture that perpetuates the worst of the past...it's been forever. It's been too long like this."

The other world was growing quickly in their data. They were half in Diba's in the middle of a busy Joburg day, and half in the wild.

Josa took her face in their hands then, watching her eyes.

Zoala looked back, unflinching, feeling the wide open channel between them. She had never lied to them. That was a first in any dalliance or union. No secrets interested her, no lies, none of those ways of shrinking herself. She wanted to be known.

The transition to the other world was almost complete. Without speaking, the two lovers stood up, and the energy shifted throughout Diba's. Zoala felt an electricity in the air around her, around both of them. She clasped their hand in hers and pulled them closer.

The televisions all shorted out at that moment, sparks flying through the air, the great noise of the room shifting from broadcast to exclamations and shock. The lights blew out an instant later.

Zoala felt calm. She looked at Josa and saw that they were in their animal skins again and seemed to be glowing in the darkness. Animal cloth brushed against her thighs. Looking at her own skin, she realized that in the darkness of Diba's, the sun from the other world was shining on them both.

Fables
&
Spells
for
Liberation

harriet is a north star

13 trips
70 people
no lost passengers
my people are free

19 trips
300 people
no lost passengers
my people are free

i can't stop thinking about harriet tubman!

i think about all the resources she did *not* have at her disposal—grants, organizations, markers and post-its, masses, privilege, a copy machine, social media, social norms, a job that could be done with recognition and safety.

she did not have a perfect language with which to critique her oppressors, a quick way to travel, time to suffer fools.

she had a vision (my people are free), a theory of change (i will physically lead to freedom those who know they are slaves), a gift for adaptation (the underground railroad was about finding the next open space in a series of precarious moves across a deadly chess board), and her body.

1 raid
700 people
no lost passengers
my people are free

i have so many questions!

i wonder if she dealt with people who were made so heavy by their own sense of being victim that they could not take the first steps north.

i wonder what happened when she faced dissent, someone who questioned her leadership. if there were people who would follow her for a week and then say they'd found a better route, a better map in the sky.

when did she tell people about her episodes, her disability?

how did she trust each group of frightened strangers with her vulnerability and freedom?

did she ever feel imposter syndrome—"oh what do i know about the way to freedom, i've only been that way twice?" if she ever wanted the recognition of the name moses, if she just longed to do her work unseen.

how did she survive the heart betrayal of her husband, who found another wife while she was working on his freedom, who rejected her when she returned for him? who else did she love, who tasted her pleasure, who saw her private tears?

how did she know to sing as a strategy? how did she choose the song, the pace? how did she sound?

when the civil war started, how did she decide to align her skills with spy work? and had she built relationships beyond her family and those she had freed, the relationships with armed white soldiers who said they were on her side? did she trust them?

13 trips
70 people
no lost passengers
my people are free

or 19 trips
300 people
no lost passengers
my people are free

freedom is the scale.

getting yourself to freedom, experiencing personal liberation, these are crucial acts, but not enough. we have to continue the risk, find the many ways to get each other free.

even when there is a price tag on our heads.

and it is not enough to know, in detail, how things are unfair. we have to know we are slaves, to see the evolving mechanisms of entrapment, to always keep one eye on the cage and one eye beyond it. we have to be able to show other people when the systems that fill the hours of their lives are stripping them of dignity and agency. we have to be impolite and disruptive. we have to move in the dark, quietly, listening for each other's heartbeats, learning as we go.

we have to be willing to pull a revolver on those who, in their fear, would risk the lives and well-being of everyone else. we have to be willing to say we will complete this journey to freedom, one way or another.

we have to give our lives to the future that comes through in our dreams. to talk directly to god, to listen directly. to be so much more than we're told we should be, to be shocking, to be myth, leaving legacy.

8 years
so many trips, in the long winter nights
so many people, directly and indirectly
train ever on the tracks
no lost passengers
my people are free

harriet guide me today
teach me generosity
adaptation and bravery
teach me the beauty of each small cluster
moving north, moving together,
moving towards liberation
teach me rigor
teach me humility
teach me to listen to the divine
directly, to let myself be well used
remind me that you did the work in hiding, in danger, hoping no one would know your name
teach me to sing when the way is clear
teach me to make freedom more compelling than the slow death of slavery
teach me to work alone and in interdependence that requires astonishing trust
break my heart in order to keep me moving

adrienne maree brown

keep my mind set on freedom
remind me that all the time
and even now
my people are free

juneteenth spell

i dedicate my life force to black people

that we may celebrate and leap forward
know freedom without waiting
that when our chance to be courageous comes
we feel no hesitation

i extend protection over our freedom fighters
pulling up from the earth mountains around each cluster of blackness

i lend speed and flexibility to our body and mind for moments of
adaptation, a river of black liberation

i cast away all effort to harm us, today and all days, may it fall away
as pollen no creature will carry

today we continue the work of burning down slavery
today we cannot be distracted from the target
today we cannot be kept from the joy
today we cannot be made small
today we can only be free

abolition spell

all that is light
break bars between teeth
grind bricks down to dust
explode a sunscale life force
in each direction
until the cages shed like dead skin

brief steamy night
slip through the cracks like rain
nourish the soil, the parents who cannot hear their children tonight
and in the dreams of the babies
let them be held
so they know to keep growing

sun sun sun
let them grow up strong, one tree,
two trees, forests that break the foundations of slave culture
burst the seams of prison walls
find home beyond the trauma of this night

all that is light
beam into the hearts of parents
who would ever let a child

any child
scream in terror where they came for safety
find the crack in the spirit and
fill it with gold

all that is darkness
abolish ice
abolish slavery
abolish prisons
abolish borders
abolish colonialism
abolish our addiction to punishing everyone who needs healing

solstice come
solstice go
solstice come
solstice go

Black August Haikus

Black August is an annual practice of honoring Black revolutionaries who have given their lives to the struggle for Black liberation, particularly uplifting the incarcerated, the political prisoners, living and ancestral. Honoring those who still fight, on all fronts. We practice together to bring awareness to the commitment—we fast, we study, we write letters to incarcerated organizers.

For several years I have also participated in a haiku practice for Black August with the SpiritHouse crew in Durham, and the Black Organizing for Leadership and Dignity community. We write and share our poems about freedom, and the challenge is to write and post a haiku as close to daily as possible. I write my haikus as brief liberation spells, letting myself feel the message of the moment. In 2021, we published a collection of our poems, *Breathing the World Anew*. Below are a few of my haiku spells.

aug 3, 2020

i matter to people who
matter to me, who
love all the ways i am free

we matter to people who
matter to we, who
love all the ways we get free

aug 4, 2020

taste the wind thru bars
become the swift tornado
tearing down the walls

catch the hidden tear
remember you are ocean
channel tsunami

flick the lighter's flame
hear the wildfire's thunder
burn each system down

stand upon the yard
ancestral bones still dancing
shift tectonic plates

...

laying in the dark
counting heroes and saviors
we pray up farmers

adrienne maree brown

pray up prisoners
who fight fires when healthy
but caught the virus

pray up the teachers
forced to watch their dear students
for symptoms and signs

pray up the nurses
and doctors who toil, tired
no respite in sight

pray up the parents
meditating thru kid-screams
loving thru danger

pray up the artists
creating for us laughter,
dreams, threading forward

bless organizers
beaming light and direction
from here to justice

this is how i sleep
counting gratitude and hearts
beating, surviving

aren't we a wonder
harnessing a tomorrow
we won't surrender

aug 21, 2020

black rest is sacred
time reclaimed, time indulged
time that is mine alone

we need time to cry
to hold ourselves, each other
and this too much world

lay down in the dark
of your own sweet mystery
and wander, amazed

particles of stars
waiting to whisper pathways
beam within your black

fill up your glass jar
press down the red dirt
water and seed your garden

dreams may beckon you
smelling of vetiver
sage visions live in sleep

humble into deep
slumber like a soul at peace
let the night hold you

adrienne maree brown

aug 25, 2020

you are meant to love
in spite of everything past
you need to be loved
you are meant for freedom
in spite of constant cages
you are still so wild
you are built to hold
in spite of the erasure
you are built for worship
you are here to thrive
this is your reclamation
your orgasmic yes

aug 8, 2020

look at the glory
standing naked in mirrors
waiting for your glance

take in the beauty
stripped of all small attention
infinite blackness

turn towards yourself
and offer that precious love
you always have you

you cannot be caught
you're never less than your soul
open your cages

stand in the moonlight
bathe, swim in that reflection
you, you are the light

aug 14, 2020

we hold multitudes
do not shrink, don't simplify
black complexity
was never for sale
we are not simple, fragile
we are whole, come true
be kind to your wild
ancestor-fed fantasies
distinction matters
oh imperfect one
what you are is so divine
don't let us miss you

aug 12, 2018

bodies melt into
one mass universe scale "yes!"
this is a greeting

"suck this breast darling
grab onto something solid"
(remember delight)

adrienne maree brown

laughter moves my flesh—
that earthquakeish movement, these
tectonic mood shifts

i can carry it
when i plant my feet earth sighs
saying "yes come home"

lovers do marvel
say "no, stay naked, feel sun"
unlearn skinny love

children dive into
these arms, this bosom, they know
they can rest deep here

a road to freedom
is held in her fat black palms
when she touches you

what is unveiled? the founding wound (poem/directive)

a body is always a body
individual or collective
(whole or in many pieces)
alive or, later, dead
a body is always vulnerable

a wound is always a wound
singular and deep
or many cuts, slowly, blood everywhere
left untreated, unstaunched, denied
a wound will always fester

the first wound happens within
the violence of birth
the expulsion from the illusion of safety
from the idea that someone (else)
will do all the labor

and some of us keep looking everywhere
for placenta, for mothering
for acceptance of our worst choices

adrienne maree brown

to be told we are so special
to be named a favorite child

some of us learn to work
we are given tools, lectures, practices
we are given the blessing of knowing
that work to nourish the collective
is a sacred path for our lives

some are only taught to eat
given the title to land that isn't ours
judged for the speck of dirt under our nails
set to race against even our own kin
for the never-ending victory of more

some of us are black
still nauseous from the boat's hold
still catching our breath from snapped ropes
still oiling our calloused field hands
and still wounded

some of us are white
still synonymous with impossible purity
still given no songs from the earth
still taught to master nothing but superiority
and still, wounded

some of us are red, yellow, brown
still made to feel tertiary to the plot
still dismissed for all we remember
still claiming we are human, not terrorist
and, still wounded

some of us are never surprised
never apoplectic when the stench hits us

what rots at the core is known, documented
it is tangible, moral, american, spiritual
it is the founding wound

gray only at the surface
brittle black where the injury began
a rainbow of bruising everywhere
green mold making life in dying flesh
but the pus, the pus bursts white

we are well past the age of turning inwards
of seeing the open wounds on our souls
of stepping into our shadows with truth light
of seeing we were shaped, and can change
of believing the wound is who we are

we know the smell of decay on breath
we see the swollen cracking flesh of infection
it is not rude to acknowledge the stink
to wonder if it is viral, venom, survivable
to look for the laceration(s)

things are not getting worse
they are getting uncovered
we must hold each other tight
and continue to pull back the veil
see: we, the body, we are the wounded place

we live on a resilient earth
where change is the only constant
in bodies whose only true whiteness
is the blood cell that fights infection
and the bone that holds the marrow

remove the shrapnel, clean the wound

relinquish inflammation, let the chaos calm
the body knows how to scab like lava stone
eventually leaving the smooth marring scars
of lessons learned:

denial will not disappear a wound

the wound is not the body

a body cannot be divided into multiple living entities (what us will
go on breathing?)

the founder's wound is the myth of supremacy

this is not the first wound, or the last

we are a species before we are a nation, and after

warriors, organizers, storytellers, dreamers—all of us are healers

the healing path is humility, laughter, truth, awareness and choice

a scab is a boundary on territory, between what is within and what
is without, when the line has been breached

stop picking at the scab, it slows the healing

until we are dead, and even when we are exhausted and faithless
we fight for life

we are our only relevant hope
we are our only possible medicine

a body is always a body
wounded, festering, healing, healed

we choose each day what body we will shape
with the miraculous material we're gifted
let us, finally, attend to the wound
let us, finally, name the violence
let us, finally, break the cycle of supremacy
let us, finally, choose ourselves whole
let us, finally, love ourselves
whole.

The Inches

If it had happened more suddenly, I might have noticed. No one would have had to point out to me, "You've changed." I would have known.

When I was a child, I had had growth spurts. I remembered once when I could suddenly see what was on the counter, and all the adults would greet me by yelling at Ma, "Wow! SO big! How old is this giant again? No way!!!"

I'd leveled out three years ago, at age fifteen, reaching a height that was somewhere around five foot seven. Except around white people—around them, I shrank. Just a little. This was something I learned without anyone ever saying it to me. It was the direction of my eyes, maybe, looking down, not just at the ground, but at my pristine Nikes moving one step at a time, each step proof positive that I was not dead, in spite of my Black skin, which offended the world so much that my ancestors were enslaved, and friends from every year of school were enslaved as well.

Ma thought I would die whenever I was out of her sight, and it was a justified concern. So, I, like every Black person in my lineage since we'd met white people, shrank.

The day I knew I was unshrinking started with denial. I woke up with my feet touching the end of the bed. Which wasn't that odd—I slept like a runaway slave, always in motion through my dreams, often waking in a tangle of sweat-soaked sheets. But that morning, I was lying straight, and I could feel the top of my head grazing the dark wood headboard. This situation, even as it was happening, was not actually possible. So, I denied it, got up, took a shower, tilting the showerhead up higher to rinse my face.

It was my brother Traywon who pointed it out in an undeniable way. He was back home, living in the basement while he got his garage up and running. I came into the kitchen for breakfast, and he was standing there in his blue jumpsuit, stained, bearded, immediately laughing.

"And what's this style called?"

He was pointing at my pants. He was right, too—they were short. My ankles showed, and a couple of inches above them, soft hair curling up the leg in odd patches, apparently my inheritance from a grandmother I'd never met. All my pants had been getting shorter, for like a month. I thought Ma had been washing them wrong, but I didn't want to say nothing 'cause then she might make me wash my own clothes, and I didn't want to do that until I absolutely had to. Dirty drawers? Ew.

"Shrank-in-the-laundry, broke Negroes edition?" I wanted to beat him to the punch. I offered to make him some cereal, some toast, something to stuff his mouth with, but he wasn't having it.

"Naw, naw—them shits ain't wool." He was laughing too hard to say more.

"Fuck you."

※

I'd found a pair of sweatpants that were usually too long for me and thrown those on, slipping out of the house on an empty belly.

I missed Ma in that moment, the kind of sharp parental need that hints of mortality and debts too great to ever repay. Ma didn't let Tray pick on me like that. She also didn't let me leave the house in clothes that didn't fit.

But she was away, being honored at a gala in DC. Ma was an organizer, always on some social justice work. Last month, the campaign she'd been working on since—I guess my whole life—actually, finally, won.

Reparations.

Ma and some other Black women had figured out a way to get reparations. Black people with enslaved African ancestry would have a set of options, and it would be part of the taxation system. For adults over the age of twenty-one by December 31 of this year, there would be options for waiving existing debt or setting up a retirement supplement to social security. People twenty-one and younger would have the additional option of supplementing college tuition at most schools. The amount we were gonna get was calculated by subtracting the national average Black net worth from the national average white net worth. White and mixed-race folks would contribute to the Reparations Fund through their taxes, based on how far above average they were, which would then be redistributed to Black and mixed-race people based on how far below average they were.

Ma was a "shaper of history" now. She was winning a ton of awards and getting even harder to deal with at home. Ma was anti-respectability but pro-standards. She wanted us to have standards for ourselves, dignity. I wasn't a sloth, but I always came up a bit short when she was assessing my standards. Me and Ma got along, though. I was proud of her.

And I had other things to worry about.

✢

A few days later, in my "Past and Future Economics" class, Delia sat next to me. Delia was a petite ink-black senior with wide eyes that always looked mom-like. But in spite of—or maybe because of—that maternal vibe, she was really pretty, smart, and she had a lot of friends. Her parents worked with Ma, so we had been revolution babies together. But her cool had come on in grade school, and mine was much delayed. Like, it was weird for her to sit by me.

I normally sat up front, shameless about my nerd life. This last week I was hiding in the back because I didn't want people to see me contort my longer legs in and out of the desk.

When Delia slipped into the desk next to mine, I looked over. She looked frantic.

She was like one of those pictures where I had to notice the differences—her big shoes looked brand-new bright. Her pants were also on the too-short side, as were the sleeves on her shirt, frills far from her wrists. And petite Delia was looking straight into my eyes when I found hers again.

After class we unfolded our long bodies and left together, quiet for a while. When we were out of the building, she stopped me with a hand on my arm.

"When did you start growing?" She scanned my length.

"Like, a month? I just noticed it this week."

"It's not normal. My mom's been measuring me. Six inches in three weeks. It's not just us either." Delia pulled her hair into a brief ponytail, then let it go. She wasn't looking at me for solutions, just data. This calmed my clueless heart.

"Who else?"

"There's seven people at school so far that I've talked to. All Black. All more than four inches of growth in the last three to four weeks." She smiled, incredulous. "It don't feel like it's gonna stop."

It had to stop. How tall could we get?

✲

Time answered that question quickly. Delia and I were among the first—Ma was convinced it was because we were children of the

Reparations Team. Traywon stopped laughing when he outgrew his uniform. Ma grew too. Delia's family too.

Every descendant of enslaved Africans currently living in the United States, over the course of about three months, grew one to three feet in height.

I topped off at seven feet, Delia at six foot nine. The tallest Black people hit eleven feet, twelve. We needed new everything—new beds, new ceilings, new wheelchairs, new shoes, new airplane seats, everything.

There were tons of theories floating around, but none of them made sense, because there was nothing that actually impacted every single Black person in the country. Nothing except for Ma's reparations. Which also didn't make any sense to me, because how could a policy make people grow?

Ma privately loved this, though. The Reparations Team made no claims publicly, and no one else seemed to connect the dots in a meaningful way. But I heard them night talking, with wine-loosened tongues and cackling laughter. "Taking the 'press' out of 'oppression!'" "We gonna need our own nation, just to raise the national standard for toilet seat height." "They gonna call this 'AR' in the history books—'After Reparations,' when we evolved right in front of they eyes!" In the midst of these jokes, they were arguing over whether to start a new campaign, or fall back, make room, live into the victory.

Me, I loved walking out into a world where every single white person I met had to look up at me. And I loved heading to Fisk knowing that the labor my ancestors had done was covering me. And the tired blood I'd been carrying around was going to get some respite. And the work it took to be small was a labor I could set down.

spell for election day

utter out loud anytime between 12:01 and poll closing where you are.

we recognize that voting
is only meaningful when we act together
as movement, as future ancestors

today we put aside our egos
we set down perfection,
and our privilege,
and our butbutbutandand righteousness

today we show up for those furthest from power
those carrying the most of our burden
those we've already lost to hate in this pale time
we say no where it is the only humane word
and yes where it is a way forward, another breath

we hold history and future in the balance.
we vote to take up our responsibility
we vote as both prayer and blessing
we open the way, widen the way, change the way
ashe

this massive rage

as we move closer to the elections
again we have to contend with
how much we will play the game
showing up and waiting in lines
people of faith as we have had to be
and always been
and really what other option is there
we come in droves
we speak amongst ourselves
if we love ourselves we know
which of these men has less tulsa in their blood
which of these men doesn't long to see us
below deck, below branches, below the unbearable weight of them
their egos, their desire for us to just take it
the violation of polite conversation
after the abuse
but before the overdue apology
and anyway
so much has been taken that justice is impossible
some days it chills my blood
how will we ever know peace
will we have to forget everything?
will we have to burn the books and make the history fiction?

how can we breathe near you
sleep near you
dream with you
when we remember
when we can be living our lives and be reminded
by griot, thoughtful essay, scathing exposé, image kept fresh across
years
by threat, or bullet, or lie, or law
how, when you haven't stopped murdering us in our beds
gleefully taking our blessings
killing our children
counting us collateral damage as you choose money over masks
over safety, over adaptation, over earth
shooting first and asking no questions, ever
all the while acting as if it were us
trying to take anything from you but our own lives
our own labor
our own right to grieve all that you've claimed
beyond your portion of miracle
you lost soul, you greedy, greedy, i lose words
i choke on the anger, even i
all the time cultivating joy in my heart
even i, seeing beyond the constructs
still
when i come across the artifact
or the present moment
or the border in my dream that says how far i can go
we can go
we can be
i remember we are not yet free
and will not be, cannot be
until you choose to be free
who designed it this way
how will we ever get beyond bitterness
how will we ever get beyond heartbreak

adrienne maree brown

how will we ever be able to tell our stories in any genre but horror
how i wonder
as we barrel towards another battle
that we have no wish to fight
as we want to hold each other
but you've made it dangerous
we want to lick each other's wounds until the scars spell new names
make different promises
fly but not like angels, not like birds, not like anything
that has ever moved through the sky before
fly beyond your touch
that's all we need
and it seems to be the only thing we cannot do
cannot get to, cannot run for
you wait around each corner of history
belly gaping with hunger, eyes pulsing with hate
demonic, vapid, wasting the precious
and only
life you will get
and you even tell your children these lies
to shape into them a foolish worldview in which
we cannot rest and they cannot feel their blessing
i have been casting spells and speaking dreams
my whole adult life
but even i feel the ways you are making me into your nightmare
without my consent
making me your enemy
when i bear no arms
making me your prey
wherever i graze with my children
it has been so long
so long i have to remind myself it isn't forever
it is so constant
i have to remind myself it cannot last
it is so small

to be a part of the sacred
it is so heavy
this massive rage
i am only able to sleep
dreaming of volcanoes
which peel away the surface and explode
and melt down what is
which decimate and steal and swallow and change
which become glass and then green island
which become breeze and beach and whale watching
and song and fruit and dance
and children and children and children
when i feel it inside me
this raging molten flow of the truth
i can only rest remembering
life comes from the eruptions
and nothing you've made will last
and my rage fills up my mouth
and our rage fills up the earth
and we can darken the whole sky
and if we can't breathe then you won't either
and our destinies are intertwined
you fools, you fools, you flesh and bone
suckle and moan
terrified to be alone
you, there, hiding behind your telephone
you will heal, or your line will end
we will heal, or we will die praying and dancing
surrendering to the joy still beating in our chests
we will find a way to live here on this earth
or she will blow us to the sky
melt away our flaws
leave only a perfect stone
full of story

papa's prayer

let it go
you will not be here forever
let it go
let it be dust blown from your palm
let it go
the mistake was made
let it go
don't build that wall of disappointment
let it go
that was your best, this is theirs
let it go
you cannot force anything real
let it go
keep only the lessons
let it go
your hands are smaller than godhands
let it go
you cannot even fully comprehend it—what a gift
let it go
be generous, you have enough
let it go
keep moving towards your joy
let it go

you can still be happy
let it go
live like a river, a long spill home
let it go
this is the only moment, the dream
let it go
with your next exhale
let it go

loving the people like fred hampton

*"i'm going to live for the people
because i love the people"
– fred hampton*

lately everything has been changing fast
and we are reminded, in case we forgot
that our blood is sacred
that it might be required
for the spell, the strategy, the next move
we are called extremists for our love
of ourselves
of our people
of our humanity

it is not enough to articulate
a radical politic
we have to declare a warrior nature
we have to embody yes-to-the-mystery
for, knowing nothing about our deaths
we must promise to give our lives

to the future
to the children
to strangers with our skin

and maybe it isn't your last breath
that is most needed right now
but, for the people, would you change?
for the people, would you apologize? forgive?
for the people, would you be honest?
for the people, would you learn, and learn?
—not for me
not for you
but for all of us?

because if you refuse to change
to look within and seek yourself out
your freest self, and your systemic self
your self which is imperfect and must grow
your harmed self who causes harm
your heartbroken self, and your resilient self
how can i trust your blood
how can i trust your work
how can i trust your love?

we do not survive when we live for ourselves
when we die our truths are forgotten
held in no heart, at most a legend
part of no wholeness, tender in no memory
when we live for the people
we never die, seeded so deeply in each other
love yourself, and the people
give your life for the people
give yourself to the people

the next economy

memory and dream weave together a net that no one can slip through.

we remember that everyone needs time to wander. we dream that everyone has comfort and a clear river on their journey.

we remember that circles hold each other through scarce times. we dream that technology will relieve us of bureaucracy.

we remember that what grows and breathes is more valuable than ashes. we dream of losing greed like we lost our tails.

we remember that constructs make us small and hungry, feeling so wrong. we dream of an economy that lets our inner realms grow beyond imagining.

we remember we are earth. we dream we are one.

boundaries and borders

boundary 1.
we need a universe between you and life

you harm us
you say our miracle
is less than yours

i know you do not believe it
you are obsessed with our magic
and you cannot contain us

border 1.
there is no separation
between in breath and out
in tide and out
sun coming up and then giving in to night

but you want to build a wall

border 2.
you exploded my life

but when i brought my babies to your door
you would not answer
because i call god by another name

this shows me
you cannot comprehend god

boundary 2.
i need to turn off the flood
but i do not know how
when i look away it doesn't stop
when i face it
i can't breathe for raging
i need lung flesh, a brand new liver and snake skin
i need, every day, dry land

boundary 3.
you want to take everything
and be safe
you only think of now
we cannot have you here
while we speak of tomorrow

border 3.
we think we are free
that is why we let you build walls around us

boundary 4.
we are supposed to be ready for this moment
prepared by our ancestors
but they learned to live in the living
and so will we

testing the abundant nature of love
we pull the edges of our hearts so thin

trying to cover the world
from you

border 4.
this is a lie
it isn't in the soil
it isn't in the river
it isn't in our blood
this is unnatural

border 5.
i am made of words
but if paper is how you police us
i say burn it all

boundary 5.
we are made of spirit
we are made of light
when you pummel us, we heal everyone
when you tear us open,
we show everyone
the way to freedom

night

the first time we howled
the moon was a sliver
a cup of light poised to pour
a stardust fascinator of gold
on the blue black

we were life moving through the forest
stepping on small branches which snapped with our weight
maple cracks sharp, oak cracks wet
magnolia cracks like fire
we sought the soft needles of pine

the moon was not bright enough
to cast truth on the borders
to say here, not here, there
all we could hear was the drum of fear
almost there, almost there

we were three miles free before we came to the endless river moving
slow
the sun rising to pull pink steam off the
glistening path
us hunched on the rocks with fingers sliding into river

it's so cold we gasp, and then we laugh
we're so free we gasp
and then
we laugh

Marla and the Creation Committee

Once again Marla was dreaming about the meta order of things. She saw the universe whole, as something without end, all of it the unfurling and curling up of a singular thing. She was considering the stuff of existence when she suddenly saw a translucent door. Marla fluttered with fear for a second. What was the point of a door?

As Marla watched, the door faded, almost disappeared. She drifted purposefully towards it and it solidified. When her hand touched it she got a joyful burst of energy. She'd half turned the knob before she thought to pause, let go, and knock. Even in dreams it was good to assume privacy.

Sounds she hadn't noticed suddenly stopped, and she stood afloat in silence. Her skin prickled in an undreamlike way. The door opened.

A very attractive creature was on the other side, and creature was the most appropriate word. There was some humanoid over-all effect—this creature had selected the best arrangement of parts from the universe and pulled together a fashion statement—lion's mane, skin some otherworldly texture, body a large and literal hour-glass in motion, a flurry of wings at the bottom. And the creature's eyes were some sort of aurora borealis caught in an almond shape. After a good moment of just considering each other, Marla smiled.

"How are *you* here, little one?"

"I'm dreaming, I think."

"Oh doubtful. Doubtful. Well anyways, come in."

Welcome can be in the tone, when the words fall short. Marla stepped through the door into a very solid place, her dream softness shut behind her.

✢

There was a massive dining table in the middle of a round room that was cluttered with seven creatures. Each of these was as uniquely crafted as the next, animal, mineral, human, fire, water, clock—all combined into beings. She took the time to just behold them as if in a dream she wanted to remember.

The round room was a big kitchen, there were mugs and pitchers all over the table, rugs on the floor, food cooking on the stove. There were eight doors, and there were eight windows, each looking out on what appeared to be a completely different landscape. For an instant everything she saw shuddered to a cold office space, all white and windows on infinite space, with the creatures leaning back in chairs floating off the ground...then she snapped back to the warm kitchen where she wanted to stay forever.

"Reality is perception, so you are crafting the place that feels most comfortable to you for this new experience. We each see it in the way that most suits us. We are excited to have you here."

"Where is here, exactly?"

"Here is the constant meeting of the creation committee. We are the makers of all worlds, the keepers of wisdom, the—"

"We're gods, Marla." The interruption came from a creature with lightning jolting across its face as expressive as a set of eyebrows.

"But not singular, and not smiting..." resumed Hourglass. "And we don't know much more than you about how things started. Each of us was invited to this place, and found it more intriguing than home. Our work is to observe and intervene in the patterns of existence."

Marla was smiling, not believing. Marla was no god. She was a single Black woman who didn't even try to keep plants alive, much less animals, or...existence. She was a hard worker at a job that she couldn't quite bring to mind right now, in a city she had learned like the back of her hand...what was it called? She, since childhood, had been and was wildly curious, studying everything that existed and the threads between it all. Recently she was trying to figure out some very basic things about love and relationship that had never clicked. She knew how to love the planet, the species, strangers in commercials, other people's babies...but one other person? In real time? Felt so stifling. A god would definitely know how to love.

Instead of getting defensive, some of the creatures smiled back, and a few of them chuckled. "We are not the best dream you ever had."

Marla's smile faded when Lightning spoke, though everyone else held a soft smirk.

"We sit here in a place where time moves out in every direction and then pulses back, and we watch the patterns. We watch existence emerge, terrify itself, destroy itself, evolve. We hold the lessons, and receive the prayers."

"And...receive visitors?" Marla was grateful her voice came out, even if it sounded a bit strangled on the question.

They looked at each other sideways before another creature—who appeared to have a river flowing down over her body as hair or a cloak and never hitting the ground, through rings orbiting around her where a waist might be—responded to her. "We've never had a new member simply appear, knocking at the door. Nothing in the pattern suggests that this is even possible."

"How were you all invited?" Marla felt waves of questions crashing up in her, and took a deep breath, thinking of calm seas.

"At the end of a life." "When I thought I was dying." "When I was becoming whole."

"Most of us," said Hourglass, "were on a path towards white light and literally felt ourselves caught out of that and ended up here, feeling just as alive as we'd ever been. We got an orientation from one of the committee, and got to work."

"Our group is always seven. When one decides to move on, to rest or travel existence, they pull in a new one." River leaned back upon sharing this, and looked around the group. They all beheld each other with openness. "Is one of us ready to go?"

Marla suddenly felt the discomfort of assumed death. "I'm not dying, am I?"

"Oh heavens no!" This from a creature who appeared to be entirely light and shadow, shaped like a luscious and very naked human with all possible sexual organs. "—At least I don't think you were. Nothing about you says death, to me."

Hourglass chimed in: "Perhaps you *are* visiting, I suppose death does come from sameness, so this is a moment of life for the committee. Separation is an illusion, which we sometimes forget here even as we play with existence."

"Love is what we call the work of being-creating. At the same time being with what is, and creating the future. If you do not act out of love, no love can find you—and love is always seeking." Hermaphrolite came close to Marla, and Marla felt pure desire awaken throughout her body at the proximity.

"I often say that what people do to survive, to live—that is love. All of it. And that is why nothing can be judged." Marla spoke softly as Hermaphrolite walked around her.

"Yeah right, wrong, good, bad, heaven, hell—the idea of a heaven or a moral code which is stagnant is a joke through all existence," Lightning smirked. "Time doesn't operate like that. The universes that are most advanced spend the least time in judgment."

"And fear—" Hourglass stood as her sand all seemed to reach the bottom and spun the bulk of herself around so the process began again, her head somehow still above it all. "Fear is the darkest act of love. It's the moment when the commitment to love overwhelms logic, and tries to overpower the process of evolution and change, to make things stop and stay as they are, or change beyond nature."

Marla felt very comfortable here, and curious. "So you know all of this, you seem very wise. But...who is in charge?"

A new one spoke, one who looked and sounded like a willow tree wrapped around a black hole.

"Everything alive can teach you, and everything is alive. But knowledge is an illusion. To understand the cosmos is to have a sense of humor—to say, I know everything! I know everything about nothing. Knowledge suggests an ending—like an experience can be finished and then known. Everything that ever was, is. And will be. What we do here is look at the patterns, learning and intervening where love is needed."

Hourglass leaned in, "The practice of love is what we maintain and observe—"

"How?"

The committee once again shared a look, and with it Marla had a flash of an entire conversation happening within one mind. Black Willow spoke aloud, "Close your eyes."

Marla closed her eyes, calmed by the stillness in her own mind. Then she became aware of the pattern of her heart beating, pulsing blood through her veins. She felt her muscles all come alive at once, and then something smaller—her skin. She felt organs active within her body, her womb quiet, her vulva still a bit flooded from Hermaphrolite's presence, her back and knees free of pain in the absence of gravity here...and then smaller—her cells.

That was where/when she became aware of a variety of feelings—oneness, separateness, splitting, connecting, all at once. She was amazed that she could feel so distinctly aware of so much all at once. And what came over her was compassion, realizing she was in this body, of it. That loving it was her work, loving it all. That the present was the place love lived.

Scale was the illusion then—the universe was this great body, comprehending itself. This committee was the soul, and the work took many minds, hearts, questions, to bring love back in, connection, relationship.

Black Willow opened all of their eyes and smiled at them, disappearing before their eyes. There was a gasp within them all. And with a quick and painless forgetting of any other purpose, Marla understood, and it was true—she was a part of the creation committee.

we are no longer surprised

we are no longer surprised
not for years
not for generations

you have tried every which way
to strip us of the miraculous
to slice it from us, the future
to leave us without the womb
into which a ncxt world can be born

you want to cover the sky
deny us the sun
we see you casting smoke against our visions
still we feel our way
you slick shit waste oil into our veins
we drag it all the way down and turn it into algae
eaten by, eaten by, eaten by the
market rate fish you overpaid for
back, back all the way into your throat
and you think it's delicious

you have no idea
what it takes to protect magic

yours was damaged centuries ago
you think it is gone
we know it is not
you are just settling for the smallest
shortest version of delight
the bloody meal in your hands
while we set a decadent table
for our children

listen
you will never, ever, ever disappear us
we are beyond borders, categories,
names you mispronounce trying to steal them
for your streets and creeks
we are beyond your bars, walls, and limitations

listen
you will never, ever, ever erase us
we are known to the roots of the trees
loved by the sediment which listens
to the stories our cells tell as they
slough off our corpses

listen
you will never, ever, ever best us
we don't retire when we die,
we come back to keep you hungry
when you're so rich you can no longer taste
to keep you lonely
when you have everything that everyone wants
to keep you working
when no effort can satisfy you
to keep you fighting
over imagined spoils

adrienne maree brown

listen
you will never, ever, ever be free
when you knot yourself to everything you touch
with the word mine, mine, mine
foolish is a lineage that tries to pass along
anything more than lessons
everything is made of everything don't you see
you are as precious as any stone don't you see
you are as sacred as any text don't you see
you are as holy as any treasure don't you feel
you are as gorgeous as any ruin

listen
run away from the cages that make you believe you have to lie to
belong

listen
the reason you will never be superior is because it is in itself the
lowest form of existence,
you are swimming towards the sewer
can't you smell yourself

listen
inside of you is a seed that can only be released
by burning down the horrific separateness
of privilege
inside of you is a prophecy that can only be heard after the words:
i was wrong

listen
i was wrong
we were wrong
our ancestors, we must say it
some of us have ancestors
who were so wrong

in so many ways
and now here we are
less and less days left in which
we can turn the tide
i feel grief welling up inside
so much grander than i can hide
for all that we've tried
as our species has bloomed
but in the same arc,
died

listen
we will never, ever, ever surrender
our story isn't one short lifetime long
your horrors are not contained by an empire
you are the shadow of our own eclipse
and you are the only one
scared of the dark

listen
we hibernate and heal during dark ages
until you forget the world used to revolve
around mothers
until you forget how a spell is just
earth and breath joined across a tongue
until you forget how a finger or a look can be a wand
and the earth can tell you how to burn
and how to grow and when to harvest
and what it is to love as mother birds,
as a lioness, as peach against teeth,
as flower following sun
how a stand of trees teaches us family
how a ghost teaches us devotion
yes until you forget that ancestors walk with us
and guide us and make us dream

adrienne maree brown

until we see the truth of it all
how we are each of us a pulse
in the singular life of the divine
unable to comprehend how beautiful
it is to take one, whole, perfect, never again breath

.

.

.

until you forget how we are all
part
of god

not busy, focused; not busy, full

this is a poem or a reset
you keep telling me you know i am so busy but...
and then you ask me for something
and i want you to know
i am not busy
no, with all of these boundaries i have space
to write.
to take care of my body.
to hold my loves tightly in my many many hands so we can somehow make it through the rest of our lives

i am so focused
on the imaginary world which is trying to whisper to me
how to write a story that unlocks a heart
to write a spell that makes us bored with punishment and immune
to capitalism
i am so full of ancestors and characters and i can't tell which is who
but they are a chorus
telling me humans are not the protagonist
and nothing i can say is more brilliant than a stand of trees or a
mycelial warning
or a newborn's first shuddering dance

or the grace of the blue heron in lustful prance across this pond
or the continuous sky flood always somewhere storming

and when the clouds are full with pending storm they are quiet
so i am studying that quiet so i can hold that storm
and when the riverbanks flood, the soil forgets it is earth and goes
flying through the water and finds a new purpose in the deep or
maybe maybe even the vast ocean
isn't every stream a boddhisatva
didn't lao tzu know it is humble to become the vastness beneath
i was running so fast and trying so hard but what i forgot was the
wonder

now my body aches to remember when i was busy
when i was so capitalist in my anti-capitalism, that is to say so pro-
ductive in my revolutionary performance
but now i am not busy
i am breathing
i am moving at the pace my body allows, ever forward, mentored
by a tortoise
i am balancing my vibrant intentions with my bemused body—
bones of betrayal, bruised by the busy i once thought was my worth
now i know my body is the sliver of earth i've been given
i am healing from the extraction
i thought gave me value
from the toxins i thought of as solace

the freedom i can experience is from the traumatic past and the
dystopic future
into the miraculous now
in which i can still find moments of respite
moments to water the garden of my home
to skim the news stopping only to witness and feel the heartache
and longing
the beauty of being so connected is that my boundless love has a

field without horizon, my heart can gallop on, loving all the people
experiencing and shaping humanity, without end

i hope to never be busy again
i owe this quiet breath to my grandmother
i am creating at an astounding rate
and some of it i even write down
some moments i get so still
i can sense how it is all connected
and that the tissue is love
and i know my love could never be wasted
or too small a contribution
i say yes when love leads
i say yes when there's enough time to do it well
and sometimes even then i am not there
because life showed me another way to love
and it was irresistible

future shaping spell

what we will see in 20 years is what we shape. right now let's shape
the future, repeat after me:

we claim the power
of our outrageous grief
our righteous anger
our responsibility for our precious lives
our interconnected individual and collective joy
and our impossible magic

we embrace our edges
that they may teach us to grow
in right relationship to the living world
our human messiness
our weird and brilliant wonders
we know how to be
in so many incredible ways

with these gifts we can
foment a revolutionary now
that centers love, care, needs
creativity and magic

we plant the seeds of radical honesty
vulnerability, authenticity
and the kindness that eases inevitable change

we will not settle!
we will grow weirder and wilder
more interdependent
for our liberation
for our liberation
for our liberation!

How to Make a Spell

Feel the longing in you, longing for a change of some sort, within you, between you and the world, in the world...that longing is the impulse to create which will spark your spell.

For a written spell, the only way to cast it is to write it:

What is true?

What do you long for?

What needs to be cleared in you, between you and the future you are casting?

What are the ingredients—from nature, from feeling, from element, from memory, from sacred sounds, from what is dead and what is being born—what aspects of life make this longing possible?

Can you speak it as if it already is?

Do you need to surrender to anything grander, vaster, older or deeper than you to seal this request?

If anyone else is implicated in this spell, do you have their permission to cast it?

Arrange all of this on a page until it feels just right. You may need to read it aloud to feel the way.

This is enough, to have felt and imagined and heard and written it.

But you *could* gather some ingredients. You could make an altar around the spell. You could bury it next to the seeds of a plant you are committed to growing. You could howl it at the moon. You could awkwardly read it to your friends. You could burn it over running water, or on the wind.

Thank you for reading this collection of magical material.

Maybe this is volume one, and I don't know it yet. More spells and fables kept coming as I was gathering this text, and I had to cast them, hear them, pray, and promise to find a place for them. All of the content in this collection served my purpose of healing towards and in love. The writer in me hopes you enjoy them. The witch in me hopes you find your own practice of listening, healing, expanding, working with the elements of this planet, focusing your intentions, and practicing your own divine shaping. Because it is a practice, listening for the spells. It is a practice, letting the stories come, wander, and find their way through us.

This work is dedicated to all the liberatory witches out there, the wizards, shamans, priestesses and priests, conjurers and medicine people, poets, healers, elders, doulas, midwives, neighbors, and friends who reach for the cedar, the juniper, the sage, the dragon's blood, the florida water, the lavender, the amethyst and tourmaline, the rose quartz and pyrite, the bell, the singing bowl, the shells, the bones, the teeth, the coins, the tarot, the oracles, the tincture, the pen, the water, fire, air, and earth.

Sources and Origins

"radical gratitude spell" first appeared in *Pleasure Activism: The Politics of Feeling Good* (AK Press 2019).

"trust the people" was inspired by the New Orleans Emergent Strategy Immersion.

"love is an emergent process" first appeared in *Emergent Strategy: Shaping Change, Changing Worlds* (AK Press 2017).

"The River" first appeared in from *Octavia's Brood: Science Fiction Stories from Social Justice Movements* (AK Press, 2015).

"a complex movement" first appeared in *Emergent Strategy: Shaping Change, Changing Worlds* (AK Press 2017).

The quote "god is change" (in "in the corona") is from Octavia Butler's *Parable of the Sower* (Four Walls Eight Windows, 1993).

The quote "the river is very fast now" (in "in the corona") is from a Hopi elder prophecy.

"spell for grief or letting go" first appeared in *Emergent Strategy: Shaping Change, Changing Worlds* (AK Press 2017).

The quote beginning "The first person that has to be impressed with..." (in "Nikki Giovanni in Space, a Portrait") is from Amy Rose Spiegel's interview with Nikki Giovanni, "Nikki Giovanni on Trusting Your Own Voice," in *The Creative Independent,* April 24, 2017, https://thecreativeindependent.com/people/nikki-giovanni-on-trusting-your-own-voice.

The quote beginning "and that is why NASA needs to call Black America..." (in "Nikki Giovanni in Space, a Portrait") is from Nikki Giovanni's, *Quilting the Black-Eyed Pea: Poems and Not Quite Poems* (Harper Perennial, 2002).

"A Moment of Integration" first appeared in *The Funambulist*, no. 24 (July–August 2019).

The August 12, 2018 poems in "Black August Haikus" were inspired by a prompt to write about the love of a fat black woman in *M Archive: After the End of the World* by Alexis Pauline Gumbs (Duke University Press, 2018).

"The Inches" was commissioned writing for *Harvard Design Review* in 2018.

"future shaping spell" was written for the 2018 Allied Media Conference closing ceremony.